Th

Co

Hill

ALSO BY EMMA DAVIES

Letting in Light
Turn Towards the Sun
Lucy's Little Village Book Club

Emma Davies

The Little Cottage on the Hill

bookouture

Published by Bookouture in 2017

An imprint of StoryFire Ltd.
Carmelite House
50 Victoria Embankment
London EC4Y 0DZ

www.bookouture.com

ISBN: 978-1-78681-351-0
eBook ISBN: 978-1-78681-350-3

To the wonderful people and beautiful places of Shropshire.
There could be no finer inspiration.

Chapter 1

Madeline peered through the windscreen at the road ahead, but all she could see were tall hedges towering above her on either side in a long dark tunnel stretching up the hill in front of her – to where, she had absolutely no idea.

She glanced at her watch anxiously and inched the car forwards. She had followed the farmer's instructions implicitly but they seemed to require a level of local knowledge she simply didn't have and, despite his assurances, she couldn't see a single turning off this lane. She must have missed the big blue sign that he'd said she couldn't miss. She was at least halfway up the hill now and becoming more nervous with every minute. What if a great big tractor appeared at the top of the narrow lane and she had to wedge her beautiful sports car up against the unyielding branches in the hedgerows beside her? So far, she hadn't got a scratch on it.

There was nothing for it, she would have to get out. The farmer had promised that the farm lane was only just around the corner after the post box, and she was right where she should be. She paused by a gap in the hedge scarcely a car's width wide and opened the car door to get a better look. She gingerly placed her heels on the ground. At least it wasn't raining; mud would be so much worse than dust and her new buttermilk suede shoes, which perfectly matched her new dress, would be easily marked. She tottered over to the gap in the hedge, and peered through the opening. Did people really drive their cars down here? She turned back to look at her pride and joy, teeth gritted. She was beginning to get a little irritated now.

Just as she was about to get back in the car, a flash of something blue deep within the hedge caught her eye, and she stopped, moving closer. She poked through the overgrown greenery, scowling as moss and dirt caught under her perfect manicure. There was definitely something in there. She pulled until a long vine came away in her hands to reveal the edge of something blue with white lettering. She stepped a little closer and peered in at the sign. She could just make out the words: *Joy's Acre*.

Relieved, she turned on her heel to get back in her car, but as she did so, one of her feet slid into a rut at the side of the road. She stumbled slightly, instinctively putting out a hand and feeling a sharp sting of nettles burn across her palm. As large white welts travelled up her wrist, she staggered backwards right into an overhanging branch that tangled itself in her hair and unravelled her elegant chignon as she pulled away. A whole section of her slippery dark hair slid out of place and flopped against her cheek.

Madeline stared into the tiny lane ahead of her. This was just her luck. After all she'd been through to get this far – the chance of a new job, and the fresh start she so desperately needed just within her reach – and now she was late and looked a complete mess to boot. So much for first impressions. She stomped back to the car and climbed inside, slamming the door. Her hands fluttered anxiously to her hair to try to fix the damage, but without pins it was hopeless. The best she could do was tuck the ends in and try not to move her head too much. She bit her lip to stop her tears from welling.

Taking a deep breath in, she fired up the engine and swung the car towards the turning. This was not what she expected at all, not even close to what had been described in her interview. Mercifully, as soon as she was through the gap in the hedge, the lane widened and the hedges lowered a little so she could see she was skirting the edge of a field, glimpses of green flashing at her through the gaps. After navigating a tight right-hand bend, she came to a wide clearing where a couple of other vehicles were parked in front of a line of fencing. Beyond, she could see a dusty yard, a large red-brick house, numerous chickens and two sheepdogs running around in circles, barking. Her heart sank.

They were simply dogs, she reminded herself, and her irrational fear of them was just that. She had never been given cause to be wary of them in the past, and these two wouldn't hurt her now, they were obviously just doing their job. It was, however, the last thing she needed today; she was nervous enough as it was. She took a deep breath, trying to calm her anxiety and remember that first-day nerves were perfectly normal. What had happened in the past was *in* the past, and no one would know about it here. This was a new beginning – she had got the job on merit and all she needed to do now was be poised and professional, just like she had been at her interview. She placed her hand on the horn, and pushed hard, flinching at the raucous note that rang out.

After about twenty seconds the front door of the house opened and a dark-haired man appeared. He looked around him and stuck two fingers in his mouth, giving a sharp whistle, which had the dogs running to his side. He scowled in her direction and strode across the yard where he stood just inside the gate, his hands on his hips.

Madeline stared at him through the windscreen. She had hoped he might come through the gate and greet her, but now that it was obvious he wasn't going to, she wasn't quite sure what to do. The lack of movement was becoming uncomfortable, and now, far from feeling like she was in control, she began to feel very foolish indeed. To her relief the man finally moved forward and unlatched the gate, giving the dogs a firm command to stay where they were. This was her cue to turn on the charm. She climbed out of the car, making sure her long legs were in full view. She stood and beamed a smile.

'I'm looking for Seth Thomas,' she said, her eyes flicking to the dogs. 'My name's Madeline Porter. I have an appointment for two p.m.'

The man checked his watch, frowning. 'Well, I'm Seth Thomas, but whoever you are, you're late.'

'Yes, I know, sorry. I couldn't find you. There's no signage, is there?' The dogs were hovering, waiting for any signal to move forward. She held both hands at waist height. 'In fact, that probably ought to be one of the first things we remedy. Easy enough to resolve; I think the hedge just needs trimming back a bit, although maybe a bigger sign would work better...' She trailed off. 'Sorry,' she said again. 'I'm getting ahead of myself. I have an appointment?'

Seth looked her up and down. 'Do you now,' he said. 'Only I don't recall ever making an appointment with you.'

'No, it was Natalie that confirmed today's arrangements. You were copied into the email, I believe.'

His mouth set in a hard line. 'Ah, well, I make a point of never reading her emails, so that might explain it.'

He stood back to let her pass through the gate in front of him.

She hesitated, wishing he would go first.

'Don't tell me you're afraid of the dogs?'

'I'm not afraid of them. I just don't appreciate them running wild and leaping up at me.'

Seth looked at the two dogs which stood placidly by the gate, and then back up at her, raising his eyebrows.

She ignored his unspoken taunt.

'I suppose you'd better come in the house,' he said, waving his hand to indicate that she should move forward, 'that is, as long as you're not afraid of the chickens as well?'

Seth's hands were back on his hips as he regarded her with an amused smile.

She whirled around to face him, a strand of her make-do hairstyle coming free and bouncing around her cheek. She tucked it angrily behind her ear.

'I bet you think that's funny, don't you?' she said. 'Well, excuse me, but your dogs were completely out of control. You might want to think about that for the future. Not everyone is comfortable around rabid dogs.'

He dipped his head slightly. 'Point taken,' he said. 'Although they are very good at keeping out unwanted visitors.' He gave a tight smile, eyes flicking to her hair. 'And you might want to think about laying off the horn in future, it only winds them up.'

Madeline's cheeks burned all the way to the front door as she hastily tried to refasten her hair.

A few minutes later she was seated at a well-scrubbed kitchen table watching Seth's back as he busied himself with the kettle. The door was firmly closed and the two dogs banished to another part of the house, but she could still hear them scuffling outside, paws scratching against the wood every now and then.

'Actually, I'll just have a mineral water please,' she said. She saw his movements stop, his back stiffen slightly and then he reached up above him to a cupboard, took down a glass and crossed to the sink.

'Tap water,' he said, placing the glass in front of her. 'Although strictly speaking it is mineral water seeing as our water comes from a bore hole.'

Madeline said nothing. She hadn't the faintest idea what a bore hole was, but it didn't sound good. She picked up her drink, tentatively taking a sip and expecting it to be warm and disgusting. To her surprise, it was deliciously cool and almost sweet.

The kettle was taking an age to boil, and Seth stood with his back to her the whole time, neither particularly tall or broad, and clad in a tatty red jumper with a frayed hem, and a hole just shy of his right armpit. She sipped her water, and waited. She fidgeted, grew hot, crossed and uncrossed her legs and still there was no sign of Seth's tea nearing completion.

Eventually, Seth cleared his throat and placed a mug on the opposite side of the table to her. Then, instead of sitting down, and to her surprise, he crossed to the door.

'Right, let's get this over and done with,' he said. 'Time for a proper introduction.'

With that, he flung the door wide open. There was a sudden, clattering skirmish as eight legs sought purchase on the tiled floor and the two dogs charged the room.

'They just want to say hello,' added Seth, 'which is entirely reasonable under the circumstances. You'll be sharing the house with them, so you might as well start as you mean to go on.'

Before she could protest, a large head pushed onto her lap, tongue lolling, spittle smearing the pristine fabric of her dress. She raised her hands as if being held at gunpoint.

Seth dropped to his haunches beside her, placing one hand on the dog's head and ruffling it affectionately, pushing the snuffling nose even further onto her lap.

'This here is Bonnie, who's a total darling, and will stand any amount of petting, won't you sweetheart?' He tousled the fur even harder.

Petting?

Seth reached out a hand. 'And this here is Bonnie's brother, Clyde, who is a little more wary to start with but guaranteed to melt your heart eventually. He's just a little shy.'

As if on cue, Clyde fell into his side, lolling up against Seth in ecstasy, his head rolling back as he tried to lick Seth's hand. Madeline all but shuddered. She had no intention of having anyone or anything melt her heart, least of all some mangy dog. She stared at Seth's jumper which was now covered in little white strands of hair. No thank you very much.

'Go on,' urged Seth. 'Just stroke them, they'll leave you alone if you do.'

Gingerly, she placed a hand on top of Bonnie's head, keeping a watchful eye on Clyde as she did so. The dog's blue eyes were distinctly wild looking.

After a moment or two, Seth straightened, rising easily to his feet.

'Come on now dogs, away.'

He moved back into the hallway, and opened the door onto the yard. Both animals leapt up and rushed outside.

'See?' he said, coming back into the kitchen.

Madeline, who didn't, simply stared at him. She cleared her throat.

'Perhaps we should make a start,' she said stiffly, dabbing away at the embarrassing wet patch on her skirt with a hanky from her bag.

Seth took his seat, finally, leaning back and watching her silently for a moment. She fidgeted uneasily under his gaze, suddenly aware of how badly this was going. His hand rose and slowly stroked the rough stubble of his chin.

'A start on what, exactly?' he said, at last.

Madeline swallowed, ripples of anxiety beginning to thread through her stomach.

'Were you kidding before, or did you really not read Natalie's email?'

'No, I didn't. I did, however, read her previous emails where I was informed at great length of my shortcomings, and told I'd left them with no choice but to enlist an *expert* to help me.' He encased the word 'expert' in speech marks with his fingers. 'At that point, forgive me, but I rather lost interest. I knew someone would be coming, but to be honest I hadn't expected you quite so soon.'

His attitude was beginning to grate on her.

'Listen, all I know is that I was to arrive today, at two o'clock, and to ask for you. I've just driven halfway across the country and—'

'This is not quite what you were expecting?' he said. 'No, I don't suppose it is.'

She ignored the sarcasm in his voice. 'Are you the caretaker?' she asked, giving his appearance another appraisal while trying to maintain eye contact.

His head shot up. 'Is that what she told you?' He muttered something else under his breath which she didn't catch. This was getting them nowhere.

'Mr Thomas,' she said firmly. 'My interview in London was quite straightforward. I have years of experience working for two top London agencies, as a consequence of which I was deemed to be the most suitable candidate from six others and subsequently offered the post of Development and Marketing Executive for Joy's Acre. After the recruitment formalities were concluded, I received my contract together with instructions to ask for you on my arrival. I gather you're to show me round the estate and help me move into my accommodation. I start work tomorrow, Mr Thomas, I'm not sure what's unclear about any of that.'

Seth turned his head away, but not before Madeline had seen a look of abject fury pass across his face. His frustration vented in a short hiss of anger, but then, without warning, he sat up straight and finished his tea in three gulps.

'No, you're right, Miss Porter, that's all perfectly clear. When you're ready I'll show you round. Excuse me for just a second, won't you?'

He sprang up from his chair and reached the kitchen door with one stride.

'Do finish your drink, though, I won't be long.'

With that, he left.

She looked around her, feeling a little more in control at last; it finally felt as if she was getting somewhere. It wasn't her fault that he was so disorganised he hadn't even been expecting her. She was beginning to understand just why the recruitment process had been conducted in London. Whoever Seth was, he was clearly part of the problem she had been brought in to remedy.

At first glance, the kitchen wasn't to her taste – far too lived-in, and with a nod to that hideous shabby chic that was all the rage in the countryside at the moment. But she could see one or two quality pieces dotted around and hidden behind all the farmhouse clutter. Not to mention a state-of-the-art coffee maker in one corner. She got up and crossed to the window, which faced out across the courtyard over which she had just walked. It reminded her of an old painting, sepia-toned, and dusty – a tired rural idyll from a bygone age.

She craned her neck to try to see past the end of the building. In front of her lay only the yard and the area where the cars were parked. Beyond this was the lane she had manoeuvred up, with its impression of fields stretching to her left. By her reckoning, she should be somewhere close to the top of the hill, so presumably there must be a view from the other side of the house.

Seth had completely disappeared, so there must be a path around the side of the house, and presumably this was where the estate complex lay; she couldn't see where it could be otherwise. Her thoughts were interrupted by the sound of shattering glass.

A minute or so later she heard the front door open again, and Seth's head appeared around the doorway.

'Ready?' he enquired. Again, that slightly sarcastic smile. Pasted on for the occasion. She gave a nod and lifted her glass, quickly swallowing the remaining water, and worried about what was in store.

★

She hadn't noticed it on her arrival, but recessed back from the main house were two outbuildings, a wide archway between them providing passage to the rear. Directly behind one of the outbuildings was an ancient greenhouse, leaning up against its warm-coloured brick walls. On the floor were three sheets of glass from the roof, smashed into huge jagged shards. She paused behind Seth, uncertain whether to stop him and point it out or not.

He seemed to sense her lagging behind and turned back. 'All I did was open the window,' he said, shrugging.

She stared inside the building, at the rows of seedlings on a table at the far side. Plants which presumably would benefit from a little ventilation alongside the warmth of the spring sunshine.

'You weren't inside?'

He stopped for a moment and looked at her as if she was mad.

'I wouldn't be talking to you now if I was. No need to, thanks to our friends the Victorians. Look, I'll show you.'

Doubling back, he rested his hand on a large handle attached to a wheel on the outer edge of the greenhouse, just above her head. It was painted dark green, generations of paint flaking off to reveal alternate colours beneath.

'See, the drive shaft runs the whole length of the greenhouse. When you turn the wheel the whole shaft turns too, winding the mechanism that opens each window. You've no need to open them all by hand, and you can do it all from outside. Canny, don't you think?'

Madeline looked at the rusting metal.

'Except it's broken the glass.'

Seth looked at his feet. 'Well, strictly speaking it didn't. The glass slipped out of the frame, that's all. It needs repairing in any case. All of this.' He shrugged again, and waved a hand at the dilapidated structure. 'Come on.'

She looked first at the greenhouse and then back at Seth, the question she most wanted to ask staying safely in her head. After all, she had no proof that the glass had slipped due to anything other than weak joints and gravity, though the large brick which sat squarely in the middle of the floor told a slightly different story.

Once past the outbuildings, the garden opened up in front of them and as Madeline walked toward it she felt her heart begin to beat a little faster. Surely this was where the complex lay? Her professional enthusiasm tingled in the small tug of a smile at the corners of her mouth.

Twenty seconds later both her smile and any trace of professionalism left her as she stared open-mouthed at the scene in front of her.

Her gaze swept from left to right and back again, taking in the full length of the gardens on either side, which looked surprisingly neat and well ordered. They were the only things that were. On one side was a small thatched cottage, set in an overgrown tangle of weeds and bushes. Lying on the front path was a pile of rusted metal that might have once been garden railings, and even from this distance it was clear to see that the roof was in as sorry a state as the windows and the front door, which sagged against its hinges.

Across to the left lay three more cottages, slightly larger than the first, and all thatched, but with whitewashed walls instead of exposed brick. However, so much of the paint had already peeled off that Madeline couldn't tell whether it had been purposefully removed in the name of restoration, or whether it had simply fallen away. An outbuilding of some sort stood forlornly behind them. The whole site had an air of neglect and if the condition of the outside of the cottages was anything to go by, then Madeline dreaded to think what she might find on the inside…

'It's what you would probably call work in progress,' said Seth, indicating the first cottage.

'Are they even habitable?' she hissed.

'Well, that depends,' replied Seth. 'For me, yes. For you? Probably not so much.' He really didn't need to say any more. 'Do you want to go on, or have you seen enough?' he said.

She wasn't sure if he said it to be unkind or not, but at that moment it felt like the final straw.

'Yes, I want to go on,' she demanded. 'At least show me the ones that have already been completed.'

Seth stared at her, an uncomfortable silence growing as he said nothing; he simply stood rooted to the spot.

'Is this it?' She rounded on him furiously. 'Are you honestly telling me that four semi-derelict cottages and an old ramshackle barn are the sum total of what Joy's Acre has to offer? I was told there would be a range of luxury holiday accommodation as well as conferencing facilities for business customers. Where are you going to put them? In a tent on the lawn?'

She drew in a breath. 'There must be some law about getting people to come and work for you under false pretences. I've come all the way down here expecting to find something really special, and what I actually find – in the middle of nowhere, I might add – are four shitty little cottages and about as much luxury as a pig pen…'

She trailed off, a sudden unwelcome rush of emotion making the breath catch in her throat. She swallowed hard. She didn't want Seth to see how upset she was, but this was still a wholly unacceptable situation. She pushed down the raw feeling inside her and glared at him.

'I'm not finding it particularly humorous either,' he said, his jaw working. 'Especially as these… shitty little cottages, as you put it, are part of my home.' He glared at her. 'I own Joy's Acre and everything in it, and the last thing I need is some trumped-up bloody know-it-all from London coming down here to insult me and worse, thinking she can tell me what to do.'

His eyes flashed with anger, but she was too concerned with her own situation to give too much thought to his feelings just now. What on earth was she going to do? He pushed past her and headed off at speed, giving her no choice but to trail after him.

As he rounded the corner back to the main house the dogs began to bark furiously again, dashing over to a tall figure standing by the farmhouse door.

'And call your hounds off, man, I've told you before.'

Seth's hands went to his hips.

'You know, Agatha, if you ever gave me some warning about your little visits, I could make sure the dogs were inside if it bothers you so much.' He gave a sharp whistle. 'Bonnie! Clyde!'

The two dogs slunk to his heel and Madeline noticed that he made no move to put them inside.

'What do you want?' he asked.

'There's a woman arriving today. My niece informed me by telephone yesterday evening, and you're to be polite to her, and make her feel welcome, is that understood? She's here to sort you out, and I will expect regular updates.'

The air between them bristled, and Madeline tried to make herself invisible a couple of paces behind Seth. This must be Natalie's aunt, who she'd been told would be on hand locally to keep an eye on things. This was not how Madeline imagined her first meeting would go and she shrunk even further behind Seth, but too late, as Seth took a huge sideways step and turned the attention towards her.

'Ah, I see you've arrived.'

Madeline tried to muster a bright, professional smile and thrust out her hand.

'I most definitely have,' she said. 'Madeline Porter, pleased to meet you.'

Her hand wavered in the air waiting to be received. Agatha let it hang there as she looked her up and down before giving a dismissive snort and turning her attention back to Seth with a scowl.

'And I'm still waiting for my hedge to be cut, three weeks after I first made the request. Perhaps you could attend to it at your earliest opportunity.'

She gave Madeline one final, very thorough look, and turned on her heel.

Madeline's mouth gaped open. Had that really just happened? What was it with these people? She had half a mind to go after Agatha, to ask her all the questions that were burning through her brain and give her a piece of her mind, but there was something about the uprightness of her back that told her Agatha was not the sort of woman you ran after. Instead, Madeline had no choice but to watch her go, the rising tide of anxiety flooding through her once again.

Beside her, Seth remained silent, his head bowed low, a look on his face that said this was not how he'd imagined today going, either.

'So that's Agatha, then,' she said.

Seth gave her a sideways glance before ushering her back inside.

'Get used to it,' he said with a tight smile.

Chapter 2

Back inside the kitchen, Seth was now sitting at the table, slumped against a chair, his legs stretched out in front of him. Madeline fidgeted nervously beside him, desperately looking for a way to restart the conversation. The silence began to grow.

All of a sudden, Seth drew in his legs and stood abruptly.

'Well, what an utterly fabulous day this is turning out to be.' He paused, looking at her. 'Coffee?'

Madeline nodded, not quite trusting herself to speak, and for the second time that day was forced to watch Seth's back while he made their drinks.

'So what exactly did Natalie say to you?' asked Seth, once they both had scalding cups of coffee in front of them. 'Would I be right in thinking that you've been given a rather different impression of this place?'

Madeline thought about his question for a moment. It was tempting to just spell it out for him, but however cross she was, none of this was necessarily Seth's fault.

'I'm just surprised that you *don't* know. You said that this is your place and made it quite clear that you don't want me here, so how come I *am* here? If you didn't want this to happen, why have we gone through the whole rigmarole of interviews, references, all of that? It makes no sense at all. Couldn't you just have said no?'

'It's not that simple,' he sighed into his coffee.

'No?' She raised her eyebrows.

'No,' he said, his mouth a thin hard line. 'Agatha and I have… a family connection, and as such she and I both have a vested interest in this place. We have an arrangement. You don't need to know what that is.'

Madeline held his look. 'Okay… but I came here in good faith. I've given up my house in London, left everything I had behind… Don't you think I deserve some sort of an explanation? Natalie spoke about a complex; a very upmarket complex. A range of luxury holiday accommodation, she said, together with leisure and business conferencing facilities. I understood it was all finished, but that now you needed input with the launch and ongoing marketing…'

Seth gave a bitter laugh.

'… and putting aside the fact that this is your home, even you have to admit that this place is none of those things.'

Seth took a sip of his coffee and then a longer swallow, watching her over the rim of his mug as he did.

'It might interest you to know that Natalie has only ever set foot in this place twice, and that was years ago. She likes to think she's something big in the city, and usually only condescends to speak to me by email.' He paused to take another sip. 'Call me cynical, but I would imagine that the set-up of the whole interview process was designed to give you the impression that Joy's Acre is rather more… upmarket than it obviously is.'

'But why? What would she stand to gain?'

Seth cocked his head to one side. 'Well, let me put it this way. If you had seen this place beforehand, or at least had an honest description of it, would you have been so keen to give up everything and come here?'

He quickly took in her expression.

'No, I thought not. You've been given an impression of Joy's Acre which sits with the vision that both Natalie and Agatha have for it. Sadly, that doesn't fit with the way I see things. This place *will* be successful, unique too, but not on their terms. So, I'm not really sure where this leaves us.'

He fiddled with the edge of an envelope that was lying on the table.

Madeline picked at a mark on her dress for a moment as it finally dawned on her just how much she'd been deceived. For what purpose, she still wasn't sure, but the fact was that she was being asked to play piggy in the middle in some ridiculous game to prove a point. The thought made her breath quicken, just a little; *not again.*

She looked at Seth's tired face. There was a lot more to this conversation than either of them was prepared to discuss, but the long and the short of it was that Madeline was now here, and she'd rented out her flat in London, so she had nowhere to go either. Even if she did, London was not as welcoming as it had once been. There was no way she was going back, not until she could hold her head up high.

She ran through her options; unexpected and unwelcome they might be, but at least she had a place to live for the time being. She also had a salary, and whether it was what she had been promised or not, there was certainly work to do.

She should have known it wasn't going to be the lifeline she'd been so desperate for. The last few months had been tough, and this first step on the road back to the kind of life she'd had before had fallen into place so easily. She had taken it as a sign that it was meant to be, but how wrong could she have been?

It was almost too much to bear. She could feel her heart beginning to beat faster and fought down the urge to cry. She needed to keep her breathing slow and shallow. Controlled. Her fingers pressed against the side of her mug. She must not give in to self-pity whatever happened – that was the deal she had made with herself.

She lifted her chin and cleared her throat, summoning the last dregs of her confidence.

'I probably ought to make a few phone calls,' she said. 'Is there somewhere private I could go… or perhaps my accommodation, now that I *am* here?'

Seth looked rather uncomfortable and the penny finally dropped.

'I'm staying here, aren't I?' she said, sighing. 'In this house? I might have known.'

Seth got slowly to his feet and held out his hand, waggling his fingers.

'Car keys?' he said. 'I'll go and get your bags. And it's not all bad,' he added. 'At least you have your own room.'

★

In fairness, the room was lovely; large, airy, and perhaps surprisingly, nicely furnished. There were huge voile drapes at the window which billowed in a gentle breeze blowing in from the garden. And yet, after fifteen minutes, Madeline was still slumped on the bed, unmoving. Her fingernails were pressed hard into the palm of her hand, but even this could not deter the onset of stinging tears. She blinked rapidly, trying to slow her breathing before a full-blown panic attack ensued. She was stronger than this, she reminded herself. She had to believe that.

Seth had carried her bags effortlessly up the stairs, pointing out his room, the bathroom and a few others before leaving her to settle in. Should she need it, he had added, then she would find the telephone in the living room. Her signal-less mobile phone lay beside her on the bed, completely useless.

What could her contact at the recruitment agency even do, she wondered. No crime had been committed – a gross exaggeration maybe, but nothing that would stand to be in breach of contract and she certainly wouldn't be the first person in the world to discover that their new job wasn't quite what they thought it was going to be. As far as Madeline was concerned she had two choices: she could stay, or she could go. It was as simple as that. Right now, she had money coming in and a roof over her head; both of which she desperately needed.

Wearily she got to her feet and unzipped one of her bags; she might as well unpack. A large oak wardrobe stood in one corner of the room and she shook out her dresses and suits one by one, moving aside the lavender sachets that hung there to fill the empty space. After that, she placed her toiletries in the adjoining bathroom. All of ten minutes had passed and there was nothing else to do. Officially, she didn't start work until the morning, but she doubted she was going to receive any formal induction of any kind. She had no idea what was required of her, or whether she would be allowed to do anything at all. But unless she wanted to hide in her room all day weeping into her pillow, she might as well go and see what she could find. She picked up her bag, slid a notebook and pen into it and pulled open the door, heading back downstairs.

Retracing her steps from earlier, Madeline went through into the garden and surveyed the scene in front of her, trying to ignore the dereliction and instead gain an overall impression of the place. Apart from the gardens themselves, which looked neat and well cared for, the whole place looked very sorry for itself, and yet… She turned her head from left to right, trying to orientate herself. If she was right, they should be somewhere near to the top of the hill.

She moved in the direction of the first cottage, standing back and peering at the exterior with a critical eye. She tried to view it dispassionately. It wasn't her cup of tea. The top-floor, ultra-modern loft apartment where she lived in London was far more to her liking, but she could see how this place could be considered charming – after a huge facelift, that is. She followed a path to her right which led around the rear of the cottage and almost gasped when she realised that, instead of simply leading to the other side of the house as she had thought, the path opened out, sweeping on to a set of large wooden gates set in the boundary fence. The view behind had been quite hidden by the angle of the cottage. Perhaps this was not the full extent of Joy's Acre after all. Her professional interest rose a notch.

It was like being in a different world. Whereas the main house seemed almost cloistered, approached from the road via the tiny lane, the world beyond the gates was an expansive sweep of fields and trees, a patchwork of colours and textures that, especially to Madeline's city-jaded eyes, seemed like a small miracle. She had lived a large part of her life surrounded by buildings and industry, roads and noise and she had never ever thought that there might be an alternative. What must it be like to wake every morning to this…? Even if just for a holiday?

As she watched, the sun broke free from behind a group of clouds and lit up the fields, light and shadow falling in turn as the breeze chased the clouds across the sun's path once more. She stood for a minute before turning around and looking at the sorry state of the building behind her. Joy's Acre might be a pastoral gem, but it was a long way from being polished.

She stared for a few moments more, lost in thought, and then made her way to sit on a bench she had noticed in the middle of the garden. It, too, had seen better days and she sat gingerly on the edge of the wooden slats, looking with distaste at the bird droppings that covered one half of it. Her dress was already stained from the dogs' saliva and some other mark she had picked up from somewhere. A nice view was one thing, but so far the countryside had proven itself to be a dirty inconvenience.

In her mind she ran back over the details of her arrival at Joy's Acre, trying to see it from a visitor's point of view. To her, it was obvious where the issues lay, and she fished in her bag for her notebook, feeling slightly more resolute. This was what she knew, what she was good at. She had filled a page before she knew it.

Lost in thought, it was some while before she became aware that a huge ginger cat had approached and was winding itself around her feet, rubbing itself against her ankles and purring in pleasure. She reached down a hand to push it away, tucking her legs underneath the bench. Undeterred, the cat simply changed position and rubbed its head against her knee instead, stretching its neck up and dribbling slightly as it pushed its mouth against her. She stood up crossly. What was it with the animals around here and their constant desire to share bodily fluids?

She took this as a cue to move on to the other three cottages on the opposite side of the garden to the first, grouped together and arranged in a semi-circle. A series of paths connected them all, linking with the main garden in front of them. A long low barn and a couple of small sheds completed the set-up.

It was the barn that most interested Madeline. She needed a feature, something stunning that would unite the use of the space and provide a focal point to tie it all together. The barn looked in a pretty poor state of repair, but if the wooden exterior was replaced with glass, a covered walkway could be extended out to pass in front of all the cottages. The combination of old and new could look amazing. She flipped a page in her notebook and sketched a quick design. The garden would have to change; it was far too kitsch, full of flowers and vegetables. It needed to be sleek and sculptural, not sweet and rambling.

There was no sign of Seth, but she supposed he had deliberately made himself scarce. Her employer's brief here was clear enough, however. Joy's Acre was to be a luxury holiday and leisure destination and, even if it wasn't yet, there was no reason why it couldn't be. All it took was imagination and money, and she had been all but promised as much of that as she needed. In Seth's absence there was no other choice but to carry on by herself. She walked resolutely back up the path to the first cottage and rattled the door handle.

It creaked, but the door swung open, and she tutted again; it was downright irresponsible leaving them open, anyone could walk in. Sadly, the interior was just as she'd anticipated: depressing, and lacking in even the most basic of facilities. On a whim she pulled her phone from her bag and checked the display. She was right about that too – hardly any signal, and nothing in the way of Wi-Fi to connect to. She stood for a few moments more, marshalling her thoughts before heading back to the house. She had a lot of work to do.

★

The time was approaching seven o'clock when she next looked at her watch and there was still no sign of Seth. She had parked herself at the kitchen table and for the last three hours had typed steadily into her laptop. Now her initial report was virtually finished and her stomach, which so far today had only had a very unsatisfactory roadside service station sandwich, was beginning to protest.

She got up, stretching out her neck and back, and went to fill a glass from the tap. No mention had been made thus far of the domestic arrangements at Joy's Acre, but it would make sense for her and Seth to eat their meals together, daunting though that sounded. She would have to ask at the earliest opportunity; it would be helpful if she knew what was expected of her.

She threw a furtive glance over her shoulder and peered quickly and hungrily into the fridge, hoping to find something that her basic cooking skills might cope with. For the most part she lived off salads or pre-prepared foods from the posh delicatessens near where she worked and lived. She had the feeling that things would be rather different here.

To her surprise, the fridge was full of all manner of things, muddy fruit and vegetables mainly, and nothing remotely like the uniform selections sitting on little plastic trays that she was used to seeing. Aside from two pieces of salmon nestled on a plate, there seemed to be little which Madeline could turn into a quick meal, and she closed the door in a desultory fashion. She was about to inspect the contents of the bread bin she had spied earlier when she heard the front door bang shut, and she jumped guiltily.

Seth stared at her laptop before glancing up at her in perplexed manner, almost as if he'd never seen her before, or perhaps didn't expect her to still be here. His hands were covered in black, grubby oil.

'Sorry, I didn't realise the time,' he said, and then, 'I should go and shower.'

Madeline gave a nervous smile. She was still standing far too close to the fridge to have been doing anything other than inspecting it.

'No, me neither. I was thinking about dinner but I didn't know...'

'Great idea, I'm starving... The fridge is full and so are the cupboards, so just make anything you fancy. I'll only be ten minutes or so and I'm not fussy.'

He turned on his heel, leaving the room as quickly as he had entered it. Madeline stared at his back and then once more at the fridge, which she now had an overwhelming urge to kick.

Of all the nerve! It was her first day here, and although she hadn't expected a three-course meal, neither had she thought she'd have to fend for herself in this way. So far, she'd been subjected to a less than enthusiastic welcome, been left on her own for hours, and now that Seth had actually deigned to return home she was clearly expected to cook for him too. Well, he had another think coming if he thought it was acceptable to treat her like a common or garden skivvy…

★

Madeline yanked the fridge door open for a second time and then slammed it shut. There was nothing in there that she knew what to do with and she was damned if she was going to start making something from scratch, even if she could. Seth would more than likely turn his nose up at anything she prepared, and she was not about to give him the satisfaction. She lifted the lid of the bread bin. He could bloody well make do with beans on toast.

Madeline stood in front of her laptop once more, and jiggled the mouse to awaken the screen. She quickly reread the last few paragraphs of the words she had written, and gave a nod of satisfaction. It was a good report – factual and to the point without being overly derogatory, and more importantly, highlighting the vast potential of the site which was still waiting to be tapped. Madeline was just the person to sell what Joy's Acre could offer, and her report would surely convince Seth of the work that was required to bring the site up to scratch.

She cast her mind back to the brief tour of the house Seth had provided on the way up to her bedroom, and remembered him saying something about a study. If there was a printer in the house, it would surely be in there. Rummaging around in her laptop bag, she found the cable she was looking for and headed down the hallway. She might not be able to cook, but she could certainly find her way around most office equipment; getting the machine to spit out her report in all its glory took her all of five minutes.

Seth reappeared ten minutes later and demolished the plate of food in front of him in minutes. Throughout, their conversation was polite but, although Madeline made mention of her report on several occasions, she was hugely disappointed that he seemed unwilling to enter into discussion about her work. Instead he asked her a series of boring questions about her family, none of which she wanted to answer in much depth. In the end, her frustration mounting, she whisked his plate away and plonked the sheaf of papers containing her report in front of him.

'It's only my initial ideas,' she began, 'but I'd like to see what you think of these for starters before I begin to add in the detail. I think it's important that we're both singing from the same hymn sheet.'

Seth stared at her. 'What's this?' he asked.

Madeline thought she had made her last statement perfectly clear and frowned.

'What do you mean, what's this? It's my initial report. I wanted to get down to things straight away, so I've done an initial assessment of the current situation, how I see things progressing and, ultimately, where I see Joy's Acre pitched in the marketplace.'

He was still staring.

'I know I don't properly start until tomorrow, but let's face it, things are far from where they should be by now, and I thought it best to make a start as soon as possible. Have a read.'

Seth picked up the top sheet, glancing at it before spreading the other pages on the table, scattering them out of order. It set Madeline's teeth on edge. He read for perhaps five seconds before replacing the page with the others.

'How can you possibly know what I want when we've not yet discussed it?' he said slowly.

Madeline was confused for a moment until she realised what the problem was; it was surprising the number of people she'd worked with before who didn't understand the importance of clear communication.

'You don't need to worry,' she said. 'Natalie has fully briefed me on the requirements already so that I could hit the ground running. I've prepared my report accordingly; focusing on the high level of finish that even the most discerning clients will demand, and backed this up with a comprehensive range of luxury facilities with service to match. I had of course already checked out what the competition has to offer and, believe me, with what I have in mind, Joy's Acre will be unparalleled in the local area.'

Madeline tapped the uppermost page.

'It's all there,' she said. 'Please do read on. Take your time.'

Seth's jaw tightened and she could see a muscle twitching just below his right cheek. He looked like a coiled spring and subconsciously she sat slightly further back in her seat. His gaze travelled up the table towards her, as if taking her in properly for the first time.

'Miss Porter,' he said. 'Do you own a pair of work boots, or heavy shoes, wellies even? Some jeans? An overall perhaps... In fact anything that you won't mind getting dirty, dusty, torn, smelly and generally trashed. If you don't, may I suggest you go into town to buy some, because when you start work tomorrow you will most definitely be needing them. What you will not be needing, is this pile of shit.'

He picked up the sheaf of papers, pushing them roughly together before tearing them in two. His chair grated on the tiled floor as he stood up.

'I'm going out now, so I'll say goodnight. I have a key, obviously, as this is my house, so don't wait up. Have a pleasant evening and I'll see you at eight o'clock sharp tomorrow morning.'

Madeline sat in stunned disbelief as his anger reverberated around the room for several minutes after he left. What on earth had she done to deserve that? She stared at the door and then around the room, almost as if she was looking for a witness to corroborate what had just happened. She was alone.

Her brain whirred with a hundred pithy comebacks which had arrived too late. Selfish pig – he'd even left her to do all the washing-up. She thought about throwing something, and probably would have if this had been her house, but instead she snatched up the papers, her own anger rapidly reaching boiling point, and ripped them into a frenzy of confetti. She threw the handful of paper away from her, watching with satisfaction as some of it fell to the floor.

A quick check of her watch revealed there was still plenty of time to pack her things and find a place to stay for the night. Even the back end of nowhere must have hotels. She could get herself a room, something nice from the bar, dial up room service for a late-night snack and then sink into a hot bath. With any luck she'd sleep like a baby, and in the morning she could drive back to civilisation and pick up her life where she had left off. She certainly didn't need to stay here and be treated like a skivvy by a rude bully who didn't know his arse from his elbow. These thoughts sustained her all the way up the stairs and into her bedroom, where she stopped dead in disbelief...

Before she'd left the room earlier, she had laid some linen trousers and a jacket out on the bed – her favourites, the ones that had cost a fortune but always made her feel like a million dollars. In the face of an uncertain day tomorrow, she had thought that this outfit, at least, would give her the confidence to meet the situation head on, and demonstrate just how good at her job she could be. But now, plonked right in the middle, and kneading the French linen with sharp claws, was the huge ginger cat she had run into earlier.

It really was the final straw. Her howl of rage gave way to choking sobs, and the startled cat shot off the bed, between her legs, and out through the door. She curled into a ball on top of the covers and shut her eyes.

★

The light outside had turned a deep violet by the time she awoke, her face red and creased from lying in a heap, taut with dried tears and snot. She lay for a moment trying to orientate herself in the strange room, with no idea what time it was and struggling even to remember what day it was. She shifted her weight slightly, grimacing as she realised that she was still fully dressed, and now another set of clothes were rumpled beyond recognition. Something warm and solid was pressed into her back, and as she wriggled again it seemed to move with her. She sat up, confused.

She hadn't even noticed the blasted ginger cat creep back into the room, never mind the fact that it had brazenly taken up a position next to her on the bed and curled itself against her spine. Two amber eyes regarded her solemnly as if challenging her to interrupt its sleep again. She sighed, and lay back down; she had no energy to protest, and her clothes were a mess now anyway, there was little more damage that could be done.

She looked over at the clock which travelled with her everywhere and whose display now glowed from the bedside cabinet beside her. It was very nearly ten at night and as she swivelled her head to listen, she could hear no movement from within the huge house. Was Seth even home? He hadn't said where he was going, or how long he would be out for, and although it was no business of hers, she was in a strange place, where she knew no one, and where things so far had been entirely different from what she had been led to believe they would be.

She knew her tears had been a release from the last few difficult months when she had been forced to keep a tight lid on her emotions, but she couldn't remember the last time she had cried like that, and she did feel better for it – washed out, but oddly at peace. She tried to remind herself why she was here. A few hours earlier she had been intent on leaving, but she'd already run away once and, despite the circumstances, she had no real desire to do it again.

One thing was certain, however; this evening hadn't gone well and tomorrow, *if* she was staying, she would have to well and truly pick up her game. Whether in practice she was working for Seth, Agatha, or even Natalie made no difference; she must not appear weak under any circumstances and she had to hope that Seth had not been around to see or hear her tears. He might be grumpy and rude, and definitely unhappy about her presence here, but even his anger was slightly more appealing than Agatha's dismissive condescension.

Chapter 3

What on earth was that infernal noise? Madeline sat bolt upright, staring around her and listening hard. It had come from outside, but she could see the sky through the open curtains and it wasn't even properly light yet. The noise came again and this time she got to her feet, padding across the room to investigate.

Her window overlooked the garden, and it was only now that she was looking down on it she realised just how large it was, and just how much was planted there. Not a spare inch of soil showed, and there were even various troughs and planters dotted around, all of which were hung with flowers or foliage. She wasn't a gardener by any stretch of the imagination, but even she could tell that it would need a huge amount of work to keep everything in its current condition. She shuddered, sincerely hoping that this was not a duty that would fall to her; goodness only knows what state her fingernails would be in afterwards.

As she watched, two huge birds wandered into her line of sight; pheasants. She had seen enough of the stupid birds lying dead at the side of the road to know what they were, and these two seemed to be no cleverer, strolling aimlessly about like they hadn't a clue where they were. A raucous screech split the morning air, accompanied by a weird shaking and fluffing of feathers as one of the birds arched its neck and flapped its wings. It was clearly out to impress. Fabulous – she was trying to sleep and the local wildlife was hell-bent on having sex. She dragged the curtains across the window and stomped back to bed.

Her head had been back on the pillow for only a few seconds when she sat up again. No, the whole point of leaving the curtains open in the first place had been to get an early start. Madeline was an early riser by nature – mornings were when she was at her best and most creative – and she was determined to start as she meant to go on. Languishing in bed wasn't going to accomplish anything and, despite a slight stiffness and woolly feeling in her head from last night's tears, she felt cleansed and energised – optimistic even.

She eyed her wardrobe despondently, Seth's words about having overalls still ringing in her ears. Pretty much everything she had brought with her was tailored and very expensive. She didn't really do casual, and she certainly didn't do scruffy. Her life in London had been punctuated by either work itself, or work-related events and activities. She dressed up for dinner with friends, and on the very rare occasions she had time to herself at home, she only ever wore jeans as a last resort. She shook her head; it wasn't happening. She might be working hard – she had no problem with that – but she was damn well going to do it in clothes that she felt comfortable in. She selected a soft pink striped blouse and a pair of navy trousers, laid them out neatly on the bed and went in search of a hot shower.

Half an hour later, with her expertly cut and highlighted hair curling gently onto her shoulders, she made her way back downstairs. It wasn't even six o'clock yet, so she entered the kitchen as quietly as she could, suddenly remembering the state she had left the kitchen in last night. Not only would the bean-covered saucepan and plates from last night's meal still be piled up next to the sink, but she had covered the table and a good part of the floor with tiny pieces of paper. She had no idea what time Seth had returned home last night, but with any luck he hadn't ventured into the kitchen, or if he had, then she could clear away the mess quickly now and neither of them would have to refer to it again.

The kitchen however, was spotless. Not only that, but the most heavenly smell of freshly baked bread was wafting over from a fresh loaf that stood cooling on a wooden chopping board beside the toaster. She leaned closer to inhale its aroma, gently touching one side with the back of her hand. It was still warm.

She checked her watch against the wooden clock on the wall, but she was not mistaken. *Who on earth gets up early enough to make bread which is ready this time of the morning?* She picked up the notepad which lay beside the bread and read the brief message. Then, with a small smile tugging at the corners of her mouth, she picked up the bread knife and cut two thick slices. *Thank you very much*, she thought, *I will most definitely help myself.*

Even after she had eaten, or rather, devoured the bread slathered in butter and jam, done the washing-up and wiped away her crumbs, there was still an hour and a half before her eight o'clock meeting with Seth. Yesterday had not gone at all well, and she had realised, somewhere in between her ranting last night and waking this morning, that she had been very insensitive in her approach to Seth and the work that was required at Joy's Acre.

Today, she would listen. She would ask Seth for his direction and give him the opportunity to explain his own vision before she tried to persuade him of her own ideas. Seth might own this place, but under the arrangement he had with Agatha he was not the one paying her salary and, as such, her loyalties had to lie elsewhere. There were, however, perhaps more tactful ways to play this out.

To kill the time before their meeting, she wandered over to the cottages again, to make a few more notes and take some photos on her phone. Whichever way she looked at it, yesterday's analysis stood firm. She really could see no other way to transform these cottages and get them turning a profit. They had to go large. Large and expensive admittedly, but it was the only way to attract big money in return. Her excitement mounted as the time neared eight o'clock and she returned to the kitchen to meet Seth.

By quarter past nine, Madeline's jaw was aching from gritting her teeth in rage as the minutes had passed. Seth had stood her up.

Her report from yesterday might have been turned to confetti, but it was still safely saved on her laptop and now she had even more to add to it. If Seth couldn't be bothered to show up to their meeting then she would simply email the whole lot to Agatha instead and, while she was at it, perhaps Agatha might also be interested to learn of Seth's shortcomings. She fired up her laptop and waited for the available Wi-Fi connections to show. She'd probably need a password to connect, but until Seth returned and she could ask him for it she could always use her phone as a hotspot.

She frowned at the screen in front of her. More specifically, at the small pop-up window which showed a total of zero available routers. This was getting to be a joke. She stood up, ready to search the house, but instead her eyes settled on her car keys which Seth had hung on one of a series of hooks by the pantry door. Getting out of this godforsaken place was a much better idea, even if it was for only a couple of hours.

★

Second time around, it wasn't as difficult to find her way around. If you turned left after leaving the narrow lane from the house (Madeline refused to call it a driveway), the road took you to the small market town which had been the last vestige of civilisation on her way down here. Or, if you turned right, the road took you to the same small market town, except that the journey seemed to take about ten minutes longer as the road climbed right to the top of the hill the estate sat on, before dropping down the other side and swinging back around. Having navigated carefully along both routes, Madeline gave up trying to get anywhere else and settled on turning the car in to a small car park by the war memorial.

An hour later, having trudged up and down a succession of streets and browsed a few shops, she pushed open the door of the Frog and Wicket and plonked herself on a bar stool. A spiky-pink-haired barmaid was at the far end of the bar, deep in conversation with the only other customer in the place. With a sideways glance at Madeline, she laid a hand on the arm of the man she was chatting to and walked over.

'Please tell me I can have a coffee or I might die,' Madeline said, not entirely sure she was joking.

The young girl looked her up and down. 'Let me guess… I reckon you're a skinny caramel macchiato?'

Madeline looked up in surprise.

'You know what one of those is?' she said incredulously.

A pierced eyebrow arched skyward. 'You're looking at Coffee Club's barista of the month, six months in a row. I know my way around.'

'What happened to month seven?'

The girl pulled a face. 'Swanky cow from the Salford branch came down, didn't she? Right know-it-all she was. Fat ankles as well.'

A laugh escaped before Madeline could stop it. 'So, did you get your own back?'

'Nah. Wasn't worth it. I mean, it's only bloody coffee, right?... So, do you want one or not?'

Madeline nodded vigorously. 'Oh, please.'

'I can do a flat white, filter or a cappuccino. Best I can do. You realise we're a pub, right...'

'So how come the macchiato then, how did you know?'

The girl gave her another appraising glance. 'Well, skinny... that's obvious, and the macchiato... well, dressed like that, I reckon you like something a bit smooth and sophisticated.'

'Which leaves the caramel?'

She pulled a face. 'Yeah well, no offence, but you should have seen your face when you walked in here. I haven't seen anything that sour-looking since my little nephew accidently sucked on a lemon wedge. Thought maybe you could do with a little sweetening up.'

Madeline burst out laughing, taking an instant liking to the straight-talking barmaid. She held out her hand.

'I'm Madeline.'

The girl rolled her eyes.

'Jeez, I can't call you that,' she said grimacing. She tipped her head on one side. 'So, Maddie, what'll it be, filter or cappuccino? I can do chocolate sprinkles as well.'

Madeline let the name play around in her head. She'd never, ever, let anyone call her Maddie in London. But then, she wasn't in London, was she? Perhaps it was time for a change.

She smiled. 'Maddie's fine,' she said. 'And I'll have a cappuccino please, if that's okay.' She glanced around the room. 'I don't suppose you have Wi-Fi here?'

There was a swift flicking of her eyes to one side. 'No, sorry. I'll just get your drink.'

Maddie sighed. Why was she not surprised? She pulled her phone out of her bag to check the signal while she waited for her coffee. She was stumped now; without an internet connection, she couldn't get any further with the Joy's Acre project. She might as well just go back to the farm. How on earth did anyone get anything done around here? She watched as her phone buffered endlessly trying to load her emails and then clicked it off with a tut just as her drink arrived. It slid across the counter towards her.

'I'm Trixie,' the barmaid said, 'and I didn't give you that,' she added, her voice dropping to a whisper.

Maddie looked down at the mug in front of her and the small slip of paper lying by its side. On it was written two words; 'Red' and 'Rum'. She stared at Trixie.

'Is that what I think it is?' she asked.

'I expect so.' Trixie winked. 'The landlord has a gambling problem, hence the password. Once you've logged on, you'd better destroy that, otherwise I'll be forced to kill you.'

Maddie looked back at the pub, indicating the tables behind her with a nod of her head. 'Is it okay if I sit and do some work for a bit?'

Trixie waved an airy hand. 'No skin off my nose,' she said. 'Though I expect you'll be wanting some food now, won't you?'

'Oh I see…' said Maddie, suddenly understanding. It was the least she could do. 'Well, yes, that would be lovely. What can I have?'

Trixie regarded her solemnly as if weighing her up. 'Do you like mushrooms?'

Maddie nodded.

'Okay, then. Leave it with me.' She waved a hand at the table. 'Go on, sit. I'll bring it when it's ready.'

She couldn't have protested even if she wanted to; Trixie had vanished through a door at one end of the bar. Alone once more, Maddie carried her bags over to the table, coffee and the slip of paper in her other hand. Settling down, she pulled out her laptop and logged on.

For a few minutes it was just like being back in London. Not only did the Wi-Fi password work, but the connection was super-fast. Maddie was in her element, calling up all her favourite websites she visited whenever she was working on a new project, and suddenly all her excitement came rushing back. This was what she was good at, she reminded herself as she began tapping away on the keyboard at a furious pace.

She was so engrossed in her work she didn't even see Trixie approaching the table.

'There you go,' she said, laying down a wide shallow dish and some cutlery wrapped in a napkin. 'Come on, put that away,' she added, nodding towards Maddie's laptop, 'it'll go cold quickly.'

Maddie looked up from her screen at the food in front of her with a startled expression on her face. Nestled in the centre of the bowl sat three thick rounds of bruschetta toast, tumbling with at least four different types of mushroom and covered in a buttery sauce. Flaked across the top were shards of parmesan, or pecorino perhaps, a sprinkling of parsley providing the finishing touch. The smell made Maddie's nostrils quiver.

She took up the cutlery. 'This looks amazing,' she said.

Trixie jutted out her chin a little defensively.

'It's only mushrooms on toast,' she replied. 'But it's *good* mushrooms on toast.'

'And I'm suddenly ravenous,' Maddie said. 'I'm sure I'll do it justice.'

She speared a fat mushroom and popped it into her mouth as if to prove her point. She nodded approvingly as a burst of garlicky juice filled her mouth as she bit into it.

Trixie left her to it, returning to the man at the bar and leaning across to chat to him as Maddie ate steadily. She hadn't had high hopes for the Frog and Wicket when she'd walked through the door, but it was proving to be a little oasis of civility in an otherwise frustratingly ill-equipped town.

By the time Trixie came to remove her empty dish some while later, Maddie had already filled two mood boards with ideas and several potential schemes, all of which she could expand on if required. She rolled her shoulders, easing the tension in her neck.

'That really was lovely, thank you,' she said. 'I was beginning to despair of ever finding anywhere I could work from. And if you carry on serving food like I've just eaten I may have to keep finding an excuse to come back.'

Trixie shrugged. 'Yeah, well, don't broadcast it, you'll get me the sack.'

'What do you mean?' Maddie asked, suddenly noticing Trixie was clutching Maddie's empty dish a little anxiously.

'Well, this isn't exactly on the menu… It's just a thing I do, okay. No big deal.'

Maddie looked around her. 'Does this pub even sell food?'

'Yeah, it does. But I don't broadcast the real menu. It's full of unhealthy over-processed cack that the idiot landlord thinks the punters will eat by the ton.' She paused momentarily, waiting for Maddie's raised eyebrows to descend. 'Sausage and chips, burgers and chips, scampi and chips, and pie and chips. Oh, and not forgetting, egg and chips and chips and chips.' Her voice was scathing.

'Oh, I see…' agreed Maddie. 'It's not exactly awe-inspiring, is it? Perhaps you should point out that the menu could do with a little… updating.'

'Well I did when I first came here, but after the eighth or ninth time I gave up. Not least because I was told very firmly to put up or shut up or he'd find a barmaid who was able to keep her opinions to herself.'

'He doesn't sound like a very enlightened man, your boss.'

Trixie leaned in towards Maddie. 'He's a total arse actually. But don't tell anyone I said that either.'

Maddie grinned, picturing in her head a beer-swilling, overweight, slack-jawed stereotype. He was probably nothing like that in real life, but the image made her chuckle.

'He does have really fast Wi-Fi though.'

'Yeah, so that he can stream porn and play on his gambling sites all day. Now there's enlightenment for you. The broadband is rubbish around here – as you've probably discovered – so he gets his beamed in via a radio signal. I mean, how sad is that?'

A tiny seed of an idea took root in Maddie's head. 'Very. But I didn't even know such a thing existed. How does it work?'

Trixie shrugged again. 'Beats me. Only thing I know is that we have a little receiver thing on the side of the pub instead of getting the broadband through the phone line.' She juggled the crockery in her hands. 'Anyway, do you want another coffee?'

Maddie looked down at her laptop; she was nearly done.

'Why not?' she replied. 'One for the road, as they say.'

Trixie grinned and turned away and Maddie watched her go, her head thrumming with even more new ideas. The barmaid's talents were clearly being wasted here, and even though she seemed resigned to her fate, Maddie suspected it wouldn't take much to fire up her old enthusiasms once more. She hoped so. Because if she could, Maddie would be the first in line to give her a job.

Chapter 4

It was late afternoon by the time Maddie returned to the farm. She had deliberately chosen to return to Joy's Acre from the opposite direction to when she first arrived. The journey took slightly longer but even though this gave her more time to review the thoughts in her head, it was not her only reason for taking this route. The approach to the farm from this direction was far more open – the road wider, and bordered by fields rather than the slightly oppressive avenue of trees, and as Maddie pulled into a passing place at the side of the road, her suspicions were confirmed. There was a perfect view of the farm from here. She got out of the car and gazed across the fields in front of her.

She could see the thatched cottage clearly, its walls glowing golden in the afternoon sun, and behind, the full extent of the gardens, dotted with colour. At the rear sat the farmhouse, looking handsome with an air of comforting permanence about it. She stood for a few more minutes letting the spring sunshine warm her back before climbing back into her car and returning to Joy's Acre.

Even here, the slanting sun had turned the courtyard golden so that the mud looked slightly more appealing than it had the day before. There was no sign of the dogs, which meant that Seth was elsewhere too. She gave the chickens a wide berth and let herself into the house.

Dumping her collection of carrier bags down onto the kitchen table, she suddenly remembered what one of them contained and she snatched it up again. It was bad luck to put new shoes on the table and she needed all the help she could get at the moment!

The room looked as she had left it. It seemed an age since she had stood there this morning, raging at Seth's non-appearance. She reminded herself that the day had turned into rather a good one after all, and she certainly didn't need to go looking for reasons to tarnish her mood, so she nipped upstairs with her bags to get changed.

When she had tried her new clothes on in the shop they had looked perfectly fine. Perhaps it was the lighting, or the fact that she was surrounded by mannequins and staff who were all dressed the same way, but back in the comfort of her own room her reflection told a different story. All she needed was a rosette and a horse to complete her ridiculous new countryside look.

She took off the padded gilet and leather boots, but even her socks looked horrifyingly jolly. What on earth had possessed her? The jeans were reasonably okay, but the polo shirt with the giant emblem was stiff and the collar scratched her neck. She grimaced at her reflection, feeling about twenty years older than she was, and yanked the top back off again, throwing it onto the bed behind her. The trouble was, between these clothes and the ones she had brought with her, she really didn't have a choice.

She reached for the shirt she had been wearing earlier, still hung neatly on the back of a chair where she had left it, and shrugged it back on. This time, biting her teeth against the horror she was wreaking on the fine cotton, she rolled up the sleeves and tied the unbuttoned ends loosely at the bottom. As she pushed her feet back into the new boots she knew they would doubtless give her blisters, but they were better than the court shoes she had been wearing this morning. Pulling the legs of her jeans down over the top of the boots, she did her best to hide the vast expanse of pristine leather. With one last look in the mirror, she undid one more button on her shirt, took a deep breath and headed back down to the kitchen.

Maddie had no idea what time the evening meal was eaten but she was determined that today would not turn out to be a repeat of the day before. If Seth *had* been out all day, then he would be starving. What better way to soften him up than by cooking him a hearty meal? Once she'd got him on side, then he'd be far more amenable to what she had to say. But what did men eat when they needed something substantial? She hadn't a clue.

Ten minutes later she had gathered an array of possible ingredients from the fridge and cupboards on the table. All she needed now was a recipe that included some of them and was easy enough for a novice like her to produce. Normally she would head straight to the internet for ideas, but that was off the cards here. She supposed she could root through the house for a cookbook, but as a visitor that seemed far too intimate an activity just now. She picked up a carrot and stared at it, waiting for inspiration to strike.

She nearly jumped out of her skin as the kitchen door was unceremoniously kicked wide open and a young woman entered the room. Her wellies were caked in mud and her hands and arms were fighting against an array of vegetables which threatened to spill from the fold of her bright blue apron. She gave Maddie a wary smile and crossed to the sink, dumping the apron's contents into it, expertly catching a potato which bounced on the rim. She turned around, hand extended.

'Madeline?' she asked, with a slightly wider smile this time. 'I'm Clara.'

Maddie took her grubby hand gingerly, feeling the roughness of the skin which met hers.

'Maddie.' She nodded, taking in the newcomer who appeared so very much at home in Seth's kitchen. Two huge blue eyes twinkled back at her, framed by a mess of freckles and a too wide mouth and a mane of messy, honey-blonde hair to her slender waist. She shouldn't have been beautiful, but she was. She was obviously Seth's girlfriend, with her matching sun-tanned face and the way she moved so comfortably around the kitchen. Funny he hadn't mentioned her before, but he'd hardly had the chance.

'Seth mentioned that I'd find you here,' she said. 'How are things going?'

Maddie wasn't sure how she could possibly answer that when she didn't know herself, or indeed what Seth might have said about her.

'Good.' She nodded. 'Well, you know, bit strange, getting used to a new place and all that. Still finding my feet.'

'Cleaning out the cupboards though?'

Maddie narrowed her eyes, suddenly realising she had strayed into someone else's territory, albeit unintentionally.

'Erm, no.' She pulled a face. 'Wondering if I should make dinner actually. Wondering *what* to make for dinner.' She looked into Clara's open face, unsure whether to continue. 'I'm not what you'd call a natural cook…'

'Oh, I see… Well, Seth's not fussy. Anything you make will be fine.'

Maddie shifted her weight onto the other foot. 'Will you be staying to eat as well?' she asked, wondering why she suddenly felt like the hired help.

Clara's response was immediate. 'Crikey no, I'm supposed to have finished work hours ago, but you know how it is. Still, delivering this lot was my final task for the day and now I'm very definitely headed for home.'

They didn't live together? Her confusion must have shown on her face.

'I'm the gardener,' added Clara. 'Not a girlfriend, or a wife, you can stand easy.'

Maddie's face flushed. 'Sorry, was I that obvious?'

'Not at all. Standing in another woman's kitchen is never an easy place to be. Perhaps it will help you to know that as far as I'm aware Seth is only ever intending to be married to this place. So if you did have a notion to clear out the cupboards you wouldn't be stepping on anyone's toes.'

'Except Seth's perhaps?' asked Maddie with a smile. 'I don't think he's all that happy with my being here at all. I was supposed to be meeting with him today but he didn't show up. I just thought that making dinner might be the way to put me back in his good books. Well, at least long enough for us to have a proper discussion.'

'Ah, well, it's one way… possibly.'

Maddie suddenly felt very exposed, and looked around desperately for an opportunity to change the subject.

'So are the vegetables for anything in particular?' she asked, eyeing the sink.

'General consumption,' answered Clara. 'I just bring whatever looks gorgeous and needs eating. The garden always produces far too much for this house alone; the rest we sell at the local market.'

Maddie's eyes fell on the familiar shape of a potato – at least she thought they were potatoes, there was a lot more mud on them than she was used to.

'So, could I use them, if I needed to…' Her voice trailed away as she trawled her brain for the few recipes it contained.

'Yes, just don't mash the spuds though, they're too new.' She checked her watch and began to untie her apron. 'I wouldn't make anything that spoils easily either; going by past experience Seth could be in any time between now and midnight.'

Maddie's face fell as things seemed to be getting harder, not easier.

'Maybe a casserole?' suggested Clara. 'They're always a good standby.'

'Right…'

Clara was walking towards the door, but she turned at the last minute, hair swishing about her shoulders.

'Listen, it's probably none of my business, but I'm guessing you're trying to make a good impression here.'

Maddie nodded.

'And, if you don't mind me saying so, you look like you could do with a little help…'

Maddie nodded again, dropping her eyes at the last minute, embarrassed at being caught so out of her depth. But deep down she knew if she was going to make a success of things here, there was one thing she needed to do, and that was to get Seth on her side, fast.

'It's just that I've come from London, and food there, well it's different. I ate out a lot…'

'So what sort of thing did you have in mind?'

Maddie dropped her head even further, expelling a slow breath.

'I have absolutely no idea,' she admitted. 'And even if I did, I'm a useless cook.'

Clara gave her a warm smile this time. 'Useless, or inexperienced?'

That was kind of her. She had no reason to be nice to Maddie at all, but whatever her motive, she was glad of it. She gave a tentative smile in reply.

'Probably both,' she said.

'Well, let's find out, shall we?' Clara dumped her apron on the table and crossed to the sink. 'First things first,' she said.

Hands washed, she swung the mane of hair over her shoulder and, in one continuous movement, plaited it into a thick braid. She fastened it with a band that materialised from nowhere and threw it backwards once more, surveying the contents of the table as she did so.

'So, I'm thinking some sort of vegetable casserole… perhaps with lentils, or beans, a bit smokey maybe… and some cheese scones to mop up the juice.'

Maddie looked at her, incredulous. 'We can do all that? Will we have time?'

'Sure. That's the best thing about it; the longer it cooks the better it gets. We'll just throw it all in the oven and when Seth gets back later it will be ready to serve, whatever the time. He'll be dead chuffed.'

'Will he?'

'Guaranteed,' said Clara firmly. 'Seth is pretty immoveable when it comes to certain things, and his passion doesn't always show itself in a good light, but I've never known him to be unappreciative of a generous spirit. When in doubt, try to remember that.'

'It sounds as if you might be talking from experience?'

Clara paused, holding Maddie's look, her expression still gentle, and yet there was a flicker of what her mum would have called backbone.

'I owe Seth a few favours, that's all, so I look out for him when and if I can. I'd hate to see him get hurt.'

Her message was loud and clear.

'So, not a wife or a girlfriend then,' said Maddie, 'and yet I still feel like I've strayed into your territory.'

There was a small smile. 'It's a long story… and one best kept for another day.' The smile grew bigger. 'But of course I also know why you're here. I've been helping Seth cut back Agatha's hedge today, and she was very vocal about the huge sums of money she's prepared to inject into this place now that she has an *expert* on board. She was also very opinionated about what she expects from you…'

She picked up an onion from the table and handed it to Maddie.

'I can see you have a lot to lose, Maddie, and quite a lot to prove if you're going to do justice to Agatha's vision for this place. Just bear in mind that this puts you in a rather awkward position; she and Seth don't exactly see eye to eye when it comes to what's right for Joy's Acre. All I ask is that you keep an open mind.'

Maddie took the proffered vegetable. 'I'll do my best,' she replied, her heart sinking at the idea of playing piggy in the middle. 'Thanks for the warning.'

'It's not a warning, Maddie, please don't think that – well, not unless you're planning on stitching Seth up, in which case I'll cut your heart out with a spoon. But Seth does need some help, so today, I'm here as a friend.' She smiled.

It was kind, but it was still a warning, thought Maddie.

'I can only imagine what Agatha has said about my role here, and I suspect it's made you rather suspicious of me. I'd have thought you'd prefer it if I fell flat on my face and crawled back to London, and yet here you are still helping.'

Clara winced. 'I'm cautious of course, but I can see possibilities and I'd like to see how this turns out. I'm a gardener, remember; it's in my nature to nurture things.'

★

Seth arrived back just after seven. Maddie heard the thump of his boots hitting the floor in the hallway just moments before he almost fell through the door, supported only by the two dogs at his side. He crashed onto the nearest chair as the two dogs rushed past him towards her, cornering Maddie by the sink as they bounced up and down, tongues lolling. Seth appeared not to have even noticed.

She tried to shrink back into the space, but any movement she made only served to excite the dogs even further. Remembering Seth's advice from the day before, she put down a tentative hand to say hello, hoping that once she had patted them they would run off somewhere else and leave her be. She snatched her hand back at the first touch of slobber, a small squeak escaping as she grimaced with distaste.

'I know, I know,' came Seth's voice, low and grumbling. 'Just give me ten, for goodness' sake.'

He looked up, slow recognition dawning on his face as if he had just seen Maddie for the first time.

Maddie wasn't sure if he was talking to the dogs, or to her. She gave a tentative smile.

'I tried the stroking thing,' she said, as he frowned at her, 'but…'

'They're hungry,' he said, eyes glazed.

'Oh…' She looked at the two ravenous beasts in front of her and pulled her hands even closer to her chest. 'I could feed them, maybe.'

'Do you even know where their food is kept?'

'No, but you could point and I—'

'Quicker to do it myself.' He sighed, lurching from the chair and out of the door again on a tide of wagging tails.

Maddie brushed at the front of her clothes and quickly turned to wash her hands, shuddering at the slimy feeling on her fingers. At least she hadn't lost any.

A few moments later Seth reappeared, taking up the same position as earlier, before sitting forward and cradling his head in his hands.

'You couldn't flick the kettle on, could you?' he asked without looking up. 'I'm dying for a coffee.'

Bugger, she should have thought of that.

'I'll make you one, shall I?' she said. 'Would you like it now, or with dinner? It should be ready.'

The hands slowly came away from his head. He stared at her.

'Dinner?'

'Yeah, I made a casserole… stew… type thing. I wasn't sure what time you'd be in, you see. It seemed the most sensible idea.'

It wasn't a complete lie, she had helped Clara to make it. In fact, after a rather tentative start the two of them had worked well together.

He was still staring at her.

She swallowed, looking nervously at him. Had she done the wrong thing? Perhaps she wasn't really allowed in his kitchen after all.

'There are some cheese scones to go with it as well… if you like them.'

A slow smile gathered on his face, which bit by bit seemed to animate the rest of him as well.

'I thought you would have eaten already.'

'No, well, I had quite a good lunch so I wasn't really that hungry. Happy to wait.'

Now that was a lie; lunch had been hours ago, and she was absolutely starving.

His eyes searched her face, but he seemed to accept what she was saying.

'I ought to go and get changed then, I'm a bit…' He searched for a suitable adjective, and then gave up. Maddie wasn't surprised, she could think of quite a few, and none of them were complimentary.

'I'll make that coffee then, shall I?' she asked, turning to the sink with the kettle in her hand. 'Was it one, or two sugars?'

'One and a half-ish, I'm trying to cut down.'

She nodded, pulling straight the smile that threatened. There was hardly an ounce of fat on him as it was, what on earth was he cutting down for?

The coffee made, she began to dish up their meal, anxiously pulling open the oven door and removing the casserole dish for inspection. She needn't have worried. The stew was rich, dark and fragrant, and as she spooned it into two large bowls she realised how satisfied she felt. It had been a very long time since she had gone to so much trouble over a meal, but the weird thing was that it hadn't felt like an arduous task at all. Chatting to Clara had only made it less so, and really it had been ridiculously simple to put together. Even the scones, which she had never made before, had outperformed all her expectations. She sniffed the heaped bowls, sending up a little prayer that Seth liked it.

They sat down opposite each other across the huge scrubbed pine table, as Maddie searched fruitlessly for a way to begin the conversation, and Seth looked, frankly, dumbstruck. He waved a hand towards the food.

'I really didn't expect this,' he said. 'But I'm very grateful. It's been a long day.'

He didn't elaborate, but then he didn't need to. Clara's mention of Agatha's name earlier was enough to help her guess exactly what sort of a day Seth had had.

Maddie gathered herself together and took a breath.

'I felt it was something I should do,' she said, 'after yesterday, I mean. Perhaps it wasn't the best of starts and I—'

'Really shouldn't apologise,' butted in Seth. 'I was in a vile mood, which wasn't your fault. I made no effort to make you feel welcome, and I'm sorry.' He took a scone from the plate in front of them. 'I do need help here, Madeline, so please don't think that I'm ungrateful. It's more that the circumstances of it are not exactly—'

'What you had in mind? Or would have chosen if you'd had any say in the matter…'

His eyes met hers. 'Yes,' he said quietly. 'Sorry.'

'And I probably shouldn't have shoved my ideas down your throat without at least doing you the courtesy of listening to what you want for this place, so I'm sorry too.'

There, she had said it. She had apologised. A line had been drawn and perhaps now they would both be able to move forward. She reached to pick up her spoon. Her ideas could wait until the morning, now was not the time.

'Do you like wine?'

The question surprised her. It seemed out of keeping with their surroundings somehow, but she nodded a vehement yes. Good grief, maybe there was some semblance of civilisation here after all.

Seth smiled, excusing himself and returning moments later with a bottle of wine, not quite full she noticed.

'Is red okay?'

She nodded again. 'Is the pope a Catholic?'

He grinned, just a little, as he poured out two large glasses.

'To Joy's Acre then,' he said once he was seated again.

She raised her glass a little hesitantly. 'To Joy's Acre.'

The wine flowed over her tongue like silk. It was good, very good.

★

It was only as she lay in bed hours later that she realised that virtually all of the conversation had been about her. He had asked her about her family, and although there wasn't much to tell, she had talked about her parents who, only last year, had sold up and moved to the Dorset coast. Her father had taken early retirement from his job as a civil engineer and now indulged his passion for wine by opening a small shop there. Her brother, by contrast, was never in the country for longer than about two weeks. As a physiotherapist under contract to the English athletics team he was regularly on tour with them and she was lucky if she saw him more than once a year. No, she had told him, they weren't particularly close.

Every now and again she had tried to turn the conversation back around, but somehow, without her even noticing, Seth had steered it back in her direction all too quickly. Perhaps it had been nerves, possibly the wine, but more than likely Seth's expert questioning, but she had babbled on incessantly about her childhood, early career in advertising, holidays, even the cars she drove, and now she realised she scarcely knew any more about Seth than she had at the start of the evening, whereas he had probably been bored rigid. She cringed at the thought.

It had been a good evening though. The wine had broken the ice, and after they had sampled the first spoonful of casserole, they were both surprised by how good it tasted and had eaten steadily. The time had melted away.

She was about to turn over and go to sleep when the soft creak of her bedroom door startled her. She must have left it ajar and it was now opening.

To her relief the tip of a ginger tail was all that came through it and she almost giggled when she felt the edge of the bed dip and soft paws slink across the bed covers. Her outstretched hand met the soft head and almost immediately a rumbling purr split the silence. The cat worked its way closer to her and, just as it had intended, tucked himself into her side as she lay down again.

She was almost asleep when she realised what she was doing. She would never let an animal sleep on her bed – the hairs, the germs! She sat up, grasping the dozing cat and, to its disgust, depositing it firmly on the landing. Closing the door resolutely behind her, she leaned against it so that it clicked shut and padded back to bed. Six minutes later she was fast asleep.

Chapter 5

The smell of baking bread the next morning could have drawn a dead man from his bed, and by the time Maddie had scrambled from underneath the duvet and hit the shower, the most tantalising smell of bacon had joined it too. It was later than she had planned, but she had slept so well that the clock had marched past her usual waking time without her so much as turning a hair. Now that she was up though, she was anxious to get going.

By the look of things Seth had already been at the table for some while before she finally joined him. His plate was empty and the coffee pot which sat in front of him was only a third full.

'It must have been the wine,' she said, moving to join him. 'I'm not normally this late up.'

Seth was warming his hands around his mug. 'I'm not sure that's true,' he remarked. 'I think you're a girl who's quite used to a drop or two of wine.' He grinned. 'More likely it was the dark that made you sleep, that and the absolute quiet. I can't imagine London being either of those things.'

He was right of course. While she was living there it was easy to convince herself that she was used to the noise, even in the small hours of the morning, but here it was easy to forget quite how insistent it was.

'Have I still got time for something to eat?' she asked, eyeing his plate.

'Sit down,' he replied. 'I'll get you a drink. Bacon sandwich to go with it?'

She hesitated. Breakfast was usually fruit and some yoghurt. If she carried on at this rate she'd be the size of a house, never mind the state of her arteries. Trouble was, it smelled so good… Perhaps if she just had it every now and again.

'I probably shouldn't,' she began, 'but just a small one wouldn't hurt, would it?'

He gave her an odd look as he rose from the table.

'I can't make them small,' he replied. 'And in any case, with the amount of work I've got planned for us today, a small one won't do you any good at all.' He was slapping rashers of bacon between pieces of bread at least an inch thick. 'Can't have you keeling over on me.'

Maddie stared at the plate in front of her and at the biggest sandwich she had ever seen. Never mind breakfast, at this rate she'd still be eating come lunchtime.

Seth was hovering by the table. 'Listen, I just need to go and have a word with Clara about something. I won't be too long, but take your time.'

She scarcely had any choice, it was just about all she could do to open her mouth wide enough to get the sandwich in there in the first place. She took a bite and began to chew. Best. Bacon. Sandwich. Ever.

Amazingly, she had nearly finished by the time Seth arrived back. She eyed the bags he was carrying, wondering what he was looking quite so uncomfortable about. She soon found out.

'Now don't take this the wrong way…'

She hated that sentence.

'But I couldn't help noticing that you and Clara were roughly the same size and… well, she has some things here, work-type clothes that she doesn't wear any more, and I thought, we thought, that you might be able to make use of them.'

She looked down at her brand-new jeans and polo top. 'But I bought...' She looked up at him. 'What's wrong with the things I have?'

He shifted his weight from one foot to the other.

'Nothing,' he said quickly, 'it's just that they're too... nice... new, even. We're going to get really filthy and you need to be comfortable.' He handed her the bags. 'Have a look and see if there's anything you like. It's not compulsory.'

She wasn't sure what worried her the most; the fact that he didn't think her new country clothes were suitable, or that they were about to get very dirty.

'Well if we're about to get filthy then the clothes I have on will cease to be nice or new-looking, won't they? Problem solved. And I'm quite comfortable, thank you.' She peered into the top of the bags. 'I'll take these upstairs and then let's make a start, shall we.'

He didn't mean anything by it, she repeated to herself all the way up the stairs. *He was just trying to be helpful. Today is going to be a good day, and nothing is going to spoil it.* She repeated it like a mantra as she laid the carrier bags on the bed and picked up her hairbrush. Getting filthy or not, there were certain professional standards to maintain, and that included the way she looked. She twisted her hair quickly into a bun and neatly fastened it with pins before reaching for her lipstick. Now she was ready to face the world. She plucked at the collar of her new top, running a finger inside to find the bit that was sticking in her, to no avail. No, she was perfectly comfortable.

★

'You have got to be kidding me?' She couldn't help herself. It was the first thing that came into her head. She stared at the pitchfork she'd just been given. If this was a joke, it was seriously unfunny. And if it wasn't a joke…

'Say that again, Seth, I don't think I heard you quite right.'

He grinned at her. 'I told you we'd get filthy.'

'You seriously want me to pull the *thatch* off this *roof*?'

'Not all of it, no. And I'm going to be doing the pulling off, what I need is you underneath to collect it up and barrow it away.'

They were standing in the garden of the first cottage that Maddie had looked at when she arrived, peering up at the roof.

'You can see the problem; these cottages are several hundred years old, and a good thatch might only last thirty years or so. This one is long overdue for replacement.'

She eyed the mess of straw, moss and cobwebs above her. 'But it's *disgusting*.'

'Hmm,' agreed Seth, 'but just imagine how it's going to look when it's redone.'

He had completely missed her point.

'No,' she said pointedly, 'I mean it's *disgusting*. I dread to think what you could catch from that. It's filthy.'

'Well, yes…' He trailed off as he lowered his eyes from the roof, looking at her for the first time. 'I think I mentioned that…' He ground to a halt.

Maddie planted her feet even firmer. 'I can't believe you think it's acceptable to even ask me to do such a thing, never mind actually expect me to do it. Can I remind you what my position is here? I'm your Development and Marketing Executive, not a builder's navvy.'

'Yes, and I'm your boss.' His eyes flashed at her.

'You're not actually, Agatha is. I'm sure when she gets to hear about this—'

'Madeline?' Seth's voice was dangerously quiet. 'Agatha pays your wages, as per our agreement. What you do here, however, is under my direction. Now, I would have thought that even you can see that it's all well and good being a Development and Marketing Executive, but there's a teeny tiny flaw in your plan...' He looked up pointedly. 'You don't actually have anything to develop and market yet...'

'I know that, I'm not stupid!' She drew herself up, standing as tall as she could. How dare he? If he wasn't careful he'd get the pitchfork right up his...

'Maybe not, but you are supposedly: creative, resourceful and a natural problem solver. A highly motivated people person, skilled in verbal communication and negotiation...'

He was quoting from her CV, the bastard. She flushed bright red.

'So, time to prove it. Tom the thatcher is coming tomorrow to make a start on this baby here, and he's expecting to be able to get going straight away. I promised him I would have the groundwork done in time. Are you able to suggest another way of removing the top layers of thatch in readiness for tomorrow, other than by actually removing them?'

'Try pulling the whole bloody place down, that should do it,' she muttered furiously.

'Ah, but then you'd have even *less* to market, wouldn't you?'

She glared at him. 'Do you know there's one thing I hate even more than a smart arse... and that's a smart arse who thinks they're funny.' She glared at him. 'Now bloody well shut up and show me what to do.'

He rolled his eyes dramatically. 'Anyone would think you were afraid of a bit of hard work.' He made a beckoning motion with his finger. 'Follow me.'

She had to try hard not to stab him in the back with her pitchfork as she followed him around the back of the cottage. They came to a halt beside a pair of ladders.

'Now listen, I'm glad you're mad at me, because this is hard work… and it's so much easier when you're angry… but anger can make you sloppy too, take risks when you shouldn't, and I can't have that.' He held up his hand as her mouth opened to protest. 'Don't interrupt either, you can have your say in a minute.'

He picked up a bag from beside the ladders. 'Masks are not optional, neither are these goggles. They don't look pretty, but thatch is dusty, and as you pointed out, full of stuff you don't want in your lungs or in your eyes. Wear the gloves too, it will help with the blisters.'

Maddie took the bag. The distance up to the roof seemed vast, and while she was extremely unhappy about the task that had been given to her, it was decidedly preferable than having to go on the roof.

Seth followed her line of sight. 'Don't worry, I'm not about to make you go up there, although I had hoped you might want to have a look. Thatching's a hugely skilled job, and I'd be happy to show you what I'm doing.'

Maddie shuddered. 'And why would I want to do that? I'm not remotely interested in how the roof goes on, or off for that matter.'

She could see that Seth had a valid point about the work that needed to be done, but this was so far removed from what she was expecting to do here, she wasn't about to give in without a fight.

'There are employment laws about this sort of thing. It's bullying in the workplace.'

'Then go home. I'll have your contract cancelled. You haven't served out your probationary period yet, so we don't owe each other a thing. You're free to go.'

He ran a hand through his hair. 'But...' He paused and took a breath. 'I really need some help here, Madeline. I'm sorry this isn't living up to your expectations, but there's nothing I can do about that right now. Someone else sold you your dream job, not me. If I'd had the opportunity, I would have been honest about what was required here. You could have come and had a look first to see what it was all about and then decided. Unfortunately, that luxury was denied to both of us, so we can do one of two things: walk away and chalk it up to experience, or try and make a go of things. What do you say?'

Maddie looked at him suspiciously. It wasn't his fault, she knew that, but he didn't have to be so rude to her. She risked a glance at his face, and was surprised to see a gentle expression there.

'Please, Madeline, we have a lot to do here, and not a great deal of time to do it in. I'd love for you to be a part of things, but only because you want to, not because you feel you've been backed into a corner. In time, I hope you'll come to understand what we're about and maybe even believe in it. The only thing that's going to give us the edge is kindred spirits working together, not Agatha's pots of money, that's for sure. She's desperate for us to fail as it is.'

She frowned. 'But that makes no sense at all. Why would Agatha give money to this project in the first place if she wanted it to fail?'

'A very good question... and let's just say if this place fails then her opinion of me will be justified. That constitutes a valid reason, in her head at least.' He sighed. 'But that's a discussion for another time, Madeline. Can we get on now?'

Despite his obvious discomfort, she wasn't about to let him off the hook just yet.

'But I don't even know what you are trying to do here yet, you haven't told me. You also haven't done me the courtesy of listening to any of the ideas I've had either. Instead, all you seem to want from me is manual labour, and you're right, that doesn't live up to my expectations at all. I'm good at what I do, Seth, and instead of dismissing that out of hand you could at least give me a chance to show you.'

He dropped his hand slightly with an acknowledging nod.

'Point taken,' he replied. 'I promise I will have a full and complete discussion with you as soon as possible. Until then, we can work until we're too knackered to speak…'

'You're not really selling this, are you?' she asked.

He grinned. 'No, that's your job.'

★

Half an hour later and the only thing that was keeping Maddie going was the thought of the shower she was going to have when they'd finished. She was certain that her whole body was crawling with insects; dust and straw had got *everywhere*. She also didn't want to admit it, but bits of her were beginning to hurt: her arms, her shoulders, back, and that damn spot on the base of her neck where the scratchy label from her new polo shirt was rubbing.

She repositioned her legs slightly, trying to relax the muscles, dropping her arms as she did so.

'So, what are your plans for the cottage then?' she asked. 'I'm surprised you're having it re-thatched actually. Don't you think it's perhaps a little twee?'

Seth looked up, a strand of straw caught in his hair. He pulled the mask away from his face. 'Say again?'

Maddie pulled off her own mask and repeated her question.

'What you mean by twee?'

'Well, you know, twee; a bit cutesy, pretty-pretty…'

'So thatch is a bad thing, is it? What would be your alternative?'

He was interested more than accusatory, for the moment at least, although Maddie was very conscious that his mood could change at any moment. She had no wish to be inflammatory, but if she was to have any chance of discussing her ideas she had to know where his feelings lay.

'I'm not sure I have one just yet, I'm just exploring the possibilities in my head… trying to see the overall look of things and where there might be opportunities for change.'

He studied her for a minute. 'How old are you, Madeline?'

Her chin came up a little. 'I'm twenty-six, why?'

'I'm just wondering why there's such a huge difference in the way we see things, but it's obviously not your age. I'm thirty-two, so only six years between us, and yet you have only one wish, it would seem, and that's to want to change things… whereas—'

'You want everything to stay the same?'

'No, I want to restore things to their former glory.'

'But old isn't necessarily better.'

'And neither is new.'

They looked at one another for a moment, a smile playing across Seth's face. Maddie sighed.

'Okay then, tell me why restoration is better than seizing an opportunity to create something unique, visionary even. What's so amazing about thatch?'

'Because it's part of our heritage, for one. It supports a tradition of skilled craftsmanship that has been passed down from generation to generation going back centuries. It's living, organic and imperfect with a character all of its own. On its own, a single strand of straw can serve no real purpose, but pull those strands together and it forms something that's strong, and enduring; it becomes something greater than itself.'

Maddie rolled her eyes. 'Oh, spare me! Did you rehearse that speech?'

Seth was about to launch into a defence when she held up her hand. 'Don't panic, I was only teasing... although you are a bit over-zealous. Has someone been giving you a hard time?'

'Don't you bloody start,' he replied, but his brown eyes twinkled with amusement. He rested a hand on top of the moth-eaten roof. 'Come on, I can sense a massive debate is about to ensue and we need to crack on. Another hour and we'll stop for a break. Then I'll share my vision for this place and you can trample all over my ideas and tell me where I'm going wrong.' He replaced his mask and motioned for her to do the same.

Maddie adjusted her grip on the pitchfork. Another hour of this might kill her, but there was nothing else for it. If she stood any chance at all of getting her point across, for the time being, she had to play the game.

★

The coffee was extraordinarily good. Or was it just that she was dying of thirst, sore, aching and utterly exhausted? Either way, it was nearly an hour and a half before they had stopped for a break and, for Maddie, it couldn't have come sooner.

Seth, by contrast, had shinned down his ladder like a gymnast and practically bounced back to the house. Maddie had to stop several times to feign interest in the plants around her just to walk at a slower pace. Now that she was seated at the kitchen table she seriously doubted whether she would ever be able to get up again.

Placing her mug back down on the coaster in front of her, she reached for a biscuit from a plate that had materialised from nowhere. She never normally ate biscuits.

'So, come on then,' she said through a mouthful of crumbs, 'you've worked me like a dog all morning, what's it all for?'

Seth joined her at the table. 'You city girls,' he grinned, 'too soft. Not used to good honest work.'

Maddie ignored him. 'An explanation of your ideas for this place, please. You promised. Besides, I spent most of yesterday coming up with some blisteringly hot plans of my own which I need to convince you are the only way if you ever want to make any money from this pile of forgotten—'

She caught the look on his face and broke off abruptly. She raised an eyebrow instead.

'Joy's Acre is essentially a farm, was a farm. Except that there's also a rather special history here and I'm trying to recreate the same environment there would have been back then. It's that simple.'

'But you're talking about the farm, which is an entirely different focus to what I've been brought here to concentrate on. I can see you have some really useful buildings here, and my brief is to market and grow the complex to upmarket holiday makers, and business people looking for well-served conference facilities. That has nothing whatsoever to do with a *farm*.'

'You keep using words like "complex"… Is that really what you see when you look around you? Joy's Acre isn't a complex, it's a collection of rundown Victorian buildings that were once home to a variety of people and, when restored, will allow them to be occupied as they once were. Admittedly it hasn't been a working farm for many years either, but I have some ideas how to address that side of things as well, and once we get some income coming in, I can start to plan how we might put these ideas into practice.'

Maddie tutted. 'Stop splitting hairs. You need to make money from these buildings, yes?'

There was a slow nod.

'So, how are you going to do that? As far as I can see, the buildings are practically falling down and need extensive work. You have an opportunity to turn them into pretty much anything you like, so what's your specification? Your timescale? Where are your designs?'

Seth tapped his head, which Maddie found infuriating.

'The "designs" are all in here because I didn't think I was going to have to explain them to anyone else. The "specification" will be subject to whatever materials are to hand, and the "timescale" starts with Tom arriving tomorrow because until the cottage has a roof on it and is watertight there's little point in doing anything else. After that, we'll work on addressing all the other issues until such time as Clara can move in and then we can look at some of the… finessing, if you want to call it that.'

Maddie bit back her response, re-focusing her thoughts on the mug in front of her. Perhaps if she stared at it for long enough her blood would stop boiling. She took a deep breath, held it and then let it out. Then she took another.

'So, let me get this straight… Apart from the fact that you seem *utterly* clueless about how you're going to achieve any of this, when you're finished, you're letting your *gardener* move in? Is she paying rent?'

Seth's eyes dropped to the table momentarily, but it was enough.

'Oh, for goodness' sake, this is ridiculous. You actually have no idea, do you?' she blazed. 'No wonder Agatha felt the need to draft in some help… In fact, does she even know about this? I can't believe she'd agree to it, not when she's paying for all the work.'

She stopped as another thought came to her. She shook her head in disbelief.

'And there's me believing Clara was just a member of staff. Well, I got that wrong, didn't I? All that friendliness was such a farce. I knew there was a warning disguised in there somewhere.' She mimicked Clara's voice from that day, '*I owe Seth a few favours that's all, so I look out for him when and if I can; I'd hate to see him get hurt...* No wonder you're so keen to get her moved in. But you know, if you want my help here, the least you could do is be honest with me, so I know what I'm dealing with – otherwise I'm going to look like a total prat.

'It's going to take months to finish the first cottage as it is, and then as soon as it's ready for occupation you're going to give it away! You need to be maximising your income at the earliest possible opportunity, not letting it slip through your fingers because your brains are in your trousers...'

She clamped her hand over her mouth. Oh Jesus, she really had gone too far this time.

She expected Seth to explode into action. In fact, she wouldn't be surprised if he picked her up and threw her from the room, but he didn't. Instead, he sat quietly, eyes fixed on her face, the only trace of his emotion in the flickering clench of his jaw. The silence filled the whole room.

Very slowly he lifted his mug to his lips and took a sip of coffee, still watching her over the rim. Then, equally slowly he replaced the mug.

'Don't ever, ever speak about Clara like that again, do you understand?'

Maddie swallowed. 'I really am sorry, I'm not sure why I...'

She wasn't sure how to finish. It was difficult when she didn't really understand it herself. The events of the last few months had taken their toll, she knew that, but perhaps she was only just beginning to find out to what extent. Clara had been a little wary with her to start with, understandably, but she'd been nothing but kind, and Maddie would never normally stoop so low. It was completely out of character. To her embarrassment, she felt tears beginning to well up and she blinked them away furiously.

'It's just that I can see how much you care about this place. My ideas are probably very different from yours, but essentially we want the same thing, and that's to make this a success. I couldn't bear to see another dream die.'

Seth stood up abruptly and Maddie was certain he was about to storm out of the room. To her surprise, he fished in his pocket and handed her a folded hanky.

'This was clean when I put it there this morning, now, possibly less so…'

She took it from him anyway. 'I'm sorry,' she said again.

His voice was gentle as he began to speak, retaking his seat opposite her.

'Right then, Miss Porter. I assume you have your laptop and plans somewhere hereabouts. Now's your chance to shine.'

Chapter 6

'It's about putting yourself in your potential customers' shoes,' she began. 'Catching their attention first, then selling them what they think they want. Most people only have an idea about what they like, but if you can present ideas and images that capture their imagination, that suggest in some way that they're only here because of their innate good taste, then flattery will take you the rest of the way.'

She angled the laptop so that Seth could see it better. 'Then you need to deliver the detail, pulling them in further with each click of the page on the website, showing them possibilities and tantalising glimpses of what's on offer, backed up by your unique selling points, until you leave them no choice but to want to find out more.'

Seth frowned. 'But websites like these cost an arm and a leg.'

'And how else do you expect potential customers to find you? They're not going to drive all the way out here just to have a look, are they? The website snares people, and then if they're convinced enough, they can go ahead and make a booking online. If not, they can give us a call for more details and that's when we reel them in ourselves.'

He wasn't at all convinced, she could see that. She pushed the laptop away, reaching into her bag to retrieve the print-outs of the mood boards she had created online. Perhaps he would be better looking at something he could connect with – the buildings themselves.

'These are some suggestions for furniture, potential colour schemes, the style and level of finish which will become your brand. The customers you're looking to attract will expect to see quality fittings and luxurious soft furnishings. Everything must be exceptionally well maintained, the connected services must be reliable and you need to think about super-fast broadband and network facilities for business users too.'

She waited as he looked between the pages of images she had shown him.

'These are just a few examples, but I think you can see what they all have in common...'

'They cost a lot of money?'

'A solid investment which will ensure a good return.'

Seth nodded. 'I think I was right the first time.'

She threw him an exasperated look. 'We need to start work on your website straight away, start building interest, sending out mailings, teasers, so that once you're up and running you'll have bookings from the get-go. The interiors of the cottages are obviously something which will have to wait, but even so, some of the more bespoke items will have to be sourced and ordered, and they'll have a lead time of several months. Right now, you should be concentrating on how you want the complex... sorry, area to look. What unifying features you'd like to see, how you're going to pull the whole thing together so that you have a cohesive development, instead of a random mishmash of odd buildings.'

To give him his due, he sat back and listened quietly until she had finished, studying the things she had shown him and taking his time looking over the images, shuffling through pages until he had seen enough. Finally, he raised his head.

'I haven't done plans or sketches of the site, obviously, but I should probably take you outside,' he said, 'so you can show me what this cohesive thingy is you're talking about.' He motioned with his head towards her mug. 'Drink up.'

Her tired legs protested as she stood up, but after a few hobbling steps she found her stride again as she followed Seth out of the door. Even so, she was quite some distance behind him by the time she reached the garden. Her heart sank as she walked over to join him; she had almost forgotten about the thatch they were supposed to be removing, and she had a horrible feeling that they would be back at it before too long.

He turned, facing away from the first cottage and looking out across the garden towards the other three.

'So, supposing I wanted to "pull all this together", what would I do?'

Maddie took a step forward.

'This was my point about the thatching really,' she said. 'You can have all the high-end fittings you like, but stick them in a building with a thatch on top and you're going to have some kind of weird fusion thing going on, and not good weird either. It'll be tasteless weird and you'll look like you didn't know what you were doing.'

'But everything should be in keeping with the character of the buildings, shouldn't it? What you've shown me is very sleek and modern. I get that it's what everyone seems to want these days, but it doesn't fit with these buildings at all.'

'Then change the buildings.'

Seth scratched his head. 'But isn't it easier to change the design of what's inside?'

'Easier, yes. Better, absolutely not.'

'I'm not sure I want to hear this, but go on…'

This really wasn't in her job remit at all, but Maddie couldn't un-see the vision she had for this place or resist the urge to share it. If Seth liked it, the rest was just a question of finances; anything was possible if your client had enough money and Agatha's niece had certainly seemed to suggest that they wouldn't settle for anything less than the best. If this went well, the end result would be more than she could ever have wished for. It would well and truly put her back on the map. It might even be enough to allow her to return to London with her head held high. There was just one thing she needed to check first.

'What are your plans for the barn?'

He gave a wry smile. 'Few and far between at the moment, I'm afraid. There are lots of things I could do with it, but it's a way down the list of priorities at the moment. Can I take it that it figures slightly larger in your plans than mine?'

This was music to her ears. The whole vision she had to unify the buildings hinged on the barn. She tried not to let her inner high-five show.

'Well in a way, that's good news, because the barn sits in a perfect position to become the pivotal feature here. It's close enough to support the first cottage, the one we've been working on today, and it also feeds directly into the garden, which in turn links it with the other three cottages.'

Seth's head swivelled back and forth as he followed her swinging arm movements. He frowned.

'What do you mean? How can the barn support the first cottage?'

Her arms spread to encompass the semi-circular view that lay in front of them. 'Imagine for a moment if the walls of the barn were made of glass... then extend the rear wall to the right to meet the single cottage, you'd have the most amazing atrium in the middle.

That's your conference centre, complete with a range of both large and small meeting rooms, breakout spaces and room for video screens and the like.'

She swung a glance at him to make sure he was following, but his face was inscrutable. She took another breath.

'Then imagine that the glass extends from the left, curving around the top of the garden via a covered walkway and leading into the garden itself and on to the other cottages. If these also had glass features the whole thing would hang together beautifully. Of course, you'd probably need to alter some aspects of the garden to gain the fullest effect, but wouldn't it look absolutely stunning?'

Seth was staring out across the space as if he was indeed imagining that very thing.

'The garden stays as it is.'

Maddie baulked at the harshness in his voice. 'But it's central to the space,' she argued. 'I don't mean rip it up or anything, but as it is now it wouldn't fit with the ideas—'

'No.' Then, as if coming to a rapid conclusion, he spun his head back towards the first cottage. 'We should get on,' he said. 'We've done well this morning, and with the two of us on the job, we'll easily get it finished.' He toed a pebble that lay at the edge of the path. 'That was a really good proposal you put together, and I can see you've put a lot of work into it, thank you.'

Maddie felt her bubble of excitement deflate. What was he saying? She waited for him to make further comment, finding herself staring at the pebble on the path as the silence stretched out. Then, she could bear it no longer.

'And?' she asked. 'Is that it? Thanks for everything, but we're just going to carry on as if the last fifteen minutes never happened?'

Finally his dark eyes lifted to hers. 'I'm sorry, Madeline, I know that's not what you wanted to hear… In other circumstances what you've described would be incredible. I'm very impressed by the breadth of your vision and imagination, but I'm sorry, what you have in mind is just not right for Joy's Acre.'

'Well, that's just fantastic,' she muttered, 'thanks so much.' She watched as Seth stiffened. 'No discussion, no willingness to even try and see how this might be the making of the place. Just a flat thanks, but no thanks…'

She was beginning to wind herself up into a fury, not because he disagreed with her, but because he was refusing to listen, or take her ideas seriously. It would be impossible for her to work with someone like that again. She couldn't stay here, that much was certain, and she had nothing left to lose. She didn't owe Seth anything. She could let him have it with both barrels, vent all her frustration, and walk away, no harm done. She was about to speak again when Seth suddenly reached forward, taking her arm, firmly, and spinning her around.

'Stick a smile on your face and shut up,' he hissed under his breath.

Maddie tried to wriggle away from him, but he held her firm. She jerked her head backwards, glaring up at him, and was about to wrench her arm away, when she caught sight of someone coming towards them.

'Please, Madeline.' His voice was low, his eyes pleading as he dropped her arm. 'Just follow my lead.' He took a step forward, finally releasing her.

'Agatha, good morning!' he called at the rapidly approaching figure. 'Beautiful day.'

He waited until she was within a few feet, a wide smile firmly fixed on his face, the rest of his body taut like a coiled spring.

'You've come at just the right moment. Madeline and I were just brainstorming some fantastic ideas.'

Maddie had wondered whether Agatha's face ever did anything but scowl, but as her gaze wandered to the cottage beside them and the heaps of discarded straw that lay in mounds beside it, her mouth curved upwards, just a little.

'Well, I'm pleased to see you've managed to spur him into action, young lady. It's about time things got going around here. And I hope you're going to tell me that once the roof is off that thing you're going to replace it with something that isn't quite so horribly twee.'

She fixed her eyes on Maddie, completely ignoring Seth.

'Well, I…' Maddie hadn't a clue what to say.

Seth took a step forwards. 'I think that's a given, Agatha. It's hardly going to be in keeping with the overall scheme of things here, is it? I mean, people will want to see luxurious fixtures and fittings, sleek design, not kitsch make-do and mend. The two are simply not compatible.'

He turned and beamed at Maddie. 'Fortunately Madeline and I seem to be agreed on this. What was it you said? Much easier to change the buildings to fit the design, rather than the other way around.'

Maddie's mouth dropped open, but she quickly snapped it shut when she felt Agatha's eyes settle on her. She had no idea what was going on here, but she could feel the tension like a force field around them.

Nothing would have given her greater pleasure than dropping Seth in it from a very great height at that exact moment, but there was something in Agatha's bullying tone and Seth's tight smile that reminded Maddie of a time she'd rather forget. She cleared her throat and lifted her head.

'It's not rocket science, is it?' she said, doing just as Seth asked and plastering a smile on her face. 'Anyone can see that the whole site is a disaster waiting to happen in commercial terms. You can hardly expect people to part with vast sums of money for something that's so…' She glanced about her as if looking for inspiration. '… *heritage*,' she finished. 'Heavens, that's what the National Trust is for, isn't it?'

Seth's jawline hardened in response to her sweet smile.

'Of course, our discussions aren't final yet, but I'm thinking that on such an open site, particularly one with the garden in the middle, that glass is the way to go? What do you think, Madeline?' he asked. 'And I'm kind of thinking on my feet here, but we could even incorporate the barn somehow, as a central focal point?'

Maddie bit her lip. If he was standing any closer she'd have kicked him.

'Sorry, Agatha, I'm rabbiting on,' continued Seth. 'Was there anything in particular you wanted?'

'Well if there was, I've clean forgotten. However, I'm pleased to hear your ideas, Seth. I was beginning to think that you had none. Now, I know I don't need to remind you why you're doing all this, or who you're doing it for, but frankly I don't care how you do it as long as it makes money for the estate. Make no mistake though, I shall not continue to throw endless amounts of money and resources at something which has no chance of succeeding. I'm sure you'll keep an eye on things for me, Madeline, and I shall expect to see some costings from you in due course.' She nodded curtly at them both. 'I'll leave you to your discussions.'

For someone of her age she walked fairly rapidly, but for Maddie, Agatha's disappearance around the corner of the house couldn't come soon enough. She was about to launch into a full-blown tirade when Seth held up his hand.

'Don't,' he said, bluntly. 'Whatever you were going to say, just don't.' He blinked rapidly, turning his face away.

She stared at him, wondering what had caused the sudden change of expression on his face, but she was too close to boiling point to process the information properly.

'You out-and-out bastard,' she hissed. 'How *dare* you?'

'Me?' Seth fired back. 'How can you complain about what I said?' His dark eyes flashed. 'I'm only repeating your own ideas, whereas you've just trampled all over mine! You say the word "heritage" like it's something to be ashamed of, when it's what gives this country its identity, its diversity. And you want to replace it with some homogenous... cohesive... crap!'

'At least they're original ideas. I'm not trying to steal someone else's and pass them off to Agatha as my own. That's low Seth, that's really low.'

He glared at her. 'I'm not trying to steal them, because I've got no intention of ever letting any of your ideas become reality here. Over. My. Dead. Body.'

'That can be arranged!'

For a moment both of them held their ground, the air crackling between them. Maddie had been riding the wave of her anger, but even as she frantically searched for what to say next she realised that it was utterly pointless. She had thought for a few minutes that her ideas were gaining some traction with Seth. He had seemed to listen, had even been generous in allowing her to share them as a peace offering after she'd been so rude about Clara. But underneath it all, she now knew he had no intention of budging from his original plans. Her emotions, which had gone up and down like a yo-yo all morning, finally snapped. With one final, disparaging look at Seth she strode off in the direction of the house.

Chapter 7

She would go and stay with her friend Beth, she decided as she yanked open the wardrobe doors in her bedroom. She had offered Maddie a bed before, when the whole thing in London blew up, but Maddie had declined, not wanting to look like she was admitting defeat. This time though, she didn't much care. A few weeks up in the wilds of the North York Moors would suit her down to the ground. With any luck she could stay in Beth's house the whole time and she wouldn't have to even speak to anyone.

She pulled out her suits and blouses and threw them into her suitcase as if they were rags. Shoes went in another bag, toiletries into a third and in a matter of minutes she was ready. There was just one final thing left to do.

On her bed she'd laid out a pair of chinos and a shirt that she had always favoured. She ripped off the polo top she was wearing over her head and dumped it on the floor, bending down to yank off her hideously uncomfortable new boots seconds later. They landed with a thump on the floor and she kicked them petulantly under the bed. Her jeans, the ones she had bought only yesterday, but which were now dusty and streaked with muck, were disposed of the same way. Standing in just her bra and pants, she looked towards the bathroom door, torn for just a moment before she reached out for her clean clothes. She would have loved a shower, but there was no way she was about to take anything else that belonged to Seth and Joy's Bloody Acre.

Dressed and ready, she picked up all her bags at once – determined to do it all in one trip – and banged and clanked her way downstairs. She had no idea whether Seth had followed her into the house or not, but she suspected he was just as keen to put distance between them as she was and would keep out of her way. And that suited her fine, she had no obligation to him; her contract was with Agatha and her niece and, once she arrived at Beth's, she would simply email her resignation.

She manhandled her baggage through the kitchen door and dumped it momentarily on the table while she scooped up her laptop and other papers, kicking open the door to widen it sufficiently for her to pass through.

Once in the yard the chickens scattered from her path and even the dogs gave her a wide berth. She flung open the boot of her car and placed her bags inside before getting in.

'Madeline, wait!' Seth's voice came from not too far behind her. 'Where are you going?'

She wasn't going to stop, whatever he had to say. She was already inside the car and one hand on the bonnet wasn't going to hold her back.

'Madeline?' he said again. 'For goodness' sake, where are you going? This is stupid.'

She wound the window down. 'What is? Leaving?' She glared at him. 'Are you sure about that? 'Cause from my point of view I'd be stupid to stay. I'm obviously not wanted and neither is my help. What possible reason could there be to hang around any longer – so I can take abuse from you, or condescending remarks from Agatha? No thanks, there's other places I'd rather be.'

Seth thumped the side of the car in frustration. 'I get that. It's not been a good start, I'll be the first to admit... but Agatha, well she...' He heaved a sigh. 'We don't get on, okay? She drives me nuts and whenever she's around I can't think straight.'

Maddie wound the window back up so there was only an inch left open. 'And that's my problem, why? I think you need to learn to get on, and that, Mr Thomas, is down to you and none of my business. Now, get off my car.'

Seth lifted his hand as if he'd been stung. He stared at her through the windscreen, his hair sticking up in tufts, no doubt still covered in all kinds of muck from the thatch.

'I heard you crying, Maddie,' he said, quiet now. 'The other night, when I came in. I couldn't help it.'

She went still, her breath held inside her body. He had never called her Maddie before. Then, without looking either left or right, she turned the key in the ignition, put the car in gear and drove off.

Her heart was beating wildly. She was mortified that she'd been heard. And why bring it up, just at the point when she was leaving? Had he known the true reason she was so upset? There was no way he could have done, reason told her that, and yet, with just a few words, he had managed to remind her of the very thing she had been running from when she came here.

What was she doing? After last time, she'd promised herself that nothing like that would ever be allowed to get the better of her again, that she would fight and win, and yet here she was running away, tail between her legs. Talk about history repeating itself. And she had done nothing wrong, it was Seth who had behaved badly, not her.

As she reached the turning out onto the main road into the village, she paused, trying to gather her thoughts. If she pulled out she wouldn't be coming back. Was that what she really wanted? She'd had such high hopes for coming here. It wasn't London, but it was a fresh challenge. More than that, she'd thought the set-up at Joy's Acre would allow her some autonomy, some escape from the politics of her past. How wrong she had been.

And yet, there was something here that she found attractive. The setting was just so perfect, or would be if... She pushed aside her doubts, reminding herself why she was currently on the verge of leaving. None of that was about to change any time soon. With a deep breath, she checked for traffic and swung out into the road, accelerating hard.

She would stop at the village and give Beth a ring while she picked up some provisions for her journey. Right now, she just wanted to feel a growing distance between her and Joy's Acre. She flicked a glance up to her rear-view mirror but the turning down to the farm was already hidden from view.

She almost didn't see the ginger streak which flashed across the road in front of her. Almost, but not quite. She stamped on her brake, but the road was too narrow and the cat had nowhere to go. Without thinking, she wrenched the wheel sideways, gasping as a wall of greenery reared up to meet her. A hideous scraping noise accompanied her passage as twigs and branches crushed against the car, screeching against the windows. The colour flashing past her turned from green to brown and the windscreen went dark as she struck a tree trunk head on.

A pain in the side of her head erupted into a bloom of white noise and light. And then it was still. No noise, no nothing. She was aware that she was waiting, for what she didn't know, but it was as if time was spinning away from her and she couldn't move to catch it.

Eventually, little by little, the feeling diminished and was replaced by a terrible need to do something. Her surroundings came rushing back into focus. She was okay, she wasn't dead. She wasn't hurt; at least she didn't think she was. But the car? And the cat? She struggled to right herself from where she had become wedged against the driver's side window, at the same time suddenly aware of her laboured breathing. The movement brought pain, a distortion to her vision and a rising sense of panic. What if she couldn't get out?

She forced herself to breathe more slowly, to relax her limbs and empty her mind of stuff that didn't need to be there. She was okay, but she needed to get out of the car and get help. She unclipped her seatbelt and pushed against the door. It was stuck fast. She pushed even harder and, although the door gave by a couple of inches, there was no way it would open further, wedged tight as it was against the wall of bushes and tree limbs. On her other side was a similar view; if she was to get out of her car at all, it would have to be backwards.

The trouble was, she hadn't bought her car for its roominess. The sports chassis sat low to the ground, the roof curved steeply around the sides giving very little headroom, and the gap between the two front seats was only inches rather than feet. She raised a tentative hand to her temple, which was beginning to throb. Sitting still and waiting it out was no longer an option. She had to try.

She managed to lever herself backwards and upwards so that she could get her feet onto the seat and wriggle around so that she was at least facing the right way. From there it was simply a matter of clawing her way onto the back seat by any means possible – which meant bum in the air. Of course, it was at exactly this moment that the back door of the car opened and an anguished face appeared only inches from her own.

'Jesus, Maddie, are you okay?'

'I will be if I can get out of the bloody car.' Her reply was muffled against the headrest. She reached forward, trying to latch onto anything she could use to pull herself forward. Her hand found the sleeve of Seth's jumper.

'Just pull, for God's sake.' She pushed her other arm forward.

'Maddie, wait, this might not be such a great idea. What if you're hurt? You could make it worse.'

She gritted her teeth. 'Get me out of this car!'

With a look of alarm, Seth nodded curtly. Twisting his own arms so that he could wrap his hands around both her elbows, he pulled.

The sensation of being squeezed in too tight a space, the possibility of sticking fast, was bringing a rapidly rising sense of panic. Her feet scrabbled on the seat behind her as she gripped Seth's arms, trying to find purchase to help propel herself forward.

After what felt like a lifetime, Maddie's chest inched over the seat and the rest of her slithered behind quickly. She landed in a heap half on the back seat, half in the footwell and inches from Seth's face.

Wriggling, she pushed at him. 'Get out of my way!'

He ducked out of the door. 'You'll have to come out backwards, feet first. There's too many branches otherwise, they'll rip your face to shreds.'

Mortified, she let him guide her legs and bum through the rear door to a place where she could finally stand.

Seth was right, there was a crush of bushes up against the car, and she had to push herself through them as they caught against her clothes and hair, scratching at her exposed skin. Eventually she reached the rear of the car and the space widened in front of her where she crashed out onto the verge at the side of the road, breathing hard.

She sat for a few minutes, her breath coming in panicked gasps as the realisation that she was free pumped a last wave of adrenaline through her body. She bent forward, both hands on her knees for support as she sucked air into her lungs. A wave of dizziness swept over. An arm went around her waist.

'Hey, gently does it. Don't breathe so deeply, try to slow it down.'

'Sorry,' she gasped.

He held her firm until the swimming in her head subsided a little.

'Better,' he said, letting go of her. 'Keep it like that, nice and slow... Try to stand up a little?'

She did as she was told, the tingling sensation in her lips easing.

'It's okay, you had a panic attack, that's all. Hyperventilating.'

Finally, she was able to stand straight, although her legs felt like jelly.

'I'm sorry,' she said again. 'I don't like confined spaces, I just needed to get out of the car.'

'I know,' was all he said.

His eyes searched hers, flicking around her face, resting on her hairline for a moment, before dropping to give the rest of her a once-over.

'You've cut your head, but I don't think it's too bad. Where else does it hurt?'

Maddie stared at him, trying to think. 'I don't know,' she said. 'I think I'm okay.'

Seth made a derogatory noise. 'Hmm, well you might feel all right now, but tomorrow you'll feel like you've been hit by a truck. We should get you checked over.'

She was beginning to feel slightly more connected with things now that her breathing was getting back to normal. She registered Seth's four-by-four blocking the lane behind them and the enormity of what had just happened came rushing back.

'I crashed the car!' was all she could think to say. Then, to her embarrassment, she burst into tears.

She felt a tentative touch on one arm, and then on the other. When she offered no resistance, Seth pulled her closer, gathering her in gently until both his arms could slide around her.

'It's okay, Maddie.'

His hug was warm and safe and she sank beneath the feel of him, eyes closed against the swimming tide in her head. Gradually the waves subsided and she moved her head a little, remembering the way he had said her name, and feeling the hardness of the muscles in his chest. She breathed in his scent, something warm and spicy…

What was she doing? She pushed him away, flustered, and stared back at the road.

'It was the cat. The ginger one. It just ran out in front of me.' She looked up at him in anguish. 'I didn't hit him, did I?'

'No, Rumpus has lived to tell the tale.' He gave a slight frown and then grimaced. 'Though, I'm not sure the same can be said for your car.' He fished in his pocket. 'Come on, let's get you home, and then I'll ring Kev the mechanic and he can come and sort out the mess.'

He led her back to his car, opening the door for her and waiting until she was safely settled in her seat before climbing into his. He switched off the hazard warning lights and pulled away.

Maddie averted her eyes as they drove past the gaping wound her car had carved out of the countryside. The reality of what had just happened hit her hard and she began to shake. She wrapped her arms around herself, realising as she did so that nothing would be more comforting than the hug Seth had just given her, so she dropped her hands to her lap and closed her eyes.

After a few moments she felt the car turn and saw that they had pulled into a farm gateway. Seth reversed and started back again the way they had come. She swallowed and screwed her eyes tight shut again, not opening them until the car drew to a halt and she knew she was back at Joy's Acre.

⭑

Half an hour later she wrapped her hands around a very welcome mug of sweet tea. Seth had called the garage, organised the removal of her car, gone back to collect her things from the boot and tended to the cut on her head. Then he had made them both a drink and was currently sitting opposite her, watching her intently.

'I'm sorry,' she said again. 'I seem to be causing you nothing but trouble.'

His expression didn't alter. 'I've had better weeks,' he said. 'But then so have you.' He scratched his head. 'And at least I'm on home territory, with familiar things around me and... you're not.'

'No,' she agreed. 'I'm not.' She raised a tentative hand to her forehead. 'Though, I'm not exactly sure where home territory is right now.'

'Would you like it to be here?'

Maddie sighed. 'That's not really an option, is it? You made your feelings very clear.'

'I was angry.' Seth frowned. 'As were you, I think. We both seem to be quite good at flying off the handle.'

She narrowed her eyes at him, acknowledging the truth of his words. 'Were you following me earlier?' she asked suddenly.

There was a slight smile. And then a bigger one.

'Guilty as charged,' he admitted. 'I didn't want you to go.'

'Why ever not? I'd have thought you'd be cock-a-hoop to see the back of me.'

He looked a little sheepish. 'Well, yes… except that it seemed wrong, for you to leave like that – upset and angry.' He shifted in his chair. 'And if you don't mind my saying, you seemed very unhappy the other day too… when I heard you crying. I know it wasn't the easiest of starts for you, but it seemed a rather dramatic response to the mix-up, especially when you'd been at such pains to appear so poised and confident. I wondered if there was something else that had upset you?'

Maddie caught the look in his dark eyes. 'I'm not sure you know me well enough to ask questions like that,' she said. 'Although, I am wondering why you're being so kind?'

'Guilt?' He smiled.

She was quiet for a moment. 'So, what do we do now?' she asked eventually. 'We seem to have reached something of an impasse.'

'Start over?' He raised an eyebrow. 'There doesn't seem to be any other course of action. Might I remind you that you've just crushed the front half of your car. I'm afraid you're not going anywhere fast.'

She stared at him, horrified, the truth of her situation dawning. 'Will it take long to be fixed, do you think?'

He shrugged. 'I have absolutely no idea, but until it is it would make sense to at least try to get along. And I could use your help. There's a lot to do here.'

'But you hate my ideas—'

'I don't,' he quickly protested. 'They're not right for Joy's Acre, but as ideas go I thought they were very well thought out.'

Maddie still wasn't sure she understood.

'But this morning you told me how you want to restore this place to its former glory, and then made me go through the whole rigmarole of telling you my ideas, even though you knew you weren't going to like what I had to say; in fact, you dismissed them just minutes later. Why bother?'

His expression was thoughtful. 'Because I wanted to see what you were made of – how convincing you could be when selling your ideas. That is, after all, what you're going to be doing here, isn't it? It doesn't much matter what this place ends up like if you can't string a sentence together, or inspire potential customers.'

He held up a hand. 'And don't look at me like that, I'm trying to pay you a compliment.' He paused for a moment. 'I thought what you had to say was very good actually. Considering how little time you've spent here, you came up with a really brilliant set of plans, full of detail and which also showed imagination and resourcefulness. That's what I need here, Maddie.'

She smiled. 'But?'

'But we've got to work together, not fight one another. And to do that you'll have to compromise on some of your principles and carry out work according to my vision of this place, putting your own aside. I'm not sure it's fair to ask you to do that… and, if I'm honest, I'm not sure you'll be able to.'

He pulled a face as if to soften the effect of his words. 'I've wasted too much time and energy here over the last few years but I am passionate about this place and what I want for its future. I'm afraid I'm not prepared to waste any more time or to let anything alter me from my course. Not Agatha. Not anyone. As long as you understand that, we'll make great team.'

'And, if I don't?'

'Then you're welcome to stay as long as it takes for your car to be fixed and then you can be on your way. No hard feelings.' He rested his chin in his hand. 'Although, I'd much rather you stayed because you want to. I need someone with your drive and tenacity.'

Maddie nodded, picking up her mug and draining the contents in a series of long swallows. Then she replaced the mug and sat back in her chair, grimacing slightly at the ache in her shoulder. She was just about to reply, when she caught sight of the tip of a ginger tail over the top of the table. She stretched up to get a better view, and Seth's eyes followed.

'Ah,' he said. 'The culprit himself. Rumpus by name, Rumpus by nature.' He bent down to run a hand along the cat's back. 'To what do we owe the pleasure?' He looked up at Maddie. 'He's a very contrary cat usually, not given to outward displays of affection.' He watched, an amused expression on his face as Rumpus wound his body around Maddie's legs, purring loudly. 'Well now, it would seem someone else would like you to stay too.'

Maddie reached down, gently pulling at the cat's soft ears. He pushed his head into her hand and she could feel his whole body vibrating. She'd never owned a cat before, or ever really had an opinion about them one way or the other, but just now she was very grateful that the cat was still in one piece. She could use a bit of comfort.

She straightened up slowly. 'I think you might be right about feeling like I've been hit by a truck,' she said. 'Everything's beginning to ache.'

Seth smiled at her. 'I'll run you a bath,' he said. 'Best remedy there is.'

Chapter 8

It was such a lovely dream. She was lying on a golden beach with a soft breeze blowing gently on her face and warming rays from the sun caressing her skin. Then she realised that it wasn't a beach she was lying on at all, but a smooth expanse of something silky, wrapped around her… She stretched out a hand to run her fingers across the surface… and opened her eyes.

The pale walls of her bedroom swam into view, a shaft of sunlight through the hazy curtain falling across her pillow. As she turned her head a fraction, a sweet-smelling breeze billowed the voile and a warm current of spring air glided over her. She went to move towards it and immediately realised the full extent of her mistake. This was no dream, it was a nightmare.

Even her fingers hurt. Her neck, her back and her shoulders she could understand. Her legs too, but her fingers? She had gone to bed feeling tired and a little achy, but soothed a little by a long soak in a hot bath. She had envisaged a slight stiffness come the morning, but how wrong could she be? Her head and neck felt like they were locked in a vice, and she realised pretty quickly that if she wanted to look either left or right then she would have to move her whole body… very slowly. She eased her legs over the side of the bed and attempted to stand.

The irony was, she had slept like a log. More soundly and for longer than she could ever remember. In fact, it was already past nine o'clock and she wasn't even out of bed. She pulled a face at her reflection in the mirror and hobbled to the bathroom.

Her bags were still on the floor where she had left them last night. It had seemed too much of an effort to unpack them all over again, but this morning, the task seemed insurmountable. She groaned. Even the thought of getting dressed seemed like an impossibility. Her eyes flicked to a carrier bag that still lay on the chest of drawers where it had been discarded. It was a long shot, but that at least she could reach.

She pulled out the pile of clothes that had once belonged to Clara and straightened them out, turning them over to see what there was. There were some leggings and a couple of pairs of jeans – pale denim worn smooth with use, but supple, not stiff and unyielding like hers were – and four tops, two of which were tunic length and two shorter, all made from the same soft jersey. To her tortured body they felt like heaven.

It took a while, but eventually she managed to put on some underwear and with a few hideous grunting noises pulled on some leggings and one of the tunics, a soft raspberry colour with a gentle scooped neckline. She felt conspicuously underdressed, almost as if she weren't wearing any clothes at all, but they fitted, and the lack of buttons, belts and hard bits of any kind was a real bonus. She eased her way down the stairs on bare feet.

The house was quiet, not surprisingly; Seth had probably been hard at it for hours, and although Maddie's stomach was rumbling her tardiness was beginning to make her feel awkward. After the truce of the evening before, it seemed wrong to be lingering here when there was work to be done. She grabbed an apple from the fruit bowl on the table and looked around for something to put on her feet.

Spying a pair of gardening clogs by the back door, she slipped them on and slowly made her way around the side of the house. As soon as she rounded the corner the sound of voices met her and, as she passed the tumbledown greenhouse, three figures could be seen sitting on the bench in the middle of the garden, deep in conversation. She hesitated, feeling very much like the outsider she was.

Seth's hand rose in the air and a shouted hello floated across to her. She picked her way gingerly down the path to where he squinted up at her, one hand shielding his eyes from the bright morning sun.

'Ouch,' he said. 'I fear my diagnosis of yesterday evening was all too accurate.'

Maddie grimaced. 'And some,' she said. 'It was indeed a very large truck. For goodness' sake, even my fingers hurt.'

Seth winced. 'I didn't really expect you to put in an appearance today to be honest, but I'm glad you have. Can I introduce you?' He smiled at the woman seated next to him. 'Clara you've already met, I think.'

She touched a hand to the hem of her top and smiled shyly, still embarrassed about her outburst the day before.

'I have.'

There was no need to say thank you, it was unspoken in the air between her and Clara's beaming smile.

'And this is Tom.' He waited until Maddie and he had shaken hands. 'Tom is our master thatcher and a very old friend. This is important, because most of the time he behaves like an irresponsible degenerate and this allows him to get away with murder.'

'I do not,' he shot back in mock-horror. 'Honestly… How could you say such a thing?' He winked at Maddie.

'I'll try and remember that,' she replied, laughing.

Tom's smile was slower than Clara's; a lazy lopsided grin, but no less welcoming. 'Pleased to meet you, Maddie. The guv'nor has been telling us all about you.'

Maddie looked at Seth, horrified, but he held her look without a trace of embarrassment.

'We're trying to formulate a battle plan,' he explained. 'One that stands a chance of being snuck past Agatha's very long nose. Now that we've got you here to direct traffic, I'm hoping we can really begin to get things moving.'

'Direct traffic?' Maddie asked. 'I'm not sure what you mean.'

'Sorry.' He waved a hand at Tom. 'Maddie here is from London, which might as well be a foreign country as far as I'm concerned, but it does mean you'll all need to use correct terminology or she won't understand what you mean.' He gave her the slightest of winks. 'Project Manager is how it's usually referred to, I believe.'

Maddie's mouth dropped open. 'You want me to project manage?'

'That's what you're good at, isn't it? And that's definitely what we need around here.'

All three heads looked at her and nodded.

'Seth's never around when you need to ask him something,' said Clara. 'So it will be great to have someone on hand who knows what's supposed to be going on.'

Maddie swallowed. Given the events of the last couple of days she'd never imagined for one minute that Seth would propose such a thing. It was extraordinarily generous.

'Maddie can schedule the work, source the materials and tie the whole project together while I'm busy with other things. That way, we won't lose any more time, Agatha will be happy – well, happier – and Joy's Acre can start to fulfil the vision I have for it.'

'As long as you tell me what that is exactly.'

Seth stood up. 'Good point,' he replied. 'I've already explained that you had a bit of an accident yesterday, and so while you're not up to much, it gives us the perfect opportunity to go back to the house, rustle up some proper breakfast, and thrash this thing out once and for all. What do you say?'

Clara grinned and Tom got to his feet, dragging his jeans back up over his hips. 'Right you are, guv'nor. Sounds like a plan.'

★

If Maddie was grateful for her elasticated waistband before, she was certainly thankful for it now. She didn't think she had ever eaten so much, and certainly never at breakfast time. Clara had made eggy bread with rashers of bacon, mushrooms and tiny sweet tomatoes drizzled in oil and herbs. There were savoury muffins too, cooked fresh from the freezer and served warm and oozing with butter. A huge pot of tea stood in the centre of the table, and for some while there was little sound apart from the scraping of cutlery against plates and contented groans. What little conversation interspersed the meal was light-hearted and easy.

She soon learned that Tom was something of a joker. While he treated Seth with an almost religious reverence, he flirted outrageously with her and Clara and, with his wheaten-coloured hair, blue eyes and day-old stubble, Maddie could see how he would seem appealing. There was no substance to his flirting though. It was good-natured banter, harmless and fun, and Maddie immediately felt relaxed in his company.

Contrary to the impression that Seth had given her yesterday, his plans for the work required on site were pretty comprehensive. Tom was merely the first in a long line of craftsmen and contractors he had lined up, the only difference being that Seth had grown up with Tom, and their shared vision for Joy's Acre had been born during a late-night drinking session at the local pub several years before. Without Tom, Seth wouldn't be in the position he was in today, it was as simple as that. As both were practitioners of traditional crafts, they were devout in their allegiance to repair and renewal rather than starting from scratch and, while Maddie could see why this mattered so much to them, she knew there was a fine balance to be weighed.

She sat back and listened for quite some time, thinking about the ideas she had put together over the last few days. It was obvious now that most of them had been wildly inappropriate; but *most* did not mean *all*, and she would need to speak up now if she wanted to get her point across.

She raised a tentative hand, causing Clara to laugh. 'Guys, will you shut up a minute, you need to let Maddie get a word in. The poor girl can't hear herself think.'

Maddie flashed her a grateful smile. 'I just wanted to mention something I found out the other day. Which, while it might go against *all* your principles, will make your lives so much easier in the long run. It will save you money and time, two resources you can't afford to waste.' All eyes turned on her. 'Please, please, please can we get some decent broadband,' she said.

Tom hooted with laughter. 'A-bloody-men to that,' he said. 'Finally, someone else who agrees with me.'

Seth gave him a wry look. 'Only because it'll mean you can check your dating app as often as you want to.'

Tom winked at Maddie. 'Nothing wrong with that,' he said. 'I'd hate for some lovely lady to miss out.'

There was a collective groan around the table.

'That, in itself, is good enough reason *not* to get broadband,' said Clara, rolling her eyes. 'It will save a huge number of poor women from utter disappointment.'

Seth was smiling, but Maddie could see it was in reaction to the comments her suggestion had given rise to, rather than the idea itself.

'I can see you're not keen,' she began, 'but can I at least say why I think it would be such a good idea?'

'Can't deny her that, surely,' put in Tom.

'No,' said Seth slowly. 'I can't deny her that.'

'Tell me first why you don't want it,' countered Maddie.

'Oh, clever!' Clara grinned.

Seth raised his hands in a helpless gesture.

'Look, will you lot shut up a minute. There are two reasons we've never had broadband here. One, is simply that we're in a really poor service area; we struggle for a phone signal as it is, and there's no way we could get a service here that is fast enough to cope with loads of people accessing it at the same time. I know, because I've checked.'

He flashed Tom a look. 'The second reason goes much deeper, and is simply that it doesn't fit with my idea of how things should be here. I want Joy's Acre to be a place where people can escape from the real world, not be tethered to it at every minute of the day.'

Maddie nodded. 'Yes, I get that and I understand it completely, but you can have both. You could set up the service so that each cottage or area of the site had its own router – that way people can choose whether they access the Wi-Fi or not. You could even control it yourself, allowing access only to certain places at certain times. That way you'd have the best of both worlds. Your business customers will be happy, but you can also create an away-from-it-all feeling too.'

Clara leaned forward, her arm resting on Seth's.

'She has a point. It would be daft to alienate people and turn away good money for the sake of your principles. If customers have a choice about whether to access the Wi-Fi or not, you won't be giving anyone an excuse not to choose this place as somewhere to stay.'

'I didn't even know you could do such a thing,' replied Seth. 'Are you sure that's possible?'

'Absolutely. I wouldn't have mentioned it if it wasn't. My main reason for suggesting it, however, is not because you'll need it in the future, but because, right now, having access to the internet could save you a fortune in sourcing materials; which materials, where to get them at the best price, etcetera. Everything you need at the click of a button. The hours you would save would make it worth its weight in gold.'

'Except, there is still one small problem,' said Clara. 'Seth's already mentioned that there's no decent broadband available here.'

Maddie grinned at the faces around the table. 'Ah, but I met someone the other day who might hold the key to that particular problem. Apparently, you can have broadband radioed in, to a dish which you put up on site, a bit like satellite TV.'

'Which will be hideously expensive, I'm sure…'

'Seth, just listen,' argued Clara, poking him in the ribs this time. She raised her eyebrows at Maddie.

'No, it's not apparently. More than the usual service, yes, but not prohibitively so.'

'And you could find out?'

'I can.'

'Right then,' said Seth with finality. 'That sounds like it's a distinct possibility. Now, does anyone want one final cup of tea before we clear this lot away? Tom, you and I have a roof to thatch.'

Chapter 9

Maddie had never driven a car so large before but, despite feeling like a doll sitting in an oversized plaything, it was remarkably easy. Effortless, even. And so much smoother than her own little sports car which hugged the road and felt every bump. Even so, her heart was going like the clappers.

There'd been no choice really, not if she wanted to go and see Trixie and strike while the iron was hot. The initial news about her own car wasn't good. If it was repairable at all, it would take some time and it had been Seth's idea that she take his car. She had half hoped that he might offer to go with her, but in reality, she knew there was far too much for him to do. Still, having him with her would have allayed a little of her anxiety, whereas now it was just her and the road…

The gaping hole in the hedgerow was still plain to see as she drove past. All she wanted to do was shut her eyes, but this didn't seem entirely sensible and so she gripped the wheel and carried on. She realised as she drove that the car's height advantage gave her a much better view of things. Nothing seemed quite as big as it had before. Perhaps it was this that made her feel safer and, as she pulled into the car park of the pub for the second time that week, she began to understand the necessity of having vehicles like these in the countryside. Chelsea tractors, they were known as in the city, but here they were a flipping godsend.

She found a parking space with ease even though it was approaching lunchtime and climbed stiffly from the car. There probably wasn't much else she'd be up for today, but if she could at least get this one thing sorted she would feel as if she were making some sort of contribution. She pulled open the pub door and scanned the inside.

The place was deserted, except for a customer who looked remarkably like the man who had been propping up the bar last time she was here. Different clothes maybe, but still the same defeated air. She glanced at her watch; bang on one o'clock and not a punter in sight.

She wandered over to the bar, perched on the edge of a stool and pulled out her phone to check the signal. It took only a moment to connect using the same password as before, and Maddie was pleased to see that the service was as strong as ever.

'She's out back.'

'I'm sorry?' She turned to see that the man had finally looked up from his pint and was staring at her.

'Bloody barmaid,' he said. 'She's out back.' This time there was an accompanying jerk of his head towards a door behind him at the end of the bar. 'You might as well go and see,' he added, 'you're wasting your time sat there waiting for her.'

Maddie slipped off her stool with a nod and headed out back and past an array of refuse bins, stacks of beer barrels and a vent in the wall blowing out steamy air. Beyond it, next to a grimy blue door, a small red car was parked, its boot raised and almost overflowing with boxes. Of Trixie, however, there was no sign.

She was about to turn away when the door beside her burst open and Trixie cannoned into her, clutching another huge box. She didn't know who was the more surprised.

'Blinkin' 'eck, you scared me!' said Trixie, bringing one knee up to stop the box from slipping. She hitched it up, adjusting her arms to get a better grip.

'Sorry... can I help?' replied Maddie.

'Nah, I'm good,' she replied. 'Just let me dump this in the car.'

She moved past Maddie and all but threw the box down in the boot. Then she turned to face Maddie, her hands on her hips, eyes narrowing.

'You're the woman from the other day, aren't you?' she asked. 'The one that liked my mushrooms?'

Maddie grinned. 'Well, they were rather nice.'

'And now very definitely *off* the menu. If you were after lunch again today, you're out of luck I'm afraid.' She glanced back towards her car. 'Once I've shifted the last of these boxes, I'm off. That fat bastard can find someone else to run his grubby little hands all over, 'cause it's not going to be me.'

She gave Maddie a rather fierce look.

'Oh.' It was all she could think of to say. Trixie certainly didn't look like the type of person who would put up with anything she didn't want to.

'Yeah, bit of a bummer, isn't it, seeing as I've got nowhere to live now either, but he can stick his job, and his poxy room.'

Maddie gave her a sympathetic look. 'What are you going to do?'

Trixie cocked her head to one side. 'Stay with a mate... for now. Not much I can do, is there?'

'But surely you could complain? To the brewery, or someone? He shouldn't be allowed to get away with it.'

'Well, you'd think that, wouldn't you? Maybe where you come from, but not here. I'm just the barmaid; probably not the first to get their arse grabbed by their boss, and probably not the last. Who's going to listen to me, anyway?'

Maddie had no answer for her. It wasn't right, not by a long stretch, but she had a feeling Trixie's interpretation of the situation was pretty accurate. She was a low-paid worker who probably didn't even have a contract.

'Listen, I had a bit of an accident yesterday so I'm not sure I can help you carry anything, but will all of your stuff fit in your car? I've an enormous Range Rover in the car park, I could help ferry stuff…'

Trixie's eyes lit up. 'Oh would you? It's all my books, you see. There's masses of them, and I can't leave them here. Only I didn't really want to have to come back for them. Once I'm gone, I'm gone, you know.'

Maddie knew exactly how she felt.

'Really, it's no trouble. I came to ask a favour of you actually, so that makes us even.'

'Oh?'

'It might be a bit of a long shot, but I've just started a new job myself and I need to get some decent broadband sorted out. I was wondering if you knew the name of the company that supplied the pub. I thought maybe I could get in touch with them.'

Trixie gave her an appraising glance. 'You're over at Seth's place, aren't you?' she said. 'I thought that might be you.'

The question surprised her. 'Yes.' She frowned. 'But how could you possibly—'

'Everybody round here knows Seth.' There was something about the way she said it that prevented Maddie from making a reply. She smiled. 'Come inside a minute.'

Maddie followed her through to a dimly lit narrow passageway which led to a large-sized kitchen. Down its middle ran a huge stainless steel table where at least half a dozen boxes still sat. Trixie had a lot of books.

Trixie crossed over to a door in one corner of the tiled room and pulled it open. On its reverse was a large cork notice board decorated with curled bits of paper. After a moment scanning the contents, Trixie plucked a card from one corner and held it out for Maddie.

'There you go. All the details are on there.'

Maddie rummaged in her bag. 'Have you got a pen?' she asked.

Trixie shook her head. 'Probably, but just take the card anyway.'

'Won't your boss need it?'

She received a long look. 'Yeah, it'll be a real shame when he won't be able to find it.' Then she broke into a wide grin. 'Come on,' she said. 'Go and bring your car round and I can shift the last of these boxes. I don't want to stay here any longer than I have to.'

Maddie dropped the card into her bag and fished out the car keys instead.

'Won't be a minute.'

★

She was back on the road less than an hour later. Trixie's friend lived only five minutes away from the town, in a house that didn't look big enough to accommodate *her*, let alone the large number of boxes that accompanied her. Maddie felt bad about not being able to help her carry them into the house, but there was no way she would be able to lift them. She was beginning to feel utterly drained again. Just standing and walking for the little time she had were beginning to take their toll.

Still, her handbag held the rewards of a mission accomplished, and not only that but she had also found out something very interesting. A quick glance inside one of Trixie's many boxes revealed not trashy fiction, as she had rather rashly assumed, but a veritable pantry of cookbooks from around the world. Trixie's guilty pleasure had certainly given Maddie food for thought as she navigated the lanes back to the farm.

After dumping her things in the kitchen, she set off to find Clara. There was evidence of her in the garden – a fleece discarded over one of the benches, a stack of canes and string propped up against it – but no sign of the woman herself.

As Maddie wandered through the pathways that bisected the space, she saw for the first time the intricacies and organisation of the planting that perfectly filled every inch of usable space. She was no expert, but through the abundance of flowers and colour, she could see that for the most part the garden had been given over to the growing of vegetables.

'Maddie!'

She looked up to see Clara madly waving, standing over by the barn across the far side of the garden.

'Come over, there's something I want to show you.'

Maddie raised an arm and did as she was asked, trying to move as quickly as possible. When she finally made it to Clara's side she could see she was frowning.

'You need to go and lie down,' she said. 'Look at you, you can hardly walk.'

Maddie would normally have argued, insisting she was fine, but there was something about the look on Clara's open face that simply made her shrug instead.

'In a bit,' was all she said. 'What did you want to show me?'

But Clara wasn't about to let it drop. 'I'm serious. I would never have called you over if I'd known you were in so much pain. You probably should have gone to hospital yesterday.'

'I'm fine, honestly. It's just a bit of whiplash, that's all. Nothing that a couple of paracetamol won't cure.'

'Then I suggest you go and take them. What are you even doing out here?'

'Looking for you actually,' Maddie replied. 'I wanted to ask you something.'

Clara grinned. 'I wanted to ask you something too. It would be weird if it was the same thing, wouldn't it?'

'It would be more than weird... I hardly dare to ask you now.'

'And I wanted to show you something too,' Clara added. 'Can you come in the barn? I know you had some ideas for this place,' she continued, once they were inside. 'Only I've been thinking about it too.'

Maddie grimaced as she looked up at the huge expanse of roof timbers above her.

'I think I got a bit carried away,' she said. 'Frankly, I'm a bit embarrassed at my suggestions now.'

She hadn't realised until she said it how true this was. It seemed ridiculous to her that only yesterday she had stood telling Seth her vision for this place, proud as anything of her ideas, and yet now, in such a short space of time, they seemed incongruous and at best inappropriate. Perhaps it was the bump to the head.

Clara smiled warmly. 'Well the whole glass thing, maybe,' she said. 'It's not really us, is it? But that aside, Seth was really impressed with your ideas for the use of the space.'

Maddie stared at her. 'He was?' she asked, feeling a little surge of pride. Maybe she hadn't got things so very wrong after all.

'Yes. I don't think he'd ever thought of being able to use the barn, but he said you mentioned some sort of communal area? Somewhere all the guests might use?'

It was the first time Maddie had been inside, and the space was much bigger that she had thought. It made her ideas about walls of glass seem ridiculous; the cost of them alone would be sky high.

'Business users was what I was originally thinking. I saw this space as a centre for meetings, conferencing, even hot-desking. I thought we could provide breakout spaces and refreshments, and from there it wasn't too far a leap to extend those services to include gourmet food for residential guests if they wanted it, so the best of both worlds.' She paused for a moment. 'I was looking for some angle that might set this place apart from the competition.'

Clara looked doubtful. 'I get that, and I won't pretend to understand what "hot-desking" is, but do you really think that's the way to go? Aren't there lots of other places where you can hire rooms for meetings?'

'There are, but none of them would have the state-of-the-art facilities that we could offer under one roof. I thought if we could attract the right sort of businesses, we could charge a fortune for additional services. The type of customer I was thinking of would be those used to the highest specification IT for example, a really bespoke service, top-quality food—' She broke off at the look on Clara's face. 'That's not going to work here, is it? I've realised that.'

'I just can't see why business people would come to our little corner of Shropshire. We're a bit in the middle of nowhere here… It's just too far a leap from where we are now, and the sums of money involved would be—'

'Astronomic. I know, it's a ridiculous idea…' Maddie scanned the roof. 'I'm thinking with my London head on and I really need to stop.'

'Not stop, just maybe refocus all those brilliant ideas in a slightly different direction. I don't think Seth had even considered that the barn might be a useful addition to what we're trying to do here, so if it hadn't been for you…'

'Now you're just trying to be kind.'

'And is there anything wrong with that?' She took Maddie gently by the arm. 'There's scarcely enough kindness in the world as it is, and yet we continue to be our own worst enemies. We beat ourselves up over the slightest thing, even when our intentions are good ones. If we can't even be kind to ourselves… well, maybe other people need to be kind for us.' She smiled. 'I've been trying to think of a use for this space that fulfils that ideal, but I'm not sure I've quite got the imagination for it.'

'Who's being hard on who now?' asked Maddie, with an answering smile of her own. 'You must have had some ideas. Come on, tell me what you've been thinking.'

To her amusement, Clara just shrugged. 'Nothing at all really. Maybe you could give it some more thought though, in a different direction from the whole business angle. Something more… communal, that all our guests could use. I mean it's close to the garden, and to the cottages themselves, there must be something.'

'That's the most unsubtle point in the right direction I've ever heard, Clara.' She tutted, but with good humour. Perhaps the daft idea she'd had earlier in the day while talking to Trixie wasn't quite so daft after all.

Clara looked shocked. 'I don't know what you mean,' she said indignantly, hand over her heart, but then she broke into a broad grin. 'Right, no messing now, let's get you back to the house for a lie-down.'

Chapter 10

Maddie's lie-down turned out to be rather longer than she expected. Left to her own devices she would probably have carried on, but Clara had insisted that she take some pain medication and go to bed. The minute her limbs sank into the soft mattress, Maddie could feel waves of tiredness begin to consume her and she let herself get lost in the feeling. It was several hours before she woke, stiff and cold down one side where her arm had rested outside of the covers. She pulled herself upright only to set her alarm and drink from the glass of water beside the bed and then she let sleep take her once more.

She was determined that the next morning would not be a repeat of the day before and even though her alarm went off as planned, she was already wide awake and mentally running through the list of things that she wanted to look at during the course of the day. Whether she would physically be able to achieve anything on this list was another matter, but a gentle testing of her muscles seemed to suggest that, while everywhere still ached, there was none of the searing pain from yesterday.

Her conversation with Clara was still very fresh in her mind and, as usual, her imagination was running on overdrive, fed, she knew, by Clara's generous hints about what to do with the barn. She was still a little uncertain how she felt about Clara – everything she did or said hinted at a very close relationship with Seth, and yet she didn't seem suspicious of Maddie at all, just genuine in her desire to help. Their discussion had solidified one thing, though; Maddie's idea about Trixie might not be quite so ridiculous after all. In fact, it might also go some way to solving another problem…

The first thing on her list, however, was to make Seth and herself breakfast. His generosity of the day before had not only taken her by surprise, but had also gone a long way to repair their relationship. The least she could do was feed the man.

To her surprise, Seth was already in the kitchen nursing a huge mug of coffee. The rich smell pervaded the room and the minute he caught sight of her he crossed to the machine which stood on the counter and poured her a cup.

'You're not supposed to be up yet,' he remarked, placing her mug down in front of her. 'How are you feeling?'

'Better,' she said firmly.

He raised his eyebrows. 'Really?'

'Okay, a bit better,' she conceded. 'A subtle, yet discernible improvement, will that do?'

He laughed. 'Still shit then.' He watched while Maddie took her seat. 'Well, I for one was in definite need of a kick-start this morning and I'm one coffee down already and still not sure I'm functioning at the required level. Do you want something to eat?'

'No, no, my turn this morning. It's the least I can do after causing everyone so much trouble. Plus, I didn't exactly pull my weight yesterday.'

'There's no expectation, Maddie. We all do what we can, when we can, and that varies from day to day. It's just how we do things here. No clocking-on times, no clocking-off times…' He dropped his eyes. 'Tom won't be around today, and neither will Clara.'

'Oh, I was going to spend some time with her today, she was going to show me...' She stopped when she caught sight of the expression on his face. 'Is everything okay?' she asked quietly.

He sighed. 'I think so, she's probably just overtired... and Tom's hungover.'

'Hungover?'

'He plays in a band,' answered Seth briefly. 'And gets a bit carried away at times.'

Maddie frowned. There was something about Seth's tone that carried a distinct warning. Now was clearly not the time to be asking questions.

'In fact, I was thinking about today,' continued Seth. 'There are one or two things I need to attend to elsewhere and I wondered whether you might like to make a start on the office? You're going to need a place to work from, somewhere we can find you. And we'll need to keep records too... something else I've been a bit lax at. I thought you might like some time to make the place your own, you know, get things how you want them.'

He gave her a sheepish look. 'It's the perfect opportunity for you to take things a little easier today... and I'm afraid it is in a bit of a mess. It's not a room I tend to spend any time in you see, other than to just dump stuff on the desk.'

Maddie picked up her mug, realising that her intention to make breakfast was rapidly losing ground, as indeed was everything else on her list for the day.

'Oh right. So you want me to sort it all out?'

'Would you? I really can't face it.'

'And you'd be eternally grateful...'

He grinned at her. 'I would.'

'Well, I'll do it on one condition...'

'Which is?'

'That once I've finished this, you let me make you breakfast.'

★

The plan had been for the full works, but Seth would only settle for a sausage sandwich before practically running out of the door. After completing the washing-up, Maddie sat for a few moments longer, before she got to her feet and went and stood in the doorway to the office.

The only time she had been in here was when she was looking for a printer. She'd been so fixated on showing off her grand plan that she hadn't really stopped to look around the room, but now that she did, her heart sank. There was stuff everywhere: the desk was piled high with papers and books, a tower of boxes occupied one corner and a bookcase overflowed onto the floor around her. She pulled open a drawer from a small filing cabinet that was pushed under one end of the desk and groaned when she saw that it was stuffed with receipts. She looked at the cup of coffee in her hand – she had a feeling it wasn't going to be her last of the day.

Maddie was well used to paperwork. In fact, she prided herself on keeping the tightest of ships when it came to running the projects she had worked on previously. It meant that her time could be better spent achieving her project goals instead of drowning in admin. Today though, it looked like she had no choice.

But, she reasoned, if she was to succeed here at all she needed to get to grips with Joy's Acre and all that it encompassed. She already knew there were several things Seth was reluctant to talk about, but he had a deep connection with the place, that much was evident, and a very clear set of ideas about how he saw things taking shape. The two were inextricably linked, and perhaps here, she might find a few answers to the story that lay behind the farm.

The real question of course was, what exactly was in this room? Was it personal, or did it relate solely to the business? If she was to make any order out of the chaos, she would need to separate the two. She pulled a piece of paper forward to use as a coaster and put down her mug, eyeing up the bookcase. You could tell a lot by the books people read.

Maddie thought back to her own bookcases at home. An avid reader, she had several, lining the walls of her London flat; a home now rented out to a friend of a friend. She hoped they were taking good care of her little library. Not particularly meticulous in how she classified her books, she did however tend to group fiction and non-fiction together, but the one thing she did do, always, was to place her favourite books right where they would be easily to hand. She looked now at the bookcase in front of her, and homed in on the second shelf from the top, the one that was exactly at eye level.

It was an interesting selection: a couple of poetry books, several thrillers from well-known authors, a weighty tome that had won the Booker Prize the previous year, and several historic texts; social histories mainly. There were books on traditional crafts, one on moon gardening, whatever that was, and a pagan book of days. She gave this a sideways glance and pulled it off the shelf, removing the auction catalogue that was stuffed between its pages, serving as a bookmark. She rifled through the book, frowning at the unfamiliar names and concepts, and when an illustration caught her eye, she began to read.

Maddie wouldn't have described herself as religious in any sense, nor was she particularly attracted to the spiritual side of her nature. In fact, she wasn't sure that she even had one, but clearly other people did. It was interesting, but it interested her more that it was on Seth's bookcase. She looked up for a moment, thinking, before replacing the bookmark.

She was about to slide the volume back on the shelf when the catalogue itself caught her eye. It was from a specialist art auction, long since gone, but the fact that it was here at all was odd in itself. She glanced around the room, but the walls were bare here, much like the rest of the house.

She flicked through the catalogue, scanning the pages. It was pretty standard stuff, not much to her taste, but then she didn't own a huge stately pile in which to display large sombre oil paintings in heavily gilded frames. She paused at a page that had its corner turned down and peered at the thumbnail illustration. It was a watercolour by an artist that Maddie had never heard of. There was something vaguely familiar about it, even though the picture was too small to make out any real detail, but at least the colours were more vibrant than those elsewhere in the catalogue. She closed the brochure, replacing it exactly between the pages of the book where she had found it, and moved on.

After a few more minutes she straightened. The books were interesting; they had perhaps shown her a little more of Seth's character, but beyond that were not especially helpful. She turned around, surveying the room, and with a nod to herself, she set to work.

It soon became apparent that the room contained three different types of clutter. Some things, like the boxes in the corner, seemed to have been put there simply because there was no other place for them. They were filled with memorabilia, the kind of things you might put aside to sort through one day with the aim of throwing most of it away.

There were other random items too: a few pieces of clothing, some jewellery, which had obviously belonged to a woman, and some bottles of perfume. It was as she reached the bottom of one of these boxes and drew out a jar of face cream that she had a sudden feeling she was trespassing on something she had no right to see. The items were too personal, and clearly didn't belong to Seth. Perhaps to a part of his past, but if they were in boxes, a part that he had packed away. They intrigued her, but there was no way she would ever ask Seth about them, not right now at any rate. They had only just begun to rebuild their relationship, and prying into his personal life was a sure-fire way to have it come crashing down again.

Among the paperwork there were things which were obviously connected to the house itself – an instruction booklet for a washing machine, piles of old electricity bills – and, lastly, there were things which Maddie could see related directly to the business side of things at the farm – receipts for raw materials and the like.

She was torn between her natural desire to make order out of chaos and the need to accomplish her primary task, which was to make some space for her to work comfortably, where she might begin to keep paperwork of her own. Besides, without input from Seth it would be very hard to know for definite which papers belonged in which category. The best she could hope for was a rough approximation and a degree of tidiness. She picked up a pile of papers and began to sort.

Another hour passed in a flash, and she chided herself for getting side-tracked once too often. There was no need to read all the documents, she reminded herself, but somehow she found herself stopping every now and then, her attention caught by a detail. She tutted to herself, and replacing a sheaf of papers in her hand wandered through to the kitchen to re-boil the kettle. Her neck and back were beginning to ache terribly, and she needed to find some more paracetamol before the pain took over her again.

The kitchen was warm and sunny and, pills taken, she wandered out into the garden for a break. She had all day after all; it wouldn't hurt to pace herself, and she didn't usually have the chance to sit and enjoy the beautiful spring sunshine. She made her way down the paths to the bench, and ran her hand along the smooth warmth of the wood before sitting down. She stretched out her legs and closed her eyes, rolling her head from side to side to try to relax the muscles. The heat of the sun was soothing on her face.

She wasn't quite sure when and how it even happened, but as her eyes fluttered open she realised she must have fallen asleep. Her limbs felt heavy and languid in the sunshine, and she blinked and looked around her, suddenly seeing the beauty of the place. It was as if time was standing still, and there was just her, sitting alone on a bench with only the sun, the breeze and the birdsong for company. She felt infinitesimally small in the space around her, but utterly at peace, as if wrapped in warm arms that held her and comforted her. It was in stark contrast to the confusion of emotions that she had been bottling up for months now. Emotions which she could never seem to find release from, but which now seemed to have dissolved and lost their meaning. Tears sprang to her eyes and she let them fall, knowing that possibly, impossibly, everything in her life was finally right where it should be. She didn't think she had ever felt this way in her whole life before.

Hardly daring to move in case it broke the spell, she turned her head a fraction, letting her eyes roam over every detail of the space around her. Whereas before she had seen neglect and a mishmash of broken-down buildings, she now saw that they were merely sleeping, waiting to be brought back to life. They were home; a place of sanctuary, a place of love. She swallowed, cleared her throat, and stood, closing her eyes once more and breathing in deeply.

Her legs felt weak, as if she hadn't used them in a while, but she walked slowly down the paths of Clara's garden, the evidence of her industry and care everywhere she looked. There was variety of texture, smell, colour, shape and size that she was sure hadn't been there before. She trailed her fingers against the foliage, feeling the coolness of the leaves and the velvet softness of the blooms and knelt for a moment to remove a stray weed from between the rows of something planted in the vegetable garden before making her way back to the bench.

She hoped that Clara was all right. Her garden would need her soon, and Maddie saw how connected their relationship was, how each gave to the other. Removing one from the equation would cause the other to suffer. Maddie laid her back against the gentle curve of the wooden bench and let her body go limp. She still felt impossibly small but gradually, as she let the sun seep into her skin, the balance shifted again until, just like Alice in Wonderland, she felt herself grow to the right size again, at one with everything around her.

And with the feeling came a rush of understanding. Was this how the others felt, when they stood here, in Joy's Acre? Because if it was, suddenly everything made sense. And furthermore Maddie now knew very clearly why she was here, and what she needed to do. She turned around and squinted at the thatched cottage behind her, just to check, but there was no sign of Seth. She checked her watch – she had a lot of work to do, and with any luck by the time he put in a reappearance later, she'd have made a good start.

★

Even with her renewed enthusiasm, it still took Maddie a couple more hours before she had sorted through enough of the discarded paperwork to feel she had made a difference. At least it was tidy and if she were asked she would know roughly where to lay her hands on things. If her assumptions were correct, the only paperwork that now filled the drawers by the desk related to the farm itself, and she could begin to keep track of things directly.

When she was finished, she went out into the hallway and peered at the only picture hanging there. She'd seen it almost every time she had passed through the space, on her way to the kitchen, or up the stairs, even backwards and forwards through the front door, but she had never actually looked at it. Now that she did, it was obvious, and she smiled to herself.

Carefully, she took it down from the wall and, walking back through to the study, propped it up on the desk. She didn't need to recheck the auction catalogue, but she collected it just the same and studied the small photograph of the painting that Seth must have purchased over three years ago.

The photo didn't do it justice; the colours were too muted and indistinct. In fact, she was surprised that Seth had even recognised it from the catalogue, unless of course he'd been looking for it...

She picked up the painting, wondering how on earth she had missed the resemblance. In reality the garden and cottages were soft in colour, warm tones of red and ochre, gentle greens and pale yellows, whereas whoever had painted Joy's Acre all those years ago had slashed the canvas with bold statements of red and purple, vivid greens and oranges. But it was unmistakably the same place, brought to life by the as yet unknown painter.

She booted up the computer and studied the auction listing while she waited for it to load. It didn't tell her much, a few lines of well-used patter urging potential purchasers to part with their cash for the opportunity to own one of the few artworks available from this little-known, but undeniably gifted Victorian artist. Maddie checked the spelling and carefully typed the name into an internet search engine: *CJ Davenport*.

Once she found what she was looking for, she supposed she oughtn't to be surprised. The painting on the desk in front of Maddie was so vibrant and joyous that she smiled to herself at her use of the word. Because joyous was the perfect way to describe it, and back in the 1880s Cordelia Joy Davenport had painted a picture of Joy's Acre, the farm she loved so much she had given her name to it.

Chapter 11

It was getting late by the time Maddie heard the front door go and she jumped at the sudden noise and intrusion into her thoughts. There was a shouted hello and she rose stiffly from the chair to make her own greeting. Seth was standing in the hallway, a plastic folder and car keys in hand, looking, frankly, exhausted.

'Hi.' She smiled warmly.

His eyes moved to the space on the wall where the picture had recently hung, a look of alarm overtaking the smile that had begun to form.

'Don't worry, I have it,' she was quick to reassure him. 'It's safe on the desk in the office. Good day? You look tired, if you don't mind me saying.'

'So do you,' he countered. 'Long day, yes. Good day… possibly. I've been in London.'

'London?' Her heart began to beat a tiny bit faster. This couldn't have anything to do with her, could it?

He grinned. 'Yeah, big place. You know, capital city? Where the Queen lives?'

'Oh, ha ha,' she retorted. 'I'm just a bit surprised, that's all, I didn't think it was somewhere you usually went.'

'Well, I try very hard not to. This was just for a meeting I have to attend every now and again. Nothing to get excited about. How about you, what sort of a day have you had?'

'I've had an… interesting day.' She couldn't help but let the sentence dangle.

He gave her an odd look, and then flicked his gaze to the wall again.

'That have anything to do with it?' he asked.

'Probably.' She grinned. 'I can't believe I didn't notice it before, or its significance. I've spent the last few hours on the internet, finding out not very much at all, if I'm honest.' She paused. 'I tidied up and sorted stuff out first, but then I got sort of hooked, trying to find out about our elusive painter. Joy doesn't seem to have been particularly noteworthy.'

Another look she couldn't decipher the meaning of.

'Perhaps you were barking up slightly the wrong tree?' He glanced at his watch, causing Maddie to do the same.

'Flipping heck, is that the time? I meant to cook something for dinner, but then… I'll go and do it now.'

Seth followed her into the kitchen, dropping his keys on the table. 'Maddie, there's no hurry. I tell you what, I'm just going to go and get changed and then we can sort something out. Maybe some fish and chips? I don't feel like cooking, and I don't suppose you do either. I'll come and have a look at the office first though.'

He let her go ahead.

'Well, I've made a start anyway,' she said. 'It's nowhere near properly organised but I think it's better than it was.'

'I'll say,' he said, peering into the room. 'That's a huge improvement. You can see the floor… and the desk.' He indicated the computer, whose screen saver was now rolling up a series of pretty landscapes. 'Do you think you'll be able to work from here?' he asked. 'If there's anything you particularly need we can sort it out.'

'A few bits of stationery, nothing major,' Maddie replied. She picked up the painting from the desk. 'I'll just go and hang this back up again.'

She got as far as the door.

'Seth?' she said, turning round. 'You said just now I was barking up slightly the wrong tree? What did you mean?'

He crossed to the bookcase and studied it for a moment. 'So, I'm guessing you found the auction catalogue or you wouldn't have made the connection with the painting, but I did wonder whether or not you'd found this?'

He pulled out a slender leather-bound volume from the shelf. 'But I guess not. You see, Cordelia Joy Davenport's story is fascinating in itself, but Davenport was her maiden name; locally she was known as Mrs Hall, and Edwin Hall's story is perhaps even more interesting.'

He handed her the book. 'Have a read while I go and get sorted.'

★

Maddie was still reading when Seth appeared a while later with two plates of fish and chips on a tray. She swung her legs out from under her and laid the book down beside her.

'I haven't quite finished it yet, but I can see why the story fascinates you so much.'

He handed her the tray and crossed the room to switch on a lamp. 'Quite something, isn't it?'

'But is it true though? This is just one villager's account of events and, heart-breaking as it is, I can see that it would have been tempting to overly romanticise the story.'

'That's a very cynical view, Miss Porter,' replied Seth, but he was smiling. 'I've found other evidence over time to back up the story.' He took his plate from her and went to sit in an armchair opposite.

'I know a lot of folk nowadays who don't handle mental health issues particularly well, but if you suffered from bipolar back then and didn't have a husband to support you, there was only one place you were going to…'

'An asylum?'

Seth nodded. 'And don't forget there were no real treatments available as there are today – when Joy's black dog came upon her she would have potentially been a very real danger to herself, and possibly others. In Edwin's eyes the only way he could keep her safe was to build this place for her. She was free to roam the countryside as she pleased, safe from the prying eyes of others, and during the good times she was inspired to paint with utter brilliance.'

'It really was a grand gesture, wasn't it? I can't imagine loving anyone that much.'

'No?' replied Seth, his eyes locking on hers for a moment. A flicker of an emotion she couldn't define rippled through them, but then he looked away, and the only indication of his mood was a slight tightening of his jawline. 'Of course, Edwin was a wealthy man, which helped. I doubt many men would have been able to carry out such a gesture even if they had wanted to.'

Maddie shook her head. 'No, I suppose not. And so Joy was able to live out her days, safe and cared for, and create her beautiful works of art.' She took a mouthful of food, thinking. 'But was it really true that all those other people lived here too? Were they relatives of hers?'

Seth shook his head. 'There's nothing to suggest that they were, but the census records certainly support the information that this was their home. The Victorians were a righteous lot and I'm sure it would have been considered quite scandalous at the time. My own view is that, in her more lucid spells, Joy decided that she wanted to help other people like herself and so she researched some likely candidates and invited them to live here, with Edwin's permission of course. We can really only guess at Edwin's motives for going along with it, but I think perhaps by then he would have done anything for her...'

'That's quite an undertaking.'

'An original philanthropist no less. I also like to ponder that perhaps these people were somehow drawn here... That can happen in certain places, where people who need help of one sort or another all gravitate together.'

She gave him a sideways glance. 'Hmm, I'm not sure about that, but it's still a lovely story. Perhaps when we start to look at how we market Joy's Acre we could use it, it would draw people here in droves.'

As soon as she said it, she could see she'd overstepped the mark. Seth, who'd been busy forking up his food, went rigid; his hand, which was halfway to his mouth, froze in mid-air.

'I'm sorry,' she blurted out, 'that was a stupid thing to say. I've still got my marketing head on and in many ways it could be the perfect angle to pin our publicity on... But I can see how it might cheapen Edwin and Joy's memories...'

She wondered whether she'd blown it by being so thoughtless. Things had been so much better between her and Seth over the last day or so, and she didn't want to change that. She could kick herself sometimes. However, Seth merely lowered his fork gently to his plate and gave her a sad smile.

'It's not that so much, just... I had a different idea in mind, but no matter for now. And you're probably right; their story would create something of a talking point.' He stared down at his plate for a few seconds, his lips pursed together. 'You said you haven't quite finished the book yet?'

'No. I'm two or three chapters from the end I think.'

'So, you won't know that in the end even Edwin's love couldn't save Joy. She killed herself the day before her forty-eighth birthday.'

Maddie's hand flew to her mouth. 'No! Oh, that's so sad.'

'There are some things we can't alter no matter how hard we try.'

The sentence dangled in the space between them, the words laying a trail to something beyond. But was it an invitation, or a warning? Maddie's eyes began to prickle as the sorrow in Seth's voice made it clear it was the latter.

'What happened?' she whispered.

'She drowned herself in a well that sits just behind the cottages. She threw herself down, knowing she couldn't swim.'

Maddie gulped as a tide of emotion swept over her, visions of Joy filling her head; struggling for breath, cold and alone and filled with despair. It was awful. She fished in her pocket for a tissue, wiping beneath her eyes. There was a clatter from across the room as Seth hastily put down his plate. In a moment he was beside her, filling the space on the settee so that his thighs were only inches from her own.

'Maddie, I'm sorry, that was crass of me.' He handed her a hanky. 'Are you okay?' He laid a hand on her arm, his eyes searching hers.

She sniffed, nodding. 'Yes, I just... it was the surprise, that's all. That poor woman.' She took a deep breath, trying to regain control of her emotions.

'I shouldn't have just thrown it at you like that. I guess for many Victorians that might have been considered a ripe old age, but that doesn't lessen its impact here. It gets to me every time too.'

And it had, Maddie could see that. Her own reaction wasn't a surprise, her emotions were still a bit all over the place and she had always cried easily, but Seth had known this story for a long while, had researched it even, and yet it still visibly moved and affected him. His dark eyes glinted in the lamplight, his expression intense; a suggestion of emotion in them she couldn't clarify. If she didn't know better, she would have said he was close to tears as well. She felt herself begin to tremble. She couldn't ask, she wasn't sure she even wanted to know, but there would be a reason for his behaviour just as there was for hers...

She was anxious to move things along. 'So what happened to Edwin?'

'He stayed here.' Seth flicked his eyes away and she felt the connection between them break. 'Don't forget, by then, there were four other people living here, all of whom were either sick or had mental health issues of their own. Edwin continued to do what he had promised Joy he would, and so time just moved on I guess.'

She gave her nose another wipe as something suddenly occurred to her. 'They lived in the cottages, didn't they, they must have?'

'Yes.' Seth smiled. 'Edwin had the cottages built, not for estate workers as would usually have been the case, but for his "guests". They're not quite as old as the main house here.'

Maddie nodded towards his chair on the other side of the room, suddenly anxious to put some distance between them.

'Sorry, I interrupted your eating. Please, go and finish your dinner.'

She received an appraising glance, but Seth got up just the same and returned to his seat.

'So what happened to Joy's paintings? I don't know much about art but she doesn't seem to have been well known, either in her own time or now. Maybe they stayed with the family.'

'Edwin and Joy had no children, so there's no real family to speak of. That wasn't quite the issue though...'

There was something in Seth's voice that made her look up. 'Oh God, what now?'

'As far as I'm aware there are only four paintings in existence. I have one, which sits in the hallway, and the other three I've been trying to track down for years. They'll turn up eventually.'

She hardly dared to ask. 'So what happened to all the others? Four paintings is not much to show for a lifetime's work, even one that was cut short.'

Seth took a deep breath. 'Joy destroyed them all. Just before she killed herself. The scourge of the creative mind perhaps; to always doubt your own talent.'

'And the four that were salvaged were elsewhere, I suppose?'

'Here in the house, I'm presuming. That's how they survived.'

She closed her eyes and nodded briefly, opening them again and resolutely spearing several chips at once.

'We should finish these,' she said. 'Before everything gets really cold.'

The room fell silent as they both ate, lost in their own thoughts. Maddie could see why Seth was in love with this place. It was beautiful, she realised; the setting, the landscape, everything. She'd been so caught up in having to move away from London that she'd focused on the negatives of living in the country, never even considering what it had to offer. But put this together with such an emotive back story, and why wouldn't you want to live here?

She felt as if she'd been walking around with blinkers on since she'd arrived, and it had taken Joy and her bittersweet story to remove them. No wonder Seth had taken such offence at her ideas; they were ridiculous. This afternoon had sown the seeds of how things ought to be here at Joy's Acre and this conversation reinforced everything.

This time, however, she was not about to make the assumption that she knew best. This time, she would make sure that she fully understood Seth and his reasons for being here. As much as she could anyway; she was only too aware that there was a lot more to him than first appeared. She finished chewing and cleared her throat.

'So in a way, Joy's Acre was a sanctuary of sorts, wasn't it? Holiday cottages aside, I'm just wondering how you see it now?'

'Ah, the eternal dilemma…' He gave a rueful smile. 'Right now, I'm caught between a rock and a hard place. You're spot on in your assessment of how I'd really like to see things take shape here, but I have to be a realist too. First and foremost we need to make money before we can think of our longer-term goals, it's as simple as that. Initially I thought along the lines of making Joy's Acre a retreat, which I think fits best with my vision of how things were in Joy's day, but they're usually partly charity funded and are either religious or have a particular theme as a space for artists, or meditation, that kind of thing. That's too exclusive and I also don't have the funds to subsidise that kind of environment. I need money coming in, not going out, and so for the time being I think the only way forward is to offer the cottages for holidays. That way we start to make money immediately, it keeps Agatha happy, and it will also allow us to develop plans for the future and guide Joy's Acre to where we ultimately want it to be.'

'I agree that Agatha's more likely to support a holiday-let business. I love the idea of the cottages being here for people who need them but I can't see Agatha going for that kind of set-up, can you? She doesn't strike me as the charitable sort.'

'She wants a return on her investment, which is fair enough. I don't like the way Agatha conducts her business, but it's her affair, and although she might be able to stipulate how things are done, she can't change how I see the world. As long as I have that, there are always ways to… bend things to make them fit.'

Maddie thought about his words. They made perfect sense and she was glad he wasn't looking for Joy's Acre to become some sort of hippie 'new age' centre, she didn't think she could cope with that. It wasn't that she had anything against people who wanted to live that way, but in her experience they were often very keen to shove their enlightened way of life down your throat in a way that was anything but enlightened.

'So, where do we go from here?'

Seth scratched his head. 'I've tied myself in knots thinking how I can achieve what I want and get the best of both worlds. Now I reckon I've been overthinking it. Because if it's going to, it will happen of its own accord anyway. I'm a firm believer in fate playing a key role. I mean, you're here, aren't you?'

She frowned at him. 'What's that supposed to mean?'

He gave her a very direct look. 'Me, Tom, Clara, and now you. We're all up shit creek without a paddle. To a greater or lesser extent, granted, but—'

'I am not!' she protested.

'No? You could have fooled me.' He held her look for a moment. 'Get to know us, Maddie, and you'll find that we all have… things in our lives… and you're no different.' He smiled. 'It's not a criticism, far from it, it's an opportunity as far as I'm concerned. That's what I meant when I said I think things here will happen of their own accord, that people will be drawn to us because they have need of us. Sure, there are people who'll come here on holiday, eat too much, drink too much, sightsee and then go home again without a care in the world, but I think, perhaps in between, there will also be people who will take something else home with them. '

Maddie stared at him.

'So, in answer to your question, I think what we do here is crack on. We need to get these cottages ready and open for business as soon as possible... and then we wait and see what happens. So if you've got some amazing ideas up your sleeve, now would be a good time to hear them.'

She thought back to her time in the garden, to the intense feelings that had swept over her as she finally realised what Joy's Acre was all about. Her time with Seth had only served to reinforce that, and she felt a rush of energy.

'Oh yeah,' she said. 'I've got some ideas all right. I'll put the kettle on, shall I?'

Chapter 12

It had taken a week, but at the end of it Maddie had felt her plans really beginning to come together. She had been tentative at first – mindful of her previous bull-in-a-china-shop approach – but as he'd listened, Seth's smile had become a grin, and that grin had only grown wider and wider. Today he was practically jumping about in excitement as he, Maddie and Clara waited for Tom to come down from the roof so that they could update him on the latest developments.

The weather was still stunning and looked set to continue for at least another week, which had given them the perfect opportunity to move on apace with the new thatching. It was nowhere near finished of course, but the weather, together with the first of the contractors coming on site, had given things a real lift and Tom had been hard at it since early morning.

Maddie waited until he had joined them and passed him a cool drink.

'So, I had some ideas for the barn originally, which were total rubbish, and—'

'Aw, they weren't total rubbish, Maddie… just a bit—'

'Yeah, they were, Clara, stop trying to be kind.' Seth grinned at Maddie. 'Sorry, I interrupted… You had some totally rubbish ideas for the barn… and?'

Maddie swung her foot at him which he evaded easily. 'Yes, thank you, Seth. And… now I've had some better ideas.

'When I first heard that Clara was going to move into the thatched cottage, I got my knickers in a bit of a twist. Purely out of concern for the financial viability of the site, you understand, and when I looked into it the numbers just didn't stack up. So I started to look at where else we might create accommodation that would give us other benefits too. Purely by chance, I had a conversation with someone who gave me the solution to how that might work.'

'Her name's Trixie,' said Seth. 'Former barmaid of the Frog and Wicket, and soon to be Joy's Acre's resident cook.'

There was a surprised look from Tom.

'Trixie was the one who put me on to the solution for our broadband problem,' Maddie explained, 'but, she also happens to be an amazing cook. With a stroke of incredible timing, I also discovered that she was moving out of the pub and about to start looking for another job. It took a while to make contact with her after that, but when we did, Seth explained what we had in mind here and she jumped at the chance. So now we're going to convert the barn and make somewhere for both Clara and Trixie to live, and at the same time create a space to use as a dining area. Trixie will be on hand to cook gourmet meals for our guests and we can make it a feature of the place; self-catering but with added wow. She's also agreed to cook for us too.'

Tom belched. 'Oh, I'm liking the sound of that. Although I've been thrown out of the Frog and Wicket before, I hope she won't hold it against me. On second thoughts…'

Clara groaned. 'Tom, is there anywhere you haven't been thrown out of?'

He scratched his head in an exaggerated fashion. 'Good point,' he added. 'But it sounds like a great idea. People always like something they don't think they can get from anywhere else.'

'Well, I hope so. Now, obviously this is work that wasn't originally planned for, but what it will mean is that as soon as the thatched cottage is ready it can be offered for occupancy, rather than having Clara move in.' She glanced at Seth for confirmation.

She had not made reference to any aspect of Clara's relationship with Seth since their first disastrous conversation about the cottage, and just the thought of what she'd said made her cringe. It was still a ridiculous idea for Clara to live there but she knew better than to ask Seth why it was so important; she just had to accept that it was. It was obvious that there was something between them, but Maddie still couldn't work out what, and neither could she work out how that made her feel. What was worse was that she couldn't work out why she should feel anything at all; after all, it was none of her business. One day she would learn why Seth felt so strongly about Clara's presence, but that would be when she had earned her place here and the trust of others. For now, it was enough to build it into her plans without further question.

Seth nodded at Tom. 'So we're looking at early June for completion on the roof.'

'That's only six bloody weeks away,' grumbled Tom. 'What if we hit a spell of bad weather? That doesn't give me much leeway.'

'No, but it might keep you out of the pub,' remarked Clara.

Tom threw her a dark look. 'Yeah, all right, all right.'

Seth patted him on the back. 'We're all with you on this one, Tom, but I'm afraid even I'm going to have to insist that it's finished on time. I'll help where I can, but I'm away next week and I—'

'What?' Maddie butted in. 'You're going away?'

Beside her, Clara shifted uncomfortably.

'Er, yeah,' replied Seth.

'Well, that's news to me. Where are you going? How long are you going to be gone for? There'll be a million and one decisions I need to sign off on, you can't not be here.'

Seth kicked at a stone on the ground. 'Well, I won't be I'm afraid, and the arrangements can't be changed.' There was something about the tone of his voice that told her he wasn't prepared to try, either. 'I go on Monday, and I'll be back on Thursday; no time at all. And I'm sure that you'll cope with whatever needs doing, or decisions that need making. Anyway, Clara has a good idea of what's what. Between the two of you, I know you'll take care of things.'

Maddie looked from one face to the next. Clara was staring at the ground, and Tom was smiling but it didn't go anywhere near his eyes. She wasn't about to get any support from either of them. There was nothing she could do about it.

'Right, well I guess that's it then,' said Seth with finality. 'Tom, are you okay with the timescale? I know it's tight, but I will help when I can.'

He pulled a face. 'Not as much time as I'd like,' he replied. 'But I'll make sure it's not a problem. The boys in the band will just have to do without me for a bit. It won't kill them.' He gave Seth a steady look. 'It won't do me any harm either,' he added.

'And the garden, Clara? Difficult, I know.'

'I'll work around everyone else as best I can. Not sure what they'll be getting, but I promise it will look nice whatever.'

Seth beamed at everyone. 'Right then, wagons roll,' he said. 'Have we missed anything, Maddie?'

She looked directly at Tom. 'Just one last thing… Super-fast broadband is being installed a week today.'

He winked at Clara. 'Amen to that,' he said. 'Look out, ladies, here I come.'

Chapter 13

Maddie looked up at the sound of furious barking. The dogs were circling the yard, running to the gate and back again and dancing with excitement. A figure stood beside it, looking around as if wondering if she was in the right place.

Maddie smiled to herself. She scarcely noticed the dogs now, but she remembered all too clearly the day she had first arrived at Joy's Acre. The thought brought a flush to her cheeks. She had behaved like a spoiled, arrogant brat, and it was surprising that Seth had even let her across the threshold. She got up to go and welcome Trixie.

She opened the front door and waved. 'Hang on a minute, I'll come rescue you!'

Perhaps Trixie didn't hear because, after returning the wave, she opened the gate anyway, entering the yard. The dogs charged over, intent on giving her a full-on welcome and, to Maddie's surprise, Trixie dropped to her knees, holding her arms wide as first Bonnie and then Clyde rubbed up against her in delirium. Tails wagging furiously, they writhed around at her feet as if they hadn't seen her for years, tongues lolling and eyes rolling in their heads.

Eventually Trixie straightened, grinning broadly up at Maddie. 'Crikey, those two can stand any amount of fuss, can't they? What are their names?'

She walked over to where Maddie was standing, the dogs close on her heels.

'The blue-eyed one is Clyde, and the smaller of the two is Bonnie, his sister.'

Trixie brushed at her jeans and jumper, shaking off a cloud of fur which had transferred onto her.

'I might have guessed. They look like a couple of scoundrels.'

She turned her head, taking in the full extent of the house and its yard. She gave a low whistle.

'Blinkin' 'eck, this is a bit of all right, isn't it? Are you really sure you want me to come and live here? I might lower the tone.'

Maddie smiled at her. 'I don't think you need to worry. There's no tone set. No one stands on ceremony here. The house is pretty big, but it's not grand at all. Besides, everyone is really keen to meet you, although Seth is away at the moment, but he gets back tomorrow and will catch up with you then.'

'Yeah, well I'll be telling him to do something with the bloody driveway when I see him. How are folks supposed to find their way down here? I couldn't see a thing, the hedges are so high.'

Alleluia, thought Maddie.

'Come on, let's go inside. Would you like a drink first or should we just go and say hello? Clara's dying to meet you.'

'I'd love a cup of tea, if that's okay, we'd got no blooming milk this morning, and I'm gagging for one.'

Maddie could feel her shoulders relaxing; Trixie was going to fit in just fine.

★

Clara was standing in the middle of a large rectangle of mud, leaning on a fork. Her face was turned to the sky and her eyes were closed, a gentle smile on her face. Her hair, blowing in the wind, billowed out around her, showing off her mass of freckles.

Maddie stopped on the path, not wishing to make her jump. Trixie, a few steps behind, came to stand beside her.

'Whatever she's on, I'll have some,' she whispered, and Maddie smiled. Clara did indeed look beautiful, peaceful and serene, totally at one with the space around her.

Clara was still some distance away, and Maddie doubted she could have heard Trixie's soft voice but she opened her eyes and looked in their direction, breaking into a smile as she caught sight of them. She wasn't at all embarrassed by having been spotted in such a reverie.

'Isn't it beautiful?' she called. 'Days like this just make you feel glad to be alive.'

The sun was warm on her skin, and Maddie realised it was lovely being able to wander outside at will. So much of her life before had been spent indoors that she rarely thought about the weather. She had certainly never been made to feel grateful for her place in the world by it. It was a nice thought.

She turned to look at Trixie, whose mouth was hanging open in wonder. 'Come and say hello,' she said.

But Clara had already thrust the fork deeper into the soil so that it would stay upright of its own accord and was marching down the path towards them. She held out her hand, covered in mud as usual.

'I've heard so much about you,' she said. 'It's lovely to have you here. I'm Clara.'

Trixie blushed a little, perhaps unused to such a warm greeting.

'I'm just amazed to be here at all,' she said, 'but it's fantastic. Look at what you've got here.' She swung around as if to illustrate her point, her gaze settling on the bed that Clara had obviously been digging. 'Do you really look after all this, all by yourself?'

Now it was Clara's turn to blush. 'Mostly,' she said. 'Seth gives me a hand with some of the heavier stuff when he can, but other than that, yes, it's my little kingdom.'

Trixie watched her for a moment. 'Is everything okay now? I read about what happened of course and…' She stopped suddenly. 'Sorry, you probably don't want to talk about it any more.'

Clara flashed Maddie an anxious look. 'Well, it was years ago and I… but yes, I'm fine, thank you.'

There was something else in that look too, thought Maddie, something she couldn't quite put her finger on. Guilt perhaps? Whatever it was, the subject matter was clearly not something Clara was keen to dwell on, or let Maddie be party to.

She gave a slightly nervous smile, pointing to the far end of the garden. 'Would you like the grand tour?' she asked.

Trixie nodded vigorously. 'Oh, yes please!'

And the moment, whatever it was, passed as the two of them moved forward.

Of course the garden held a lot more than just vegetables, but as they walked around it was clear to see where Trixie's interest lay. In fact, she and Clara were chatting as if they'd known one another for years, and in many ways their combined interests fitted together perfectly. Clara was a knowledgeable and instinctive gardener and Trixie a natural and intuitive cook. So, as Clara explained the various crops and how she grew them, when they were at their best, and what varieties she used, Trixie provided a running commentary on how she might use them in her recipes, what worked well with what and asked endless questions to check what everyone liked.

'I feel like I've been let loose in a sweet shop,' she said as they made their way back to where they started. 'Honestly, I've never seen so much variety, imagine what it will be like come the summer.'

Maddie could see Clara swell with pride as she showed off her hard work.

'We'll probably get a glut of certain things, that always happens. One hundred and one ways to use a courgette, now there's a book someone should write.'

'I guess,' replied Trixie, clearly thinking. 'But that's what's so amazing too, being able to use fresh ingredients, but more importantly seasonal ingredients. A while back I used to live above a greengrocer's shop and I often had just enough time when I got back from work to pop in before he closed and grab whatever was left. It was much cheaper for one, but because I didn't always have a choice it made me try out new recipes, things I probably would never have attempted before. It was good experience, I suppose.'

Maddie stood back, enjoying the ripples of excitement and enthusiasm that were coming off the pair of them in waves. Whatever doubts she might have had about them not getting on had vanished in an instant. Their mutual love of food, one in growing, the other in cooking, would stand them in very good stead.

'And of course if there's anything you particularly like, let me know. It's key sowing and planting season over the next couple of months, so if I've missed anything just shout.' Clara pointed over at the bed she'd been digging. 'New potatoes are just about to go in there, and I've got leeks, broad beans and parsnips lined up. Plus, the ubiquitous runner beans, which will be coming out of our ears in late summer.'

'But they're great preserved, have you ever tried it?'

Clara shook her head. 'I've often thought we should be doing more of that, but I haven't got the time, and what surplus we have at the moment I sell at the local farmers' market.' She frowned. 'Which is fine, but what *we* have a glut of so does everyone else, so produce often ends up getting sold much more cheaply than it should.'

'Could we add value by offering preserves or homemade savouries, cakes, soups even perhaps?'

'Definitely! Would you be up for that?'

Trixie grinned at her. 'Try and stop me,' she said. But then she pursed her lips, anxiety flooding her face. 'Bloody hell, would you listen to me? Sorry, Maddie, I'm shooting my mouth off; I haven't even moved in yet and I—'

Maddie gave Clara an amused look. 'Should we go and show her the barn now, do you think? That will totally blow her away.'

★

'I can't believe I'm even here, let alone that you're doing all this for me. I mean, you don't even really know me.'

They were standing in the open space of the barn, looking up at the timbers above them.

'True, but I'm a great believer in going with my hunches.'

She received a sideways glance. 'You really did like my mushrooms, didn't you?'

Maddie thought for a moment. 'What I liked was the fact that you had a shitty job, in a shitty pub, serving shitty food, and yet you weren't happy to settle for that. You made me the most beautiful mushrooms on toast, not because anybody was paying you to, or because it would have done you any favours, but because you could, and because you wanted to. I liked that about you. You had your own standards to maintain whatever the circumstances, and that takes integrity.'

Trixie flashed her a wide grin. 'Not sure I know what that means, but it sounded like a compliment, so thank you. And you're really going to put a proper kitchen in here, and a place for folks to eat?'

'That's the plan,' replied Maddie, 'which is all going to take a little time. The builders are going to be working morning, noon, and night. Meanwhile, you'll have to slum it with us in the house.'

'Are you sure I won't be in the way?'

Maddie gave her a pointed look. 'Trixie, I'm not being funny, but you don't actually have anywhere to live, do you? And coming here will be doing us a massive favour. It's a win-win situation as far as I'm concerned.'

She gave her watch a quick glance. It was nearing half past ten. Clara caught her look of frustration.

'No, I haven't heard from him, either,' she said, knowing exactly what Maddie was thinking. 'Although, if I know Tom, he's probably still lazing in bed.'

'I was hoping to introduce him, that's all,' she remarked. She turned to Trixie. 'Tom is our thatcher,' she explained, 'and he's a tad unreliable at times,' she added, seeing Clara's look of disapproval.

He'd been completely unreliable while Seth had been away, but she didn't want to moan about him when Trixie had only just arrived. She'd save that for when she and Clara were alone. It was just one of the reasons why she'd be glad to have Seth return in the morning.

'Anyway, why don't I show you the rest of the house and where your room is going to be? There's a bit of a junk room downstairs that we're planning to clear out – not done yet, I'm afraid, but hopefully it will be ready by the time you move in. We thought you could put your books in there.'

Trixie beamed. 'You really don't need to go to so much trouble, and I'd be more than happy to clear out the room myself, it's the least I can do.' She gave them both a rather shy look. 'I haven't got to rush off anywhere today, so I wondered whether you might like me to stay and cook tea?'

★

It was late by the time Maddie was ready to turn out the light and go to sleep. After helping Clara dig the garden for several hours in the afternoon, Trixie had made them both the most sublime risotto, and coupled with the rest of the white wine that hadn't made it into the dish, they had stayed parked at the kitchen table for hours, talking. Parts of Trixie's past were colourful indeed but they made for entertaining listening.

Lying in bed, Maddie was just about to put her book to one side when a scrabbling noise at her door caught her attention. She pulled it open, only to see a flash of ginger streak past her.

'Oh, no you don't,' she said, picking up Rumpus, ready to deposit him back outside the door. He was warm and heavy in her arms. She sighed. 'Okay then, just this once… and only because the master of the house is away.'

The cat needed no further invitation. The moment she put him down he jumped on the bed, where he waited for her to climb under the covers again. He turned around several times before finding a spot sufficiently warm for his liking and settled down. Within minutes both Maddie and Rumpus were fast asleep.

Chapter 14

At least Tom had turned up for work this morning. If she were being cynical, Maddie would say that it was because Seth was coming back today, but Tom would only smile and say that it was just pure coincidence. Whatever the reason, Maddie was happy to see him. Work was progressing well inside the cottage and she was adamant that they stick to their deadline.

She called a greeting to him as she passed by to speak to Clara.

'How's it going, Tom?'

He gave her a thumbs up. 'She's coming along nicely, I reckon. I could do with Seth making up the spars for me, then I wouldn't have to keep stopping, same with the yelms, but beggars can't be choosers, I'll manage.'

Maddie squinted up at him. 'Sorry, I have absolutely no idea what you're talking about.'

Tom pulled out a vicious-looking two-pronged stake from where he was working.

'That's a spar.' He grinned. 'Made from a hazel twig, and twisted in the middle, it's essentially a big staple and is what's holding this baby together. I'll get through several hundred by the time I'm done... And you don't buy 'em, you make 'em.'

'Oh,' she replied, surprised. 'Do you know, I never even thought about that. I don't know what I thought really, probably not much if I'm honest.'

'Aye, not much thatching in London, I reckon, least not nowadays.'

'I hardly dare ask, but what was the other thing you mentioned, yams was it?'

Tom laughed. 'Not quite,' he said. 'Y-e-l-m-s – yelms, an altogether different thing. To put it simply they're bales of straw, shaped and strung, and you have to make them too, maybe six hundred or so.' He leaned backward, patting a second ladder that lay on the roof beside him. 'Do you want to come up and have a look?'

Maddie wasn't sure if her legs would take the height, but it seemed rude not to. 'Erm, I'm not actually sure I can, how do I do it?'

It sounded like a ridiculous question, but she'd never been up a ladder in her life before, at least not one that high.

'Hold up,' shouted Tom, 'I'll come to you.'

He was on the ground in seconds, the ladder bouncing alarmingly as he shot down. 'I'll follow you up.'

For one awful minute she thought he meant he would literally follow behind her, and she didn't think she knew Tom well enough yet to have him in quite such close proximity, but to her relief he merely held the ladder until she was a few rungs up and then began to climb his own, keeping pace with her ascent.

'Best not look down if your knees do that weird jelly thing,' he said. 'Just lie against the ladder.'

She was breathing rather more rapidly by the time she got to the top, but she had done it. And then she looked up and what little breath she had left was taken from her. From her vantage point close to the roof's apex, she suddenly saw the whole of Joy's Acre spread out before her.

She felt like she was flying. To the front of her lay the swoop and sway of the fields and hedges, beginning to turn every shade of green in the spring sunshine as they descended the hill into the distance. Closer at hand were the estate gardens, filling the landscape with colour and texture in ordered shapes and pattern, and then behind her the warm solidarity of the handsome farmhouse, its windows glinting in the light. It was a magical feeling to be able to gaze upon it all, and she felt humbled to be at its centre. She turned to look at Tom, who had a broad grin on his face.

'No finer view, is there?' he said. 'Doesn't matter where you are, things always look amazing from up on a roof. It gives you a whole different perspective on life.'

And Maddie could see that it was true. She gave a wry smile and looked back down at her ladder, which was lying against a patch of roof that had yet to be re-thatched. It looked a complete mess if she were honest.

'That's where Seth has taken off the top layers already,' indicated Tom. 'You're looking at one-hundred-and-twenty-five-year-old thatch underneath, give or take a few years.'

Maddie stared at the roof in front of her. 'Is that the god-awful mess I was helping Seth to cart away the other day?'

'Aye, Seth mentioned he'd got you working on that.' There was an amused twinkle in his eye. 'Pretty grotty stuff, isn't it?'

'Yeah, but…' She paused. 'I never realised there was quite so much to it. I thought you just took off the old roof and put on the new one, but this… it's like a slice of living history.'

Tom grinned at her. 'Now you're getting it,' he said. 'This section of thatch was laid in Victorian times, probably when Joy and Edwin were living here, imagine what that must have been like.'

Maddie risked a glance around her. 'The place probably looked nothing like this then.'

'No, I don't suppose it did, but to be honest thatching is not much different now, we still use all the old traditional methods.' He pulled a spar from the roof and handed it to her. 'Just the same. How many things can you say that about today?'

She stared at it, mesmerised, suddenly understanding why Seth and Tom felt so passionate about this. Seth must have wanted to slap her when she'd been so scathing about the word 'heritage'.

'I am the biggest idiot,' she said.

Tom shrugged. 'Different lives, is all,' he said. 'If you've never come across it, why would you think about it? I just consider myself lucky that I get to carry on the tradition. As long as we keep doing that, nothing is lost.'

'And that's why you're training Seth? So that there's someone else who can carry this on too?'

'Pretty much. How long does it take to learn, do you reckon?'

Maddie thought for a moment. 'I've no idea,' she said. 'And knowing me, I'll probably say something really offensive.' She grimaced.

'Well then, how long does it take a doctor to train? You must have an idea about that.'

'Five years or so?'

'Right. And it takes an apprentice thatcher four years to learn his craft, then another couple before they're any good...' He let the sentence trail into the air.

Maddie could feel her cheeks beginning to burn. 'Like I said, I really am the biggest idiot. I'm sorry, Tom, I think it's pretty obvious I had no clue before, and I've been horrendously rude as well. But I do get it now, I honestly do... and I think it's amazing. I'm not just saying that.'

Tom patted her hand. 'Aye, I can see that.' He winked at her. 'We'll have you making the spars next.'

She laughed. 'Don't push your luck. Besides, Seth's back today, and I'm pretty certain I'd be rubbish at it.'

'Don't be so hard on yourself, you never know. And it will take Seth a few days before he's up to much, I may well be knocking at your door.'

He indicated that they should go down again, but she caught hold of his arm. 'Why? I thought he was just away on a business trip.'

A look of alarm crossed Tom's face. 'Yeah, that's right.'

His reply was nonchalant, but Maddie wasn't about to let it drop. There had been altogether too much secrecy surrounding Seth's few days away, and it felt as if she was the only one who didn't know what was going on.

She narrowed her eyes at him. 'So why won't he be up to much then, Tom? If it's just a business trip.'

This time he groaned. 'Shit, look, I shouldn't have mentioned anything, okay. Forget I even said it.'

'I couldn't possibly,' she replied, holding his look. 'Come on, Tom, what's the big secret?'

Tom passed a hand over his face. 'Maybe ask Clara, I dunno, but I'm saying nothing.' His look was apologetic. 'I'm sorry, Maddie, but I promised. My mouth has got me into all sorts of trouble in the past, but not this time. If Seth wanted you to know where he was going he'd have told you himself.'

She relented. It wasn't Tom's fault and he was trying to be a good friend. Besides, she didn't want to spoil what had been a very revealing few minutes. Tom might come across as lazy and unreliable at times, but there was a deep passion that ran under his skin, and he'd been generous enough to share some of that with her today.

'Ah well, perhaps you *will* have to call on me to make some spars for you then, after all.' She took a final look at the roof and the amazing view. 'Thanks, Tom. I mean it, I learned a lot today.'

They both knew she wasn't just referring to thatching.

Tom followed her down to the ground and then began to re-climb his ladder.

'Catch you later,' he said, and winked in farewell.

The trouble was that Maddie understood Tom's stance perfectly well, but that didn't remove her desire to find out what was happening. She was just beginning to find her feet here, to feel as if she belonged in her own right, and she knew from bitter experience that miscommunication could lead to disaster. She had hoped that she and Seth had got over their rather disastrous start, but it rankled that he was still keeping things from her.

She also knew that the reason she was headed back into the garden was not because she wanted to admire it, or to pause a moment in the sunshine, but because she knew without a shadow of doubt that Clara would know exactly why Seth had gone away. The only question was, whether she would be willing to reveal anything.

Clara was on her knees, a tray of fledgling plants beside her. She looked up as Maddie approached, a warm smile on her lips.

'Runner beans,' she said. 'Had to be done. I'll be heartily sick of them by the end of the season, but the anticipation of the first ones is always enough to make me plant them year on year.' She scooped out another ball of soil and popped a plant into the hole she had just made. 'With any luck I've just got time to get these in.'

It was an odd sentence, coming from Clara, for whom time didn't seem to hold the same boundaries as other people. Maddie gave her a quizzical look.

'Seth's train gets in in just over an hour,' she said by way of explanation. 'And I said I'd pick him up.'

It was the perfect opportunity that Maddie needed.

'Oh, I know where the station is. I passed it the other day with Trixie,' she said. 'And now that I've finally got my car back again, I can pick him up if you like, save you the bother of having to stop.' She sighed. 'To be honest I'm at a bit of a standstill this morning, there's not much I can get on with until Seth gets back, and I've got a list of questions to ask him as long as your arm. The poor man is going to get bombarded.'

Clara's response was immediate. 'It's no problem, honestly. These will only take me a few minutes to pop in and the break will make a welcome change. All that digging yesterday afternoon is beginning to take its toll.'

'That, and a late night with several glasses of wine, I bet. I still feel half asleep myself, and I didn't do nearly as much as you.'

'It was a nice evening though, wasn't it? Trixie's lovely, and I know she's going to fit in well with everyone. It will be a real treat having her cook.'

Maddie nodded. 'I said I'd give her hand to tidy up the spare rooms later. Then she can bring her books over too; just somewhere to store them until we can get sorted. In fact, that's something else I need to speak to Seth about. I haven't a clue what's in that room, half of it looks like junk that's just been shoved in there.'

Clara began to pat the soil around the new plants and she spoke without even looking up.

'No, I wouldn't have a clue either, I'm afraid. Although perhaps you might wait to tackle Seth about these things until tomorrow. He'll be very tired, I expect.' She carried on with her task.

Maddie was getting nowhere and she was beginning to feel a little irritated. She dropped down to her haunches so that she was the same level as Clara.

'Can I ask you something?' she said. 'Only Tom also mentioned that Seth wouldn't be up to much when he got back, and I wondered whether I'd missed something. He has just been away on business, hasn't he?'

'Why? What did Tom say?' Clara's head jerked up.

'Nothing in particular… in fact he wouldn't say anything else when I asked him, but he seemed a bit… I don't know, uneasy maybe? Is there anything wrong?'

Clara sat back on her heels and picked at some soil that clung to her fingers. 'Look, I'm sorry, Maddie. I did mention to Seth that he ought to tell you, but he's very funny about it, okay. He doesn't want anyone to know, not after last time, and if he won't tell you, it's not my place to.' She looked genuinely contrite.

Maddie nodded. 'That's pretty much what Tom said too, but I'll be honest, Clara, keeping me in the dark when both you and Tom know what's going on is beginning to make it seem even more worrying. What doesn't Seth want me to know?'

She bit her lip. 'He's had a routine medical procedure, that's all I can tell you. It's nothing serious, he's not ill or anything, but he might be out of it for a day or two… and if I know Seth he won't want anyone to make a fuss.'

Don't ask any questions, in other words, thought Maddie. Another warning. Clara was trying to make light of it, but Maddie wasn't fooled. In fact, she was surprised at how ill at ease it was making her. And even a little jealous…

'You seem as if you know him pretty well?'

She caught the surprise in Clara's eyes. 'Maddie, don't be angry, please. Seth and I go back a bit, and yes… we're very close. We have some things in common, and I owe him a great deal for many reasons, but we really are just good friends. You don't have anything to worry about.'

Maddie flushed red. 'No, I didn't mean…' But she wasn't sure what she meant, and trailed off.

Clara laid a hand on her arm. 'This is important to him and I have to respect his wishes.' She looked at her watch. 'I need to get going, but I promise I'll do my best to persuade him to talk to you about it.'

With that, she got to her feet and, mindful of her dirty hands, gave Maddie a hug.

'This is nothing personal, I promise.'

She gave her a final squeeze, picked up the tray of plants beside her and walked back down the path to the greenhouse. Maddie was left with no choice but to return to the house.

She filled the kettle for something to do and went through into the office to switch on the computer. She stood staring at it for several minutes while it loaded, deep in thought. Something Trixie had said yesterday when she first met Clara had just come back to her. Trixie had asked Clara how she was, saying she had read about what happened. Clara had been just as evasive about events then, and in light of the conversation they'd just had, Maddie wondered whether the two things were connected. Was this the thing that she was indebted to him for? The thing that had created the special bond between them?

If Trixie had read about what had happened, then it meant she had either seen it online or in a newspaper. Either way it would probably take only a matter of minutes for a search engine to find some reference to it. Thinking back, Trixie had also mentioned that everyone locally knew who Seth was. So was that down to them living in a small community where everybody knew everyone else, or had what happened been reported widely enough for him to have become a talking point? It was very tempting to find out, but it would also be a huge betrayal of trust. She reached over and shut down the computer again.

Tutting at herself, she walked from the room. She was annoyed because she felt as if no one trusted her enough to let her into their secrets, and yet here she was on the verge of betraying their privacy. Which only really served to prove the point, didn't it? And as for Seth and Clara, for goodness' sake, what did it matter if they were bonking each other senseless; it was none of her business and they were nice people, surely they deserved some happiness? Anyone would think *she* had feelings for Seth...

She banged a cup down on the side, throwing in a teabag and staring out of the kitchen window. She had no idea what to do now, except wait, and she wasn't a particularly patient person at the best of times. She needed an activity to take her mind off things.

While her tea was brewing she wandered through to the spare room that lay at the back of the house. In effect, it was a second sitting room, larger than the one they used but without the same cosy charm. By his own admission Seth hadn't really bothered with it for years, but it was a bit austere, and over time had become a dumping ground for all the things that people hung onto *just in case*. Some of it was even still in boxes.

She poked around in a desultory fashion for a few minutes, opening some drawers in a large ugly dresser that stood against one wall. A waft of camphor hit her as she peered at layers of tablecloths and other linens, crammed into the space. They were all uniquely hideous. A second drawer heralded a multitude of tarnished cutlery and sticky place mats and, as she pulled open the last drawer, she almost didn't bother to look at the contents, but something made her lift out a few papers to see what was underneath.

Twenty minutes later, her tea now cold, stewed and totally forgotten, she was still sitting on the floor with a lap full of coloured catalogues when a furious banging on the front door broke into her thoughts. Puffing with irritation, she placed the catalogues carefully to one side and walked the length of the hallway.

'Just a minute,' she called out, struggling to make herself heard above the cacophony of barking that ensued. The ferocious beating of the door continued.

The door wasn't locked, but whoever was on the other side was clearly in a state and their angst transferred itself to her. She fumbled with the catch at the same time as trying to contain the two wildly leaping dogs.

Eventually, she got the door open and did her best to paste on a bright smile as she registered the furious face in front of her.

'Agatha, what can I do for you?' she asked stiffly, very tempted just to let the dogs go.

Agatha ignored her and stared down the hallway over Maddie's shoulder.

The silence grew unbearable.

'Seth isn't here, I'm afraid.'

Still nothing. Agatha's eyes narrowed in suspicion.

'You can come in and look for yourself if you don't believe me.'

Maddie's words suddenly seemed to unlock something within Agatha.

'And why, may I ask, would I believe anything you say?' Her face was sour and unyielding.

Maddie tried to recall the detail of their last conversation, but as far as she could remember, Agatha had gone off happily enough – for her. The unfairness of her comment rankled.

'Seth will be back later on today. Would you like me to give him a message?'

'No, thank you, I'll wait. I'll have a cup of tea.'

She pushed through to the hall and marched into the kitchen. Maddie let go of the dogs who, obviously catching the bad vibe, slunk off down the hallway, leaving Maddie to follow her boss to the kitchen alone.

Agatha was already seated at the table when she entered. 'I take my tea with milk and one sugar.'

Maddie tried to politely ignore her. 'I really have no idea when Seth will be back. Wouldn't you be better to come back later? Or tomorrow, when I know he'll be free.'

'Yes that would suit you well, wouldn't it? However, this can't wait and I've no intention of giving you the opportunity to get in with your sad little sob story first.'

Maddie thought she must have misheard her. The accusation had come from nowhere and she had no idea what Agatha was talking about.

'I beg your pardon?' she said, her cheeks flushing red in agitation.

But Agatha hadn't finished; she pinned Maddie with a fierce glare.

'I suppose you thought it would be easy to pull the wool over Seth's eyes, and mine for that matter; a couple of country bumpkins who knew no better. My niece, however, is altogether a different kettle of fish, Miss Porter, and she is very well connected in London.' She leaned forward. 'She knows a *lot* of people.'

Maddie could feel the colour draining from her cheeks at the very mention of the word 'London', a place that now seemed so much further away than ever before. She'd been promised that no one would find out what had happened, but the gleeful look on Agatha's face would seem to suggest otherwise. Maddie clenched her fists, trying to draw in a surreptitious deep breath.

'Agatha, I'm sorry, I'm not sure what the problem is, but I really don't think—'

A toot from a car horn cut across her and Maddie's heart sank even further. From her standing position she could see exactly who had just pulled into the yard, and there was only one way this conversation was going to go, and that was badly.

Agatha craned her neck, and flashed a satisfied smile at Maddie as she spotted Seth and Clara.

'Well, perhaps I won't be needing that cup of tea after all, although if I were you I would make use of the extra time and go and pack your bags.'

Chapter 15

The dogs had set up another round of barking and Maddie went to the door to let them loose. She couldn't think straight with all the noise. She watched as they dashed across the yard, scattering chickens in their wake.

Clara was first out of the car, waving at Maddie. She lifted a hand in reply, although if she could have semaphored the sign for danger she would have done. Mindful of what Clara had said, the last thing Seth needed right now was Agatha shouting in his face.

It probably didn't matter at this juncture whether she got to Seth first or not. Her fate was pretty much sealed. She'd already heard the scrape of the kitchen chair across the floor as Agatha rose from it, and as she took a tentative step outside, Agatha's tall, thin figure pushed past her. For a moment, Agatha blocked Maddie's view of the car, but as she trailed behind, Maddie was astonished to see that Clara had one arm around Seth. She had obviously helped him from her car, and was now supporting him as he walked slowly to the gate.

He looked dreadful. His face was almost white from pain, his eyes and the black stubble of his beard stark in contrast. Even the dogs had stopped their greeting dance and walked slowly by his side.

'Maddie, could you get Seth's bag from the car?' Clara held out the car keys with her free hand.

Maddie did as she was asked, her eyes resting on Seth as she moved past them, but his stayed resolutely on the floor. It was Clara who held her look, a slight shake of the head warning Maddie not to say anything. She fetched the bag, dropping the boot closed and re-locking the car before bringing up the rear.

She could see Agatha wavering with indecision. Seth's appearance had rather taken the wind out of her sails, but she had important news to impart and would not be deterred. She opened her mouth to speak, just as Clara cut across her.

'Agatha, whatever it is, it can wait. Not today.'

But Agatha clearly didn't take direction from the gardener.

'I'll wait until you're inside,' she said to Seth, ignoring Clara. 'This won't take long, but I'm afraid it really can't wait.'

From behind, Maddie couldn't see Seth's response, but his slow shuffle halted momentarily before he moved off again, slightly faster than before. It seemed to take an age before they reached the threshold of the house, Agatha hovering just ahead of them. She would have entered the house first had Seth not put out an arm to stop her. Even in his diminished state he was determined not to let her have the upper hand. It almost made Maddie smile. Almost.

Whether it was deliberate or not, it seemed an age before Seth reached the kitchen table, lowering himself gently onto a chair, in obvious pain, and clearly favouring one side. Agatha was itching to speak but the air almost crackled with an unspoken dare to break the silence and suffer the consequences. The look on Seth's face was fair warning. Maddie moved a fraction closer. There was nothing she could do and she knew her face was a combination of abject apology and utter helplessness.

Seth raised his head and stared directly at her for perhaps a couple of seconds. It was enough to turn her insides to liquid. Then he looked at Agatha.

'Right then,' he said. 'I can see you're dying to get something off your chest, Agatha, but as Clara has already mentioned, now is not a good time. I'd like you to leave.'

It wasn't what Agatha was expecting, Maddie could see that. Her mouth opened and then closed abruptly.

'Then I'll be brief,' she said. 'I'm terminating Miss Porter's employment with immediate effect. It's come to my attention that she gained this position by falsifying her references, and that far from being the blue-eyed girl in her last company, she was actually dismissed for gross misconduct for stealing a colleague's ideas and passing them off as her own.'

There was a sharp intake of breath from Clara and Maddie felt a wave of nausea pass over her. Her stomach contracted violently and for a moment she thought she might actually be sick. She closed her eyes, trying to drag air into her lungs.

'I see,' said Seth quietly. 'I believe I asked you to leave, Agatha.'

'Didn't you hear what I said?' she retorted, her voice shrill with indignation. 'The girl lied to us.'

There was no point trying to defend herself. No one had believed her then – not colleagues she had worked with for years, not people she had thought respected her, not even those she considered friends who had dumped her at the first sign of trouble. There was no way people she barely knew were going to believe her. And Agatha's accusation was as damning as it was succinct. She had finally lost.

'Get out of my house,' said Seth in a quiet voice, hard with steel.

Maddie could hardly contain the choking sob that was rising in her throat. She was about to turn and run for the door when she felt a soft hand on her arm, a gentle but protective restraint. It was Clara.

'He doesn't mean you,' she said, and now that Maddie dared to look she could see that Seth's eyes were fixed on Agatha.

'Well, honestly! Are you really just going to sit there and—'

'It would certainly seem so. Now, do I need to say it again? Or are you leaving?'

Agatha looked between Seth and Clara, and back again, finally turning her glare on Maddie with a noise that sounded like a hiss. The front door slammed as she left, the kitchen windows rattling farewell.

Maddie felt as if she needed a pin to burst the tight bubble around them and release some of the tension from the air. She stood quietly, trembling, her heart beating in anticipation of what would come next. She knew she ought to explain herself, just as she knew she would soon be asked to leave, but she couldn't bear to go leaving Seth and Clara with such a poor opinion of herself. It was hard to know where to begin.

'I'm so sorry, Seth,' she began. 'Agatha just barged her way in here. I couldn't stop her, but I didn't want you to find out like this, and I—'

Seth visibly slumped against the table, his head resting on his arms. One hand however was turned, palm uppermost, his fingers splayed as if warding off a blow. He stayed that way for several seconds, before dragging himself upright.

'I'm sure I have a million questions, just as you, presumably have a million answers, but I can't do this now, Maddie, not this afternoon, not this evening, not today. I'm sorry.' He gave her what might have been a smile. 'Clara, could you help me upstairs please.'

★

Half an hour later Maddie was still sitting at the kitchen table, the tissues clutched in her hands almost shredded. Clara had reappeared, eventually, looking pained and anxious herself. Maddie had crossed the kitchen to fill the kettle and make a drink for them both, but now she was sitting hunched, hands wrapped around her mug, hoping the warmth would provide the comfort she desperately seemed to need. Neither of them knew what to say.

Maddie wanted to cry. She wanted to tell Clara how wrong Agatha had got things, how her accusations weren't the whole truth of what had happened at all. She wanted to beg Clara not to think poorly of her, and to seek from her some crumb of comfort that might mean that things were not as bad as they appeared. But she couldn't say any of those things, because Clara was lost in her own world of hurt and anxiety and to do so would seem to suggest that Maddie's problems should take priority. She bit back her tears.

'Is Seth okay?' she began. 'I mean, I can see he's not okay… and I know that you don't want to tell me the details and that's okay too, I just…' Her distress was making her garble. '… Wondered how he was…'

Clara gave her a wan smile. 'Yeah, he's okay, well, he will be.' She made an exasperated noise. 'God, he's so bloody stubborn, it makes me mad. He's so determined that he doesn't want anyone to know about this that he refuses all offers of help.'

She threw Maddie a fierce look. 'And he would have been fine if he'd listened to medical advice. He was supposed to get a taxi from the hospital to the station, but because it was a little late and traffic was heavy, he decided to walk. Now his back is killing him, stupid bugger.'

'He did look like he was in a lot of pain.'

'Yes, and it will take him a lot longer to recover now as a result. I love him dearly, but honestly, sometimes I could kill him myself!' She put her mug down on the table, its contents slopping dangerously close to the rim. She swivelled in her chair to see behind her. 'Are there any biscuits?' she asked. 'I need something sweet.'

Maddie got up to fetch the tin from the side. 'A few, I think.' She pushed it towards Clara, the thought of eating anything at all making her feel slightly sick.

Clara prised the lid off the tin, pulling out two of the homemade cookies that Trixie had somehow found the time to bake. She ate them both without stopping, so quickly that Maddie doubted she had even tasted them. Then she slumped back in her chair as if consumed by lethargy.

'He's always been the same, ever since I've known him,' she said. 'Absolutely consumed by things. Once he's got hold of something, he's like a dog with a bone, he won't let go until he's finished it.' She shrugged. 'It's one of the things I most admire about him actually… but every now and again it's the most irritating thing ever. It's a coping mechanism of course, we all have them, don't we? And in Seth's case I totally understand it, but…'

Clara wasn't helping. Maddie knew that she was simply offloading, giving voice to her frustrations in order to lessen them, but for Maddie all this achieved was to make her feel even more isolated. Clara and Seth shared a history she knew nothing about, and the more she heard about it, the less she felt as if she belonged at Joy's Acre at all. In fact she wasn't even going to be here soon. Her predicament came rushing back at her with force, and she gave an involuntary shudder.

'Oh God, Maddie, I'm sorry.' Clara's response was immediate. 'Here's me rambling on and you've been… well…'

'Fired?'

Clara flinched. 'I'm sure Agatha didn't mean it. She'd obviously got a bee in her bonnet about something, but I'm sure it's just a case of crossed wires. As soon as Seth is up and about again, he'll sort it out, I'm sure. Besides, what would we do without you now? You're part of the team here.'

Maddie gave a sad smile. 'That's kind of you to say, Clara, but we both know that's not true. Agatha has got her wires crossed but it won't make a jot of difference. She's my boss, not Seth, and there won't be a thing he can do about it, even if he did want to. It's been an interesting few weeks, but this is where it ends I'm afraid.'

She looked up at Clara, wondering whether to continue. It would sound all wrong, she knew that, but she was hurt too.

'Whatever is going on with Seth, he's lucky he has you, but he obviously doesn't trust me enough to let me be a part of things properly, so perhaps it's for the best.'

As expected, Clara sighed. 'Maddie, please don't take this personally, Seth is like this with everyone—'

'But, Tom knows!'

Maddie knew she was being difficult but she was almost past caring. She was also shocked by how much the sight of Seth in so much pain had affected her, and she was finding the thoughts she was having about him hard to admit to. The fact that this might prove to be the biggest irony of them all was not lost on her.

'Yes, Tom does know, but that's different... circumstances.' Clara broke off, reaching out a hand towards Maddie. 'Look, things can be a little complicated around Seth sometimes, it's partly the reason why we're all here, the things we all have in common, but I can't tell you what that is, Maddie, it wouldn't be fair. Seth will tell you, one day, I'm sure of it.'

'But he's not going to get the chance, is he? I've been sacked, remember.' She held Clara's look defiantly until she dropped her eyes.

'No, possibly not. I am sorry, Maddie. I really like you, I want you to be a part of things here. I think you're good for Seth, and you—' She broke off abruptly. 'No, it doesn't matter. I'll talk to him, I promise. I said I would. But in the meantime, you have to let me handle it. I've already told you how stubborn Seth can be, and the one thing I've learned is that if you push him in the wrong direction he just digs his heels in even further.' She took hold of Maddie's hand and gave it a squeeze. 'Please.'

Maddie left her hand wrapped in Clara's for a few moments to show her agreement. It wasn't what she wanted to hear but she had no choice, not if she wanted to stay, and Clara had been a good friend so far. She had no reason not to believe her.

'I'm sure we'll think of something, Maddie, but… what will you do if we can't? Do you have somewhere you can go?'

'A friend's,' she replied. 'That's what's so ironic. Not that long ago I would have gone there quite cheerfully without a moment's hesitation. Now that I'm being forced to go, it's the last thing I want. And I've no idea what I'd do either. My friend lives in Yorkshire, in a tiny village where she's a primary school teacher. I can't see there being any call for what I do. It's in the middle of nowhere.'

'A good place to lick your wounds perhaps, until you're ready to go back to London?'

'Yes, but I can never go back, not to my old life anyway. Those bridges have been well and truly burned.'

Clara prised the lid off the biscuit tin once more. 'Trixie will probably shoot me 'cause I won't eat any tea at this rate, but sometimes… needs must.' She moved the tin to Maddie's half of the table. 'Come on,' she said. 'Chocolate chips make everything seem better.'

Maddie smiled and took one this time.

'Was your old life so good that there's no alternative to wanting it back?' asked Clara gently. 'Isn't there room for a new start?'

'Perhaps. Not in London though. The business I work in is very incestuous. Everybody knows everybody else, and believe me, after they'd finished with me there are no new doors left to open. And I don't have experience in any other fields. I'd end up in some dead-end admin job, and no disrespect to anyone who does that, but I couldn't go back to London under those circumstances, it would break my heart. There's too many reminders of what I had, too many so-called friends who when it came to it weren't friends at all.'

'So go someplace else to start over. You could go anywhere.'

Maddie pursed her lips. 'I thought that's what I had done,' she said.

'Oh God,' said Clara, her lip trembling. 'I'm so sorry, Maddie.' They were back to square one and they both knew it.

Maddie shrugged, lifting her shoulders and biting into her biscuit. 'Never mind, I guess I'll just have to do it all over again.'

Clara was silent for a moment. 'I will speak to Seth,' she repeated. 'And I'm not going to allow him to let you slip through his fingers. I mean that, Maddie. I don't want to know what happened in your last job, because Seth should be the one to hear that first, but I can see what it's done to you, and I know that after you've spoken to him, when you're ready, you'll tell me one day too.'

She gave Maddie a warm smile. 'I just want you to know that I trust you, Maddie...' She took a deep breath. 'And that's why I'm going to tell you how I met Seth and what all this bloody secrecy is about.'

'Clara, you can't do that!' shot back Maddie. 'It's my fault; I've backed you into a corner, and made you feel like you should tell me, but you made a promise to Seth. Don't break that just because of me.'

'I'm not. I've already said that sometimes Seth is far too stubborn for his own good, and this is one of those times. I think you deserve to know, and if Seth stops to think about it logically he'll think so too.'

'If?'

'Leave it to me,' she said. 'I'll make sure he does.' She fished the last two biscuits out of the tin. 'Come on, let's go for broke.'

'Seth's going to kill you when he finds out.'

Clara stared at her for a moment, and then burst out laughing. 'Oh, that's so funny.'

It was probably the stress of the situation that was making Clara find the comment so amusing, because it really wasn't that funny, but she was caught up in a fit of giggles which didn't want to stop.

'What?' demanded Maddie. 'What have I said now?'

'Only that killing me is the last thing he'd do, not after the lengths he's gone to to keep me alive.'

Clara suddenly sobered as the reality of what she'd just said sunk in.

Maddie's eyes widened. 'Do you mean that?' she asked. 'Has Seth really saved your life?'

There was a small nod. 'Four years ago I was dying from acute myeloid leukaemia… and now I'm not.'

'Leukaemia?' And suddenly it all made sense. The trips to London, the operation, the pain in his back… 'Seth's a bone marrow donor?' she whispered into the hushed room.

Clara nodded. 'Yes,' she said simply. 'He donated stem cells to me and without them I would have died. I have to have regular check-ups and take certain medicines for the rest of my life, but I have a life, and without Seth I would not. At the time, we didn't even know each other. He was an anonymous donor on the bone marrow register and we scored a match. The rest, as they say, is history.'

Maddie's thoughts utterly deserted her. Her brain was searching frantically through her bank of stock phrases, searching for anything she could say that didn't sound trite, or bland, or wholly uncomprehending of the enormous generosity that Seth had shown to a total stranger. In the end she said nothing.

Clara smiled. 'Bit of a conversation stopper, isn't it? Don't worry, there's not a lot you can say, but the look on your face tells me you get it.'

'Bloody hell…'

'Yep, that just about sums it up.'

The two women stared at one another for a moment. 'I had no idea, but… blimey, I think I'd walk over hot coals for him too.'

'Well, I wouldn't go that far, but yes, it makes for an interesting relationship. I will always be indebted to him, and now that Joy's Acre provides my employment, and soon my home also, even more so.'

Maddie nodded. 'But I thought there were protocols and stuff, so that donors remained anonymous?'

'There are. And counsellors, and a whole host of people who talk these things through with you, so that if you do decide you want to contact one another you know what you're letting yourself in for, and believe me when I say it's quite a ride.' She grimaced at the memory. 'There's absolutely no possibility of contact for the first two years for exactly that reason, but after that the donor can request to make contact. You're supported through it very carefully.'

'So, that's what Seth did?'

'He did, and I was really struggling at the time, emotionally and financially; I'd lost my job because of all the time off I had to have, and so I thought very carefully before I agreed to meet Seth. I mean, he'd done enough for me as it was and I knew that I would be in danger of using him as some kind of crutch.' She stopped for a moment to compose herself. 'Of course, in a way, that's exactly what did happen. It happened to us both… for different reasons, and that was hard to come to terms with.' She frowned. 'Really hard.'

'How come?'

'Well, for one thing, the local press had a field day with it. You know what they're like. They tried to throw us together at every available opportunity, citing Seth's motives as purely romantic… It almost became an expectation we had to live up to, regardless of the fact it wasn't true. Bizarrely though, it did sort of push us together – dealing with the fallout of the papers' interest was hard and we supported each other through that too. But when that all died down I was scared that once we'd stopped needing one another, we'd discover that's what our entire relationship had been built upon, and that would be the end of it.'

Maddie thought for a moment. 'I can understand that, up to a point,' she said. 'But why was Seth so dependent on you? There was no reason for him to be, surely.'

For a second Clara looked like a rabbit caught in the headlights. She dropped her gaze quickly, her hands twisting together in her lap.

'That probably came out wrong,' she said, recovering herself. 'What I meant was that when two people get thrown together in unusual circumstances the emotions can be pretty intense. That's what all the safeguards are in place for. Once we'd worked out that there was never going to be anything romantic between us, things were fine.'

'So, no regrets?' said Maddie gently, ashamed to say she felt an almost overwhelming relief.

There was a soft smile in reply. 'I think there might have been once upon a time; I had a bit of a crush on Seth.' She looked up with a grin. 'Okay, a fairly major crush, but I got over it, and given the circumstances, it's definitely for the best. I still love him to bits of course, but platonically, simply because of who he is, and without all the emotional stuff getting in the way.'

It was on the tip of Maddie's tongue to ask what the given circumstances were, but she bit back the question. Clara had been extraordinarily open and generous in sharing her story with Maddie and it would be churlish to probe any deeper.

'So did all this happen before or after you came to live round here?'

'Oh before, thank God, I don't think I'd still be here otherwise.' She rubbed her eye. 'We had a very long chat once we figured out what was going on. Did the "no hard feelings and all that" routine and then to my amazement Seth invited me to live here. Of course, what he actually needed was a gardener to bring some sort of order to the chaos that was here when I arrived, but he dressed it up very nicely... and so, here I am. For a while I stayed here in the house, but I had my own life to rebuild and so with my parents' help, I was able to move out to a little rented cottage in the village where I could live more independently.'

'And are things okay now? I mean you're going to move back on site, so does that mean you're not fully recovered?'

'No, I'm okay,' she said, laying a hand on the table. 'Touch wood,' she added. 'There's no guarantees. Even now my body could still reject the transplant, and the drugs I take to help combat this suppress my immune system so infections can be really tricky. I've had a couple of those recently and it made me realise how scary it can be on your own. Plus, I'd much rather be on site and in the thick of it all, particularly now with everything going on. But I'm lucky; I work outdoors instead of in a stuffy, germ-laden office, so things are pretty good. Seth can be a bit over-zealous at times if he thinks I'm overdoing things, but I can hardly complain.'

Maddie regarded her solemnly. 'Thank you for sharing this with me, Clara, really; it explains a lot. I just hope I haven't put you in too difficult a position. There's obviously a great deal I need to talk to Seth about, things that happened before I came here, but I promise I've done nothing wrong. If I had, I wouldn't still be here.'

'Like I said, Maddie, I trust you...' She trailed off, her mouth curving into a grin. 'But do anything to hurt Seth and you're a dead man... woman.'

Maddie wasn't entirely sure if she was joking.

Chapter 16

It wasn't a surprise that Maddie couldn't sleep, but it was damned annoying. Clara's revelations that afternoon had been going around her head for hours, as, of course, had her own predicament, and just when she felt herself losing the iron grip she had on her thoughts enough to let her sleep, another thought would arrive centre stage and she'd be back to square one.

The trouble was, the more she thought about Seth and Clara's story, the more she wanted to stay at Joy's Acre, and because of that, perversely, it was only too easy to convince herself that she was on her way out. Her recent history had only proved that honesty and integrity were lost in the world and, yet, here were two people who seemed to live their lives according to these principles.

The insight that it gave into each of their characters also intrigued her. She couldn't comprehend what it must be like to have death stare you in the face like that. The worst she had ever suffered was the occasional bout of flu and a broken arm from falling out of a tree as a child. And yet, Clara's whole adult life had been punctuated by ill health, and her crisis had come when she was only in her late twenties, the same age as Maddie was now. It was no wonder that Clara surrounded herself with living things, anything in fact that she could nurture and grow, and Maddie got the feeling it was not just plants that she turned her attention to.

Seth, by contrast, was a very driven person. He was tenacious and unceasing in his desire to achieve the things he wanted, but Maddie knew from experience that this often came in place of something that was missing, an overriding yearning to fill a gap – left by what, in Seth's case, Maddie had no idea. He was also a very private person, made into somewhat of a local hero following the widely published account of his saving of Clara's life, and this had obviously not sat easily with him. His current desire to keep the latest outing by his white knight persona quiet was understandable, but again she had the feeling that his keeping things under wraps was serving some other purpose.

She plumped the edge of her pillow in frustration and then picked it up, turning it over in an attempt to find a cool, wrinkle-free spot. She nestled her cheek against the cotton and closed her eyes again, willing her mind to quieten. She had a multitude of questions but none would get answered now, in fact, they might never get answered at all…

A sudden thud sounded in the quiet night. Maddie raised her head, listening. It had come from somewhere close, inside the house she felt, rather than outside. She raised herself onto her elbows. It wasn't the sound of a door opening, and there were no tell-tale footsteps across the landing. Beside her, Rumpus was curled in his now habitual place at the foot of the bed. All quiet.

She swung her legs out of the covers and sat up, sinking her toes into the soft, cool rug. A big part of her was keen to climb straight back into bed, but she'd tossed and turned for so many hours, the thought of walking about and stretching was quite appealing. She stood up and walked to the bedroom door, silently pulling it open and peering out onto the landing. A stifled expletive floated down the hallway.

Maddie had never been in Seth's room before and the door was always closed. However, at some point during her conversation with Clara had sprung the notion that she would very much like to find out more about him, and her hand was tapping lightly on his door before she could stop herself.

A soft light lit the room; it was large and airy and, like hers, overlooked the garden. One of the two windows was wide open and the curtain stirred gently in the breeze. Seth had obviously been propped up in bed, but was now slumped to one side, a pained expression on his face. He looked extremely uncomfortable. A dark patch was clearly visible on the carpet beside the bed, an upturned glass by its side.

Seth looked up, startled, his expression rapidly turning to annoyance. He practically growled at her as she approached the bed and bent to pick up the glass.

She hovered uncertainly for a moment. Knowing the things about Seth she now did, it was obvious that he would feel very uncomfortable about her presence, and yet how could she possibly ignore his obvious need for a drink? Particularly when she spotted the packet of painkillers on the bedside cabinet, an untouched sandwich lying beside them, dry and crusty-looking. She refilled the glass from the jug of water that had also been thoughtfully left by Clara.

He tutted. 'I can get it myself.' His voice was harsh with irritation.

Normally Maddie would have been tempted to replace the glass on the carpet and watch him struggle, but instead she sat gently on the edge of the bed.

'Probably not,' she said. 'By the sound of things you're in need of painkillers too. Can I get some for you?'

Seth closed his eyes and laid his head back against the pillow. He licked his lips.

'They're in that packet, there. Thank you.'

She checked the dosage and popped out two tablets.

'How many of these have you already had?' she asked. The packet was half full.

'Not enough,' he replied, his eyes still closed. 'And don't lecture me, you're as bad as Clara.'

'I haven't said a word!'

He opened one eye cautiously, and then the other. 'No, but you were going to, I can tell.'

Maddie smiled, knowing how right he was. Not that she would ever admit it of course.

She held out her hand. 'Here,' she said, dropping the tablets into his open palm. She watched as his fingers curled slowly over them. He made no further move. 'Do you need some more help?' she asked. 'To sit up, I mean.'

There was a sigh of frustration. 'I can manage,' he said.

She ignored him, getting up and crossing to the other side of the bed. She knelt on the vacant side, slid an arm around his shoulders, and gently pulled him into a more upright position. The skin around the edge of his tee shirt was hot and damp. Then she wedged a couple of pillows behind him and one to the side to try and support him.

'Better?' she asked. He ignored her.

She moved back to her original position on his other side and picked up the water.

'Right, come on then. You need to take those.' She held the glass against his other hand, pushing it so he had no choice but to take it.

Eventually he lifted the tablets to his mouth and followed them with the entire glass of water.

'The word you're looking for is thanks,' she said.

'Maddie, I didn't ask you to come in here...'

'No, you didn't. But now that I am, you could at least be civil, I'm only trying to help. Not that you need any help of course, I know that.' She held his look. 'And before you say anything else, I know you're in a lot of pain. I also know why.'

There, she had said it. She had nothing to lose, and whatever happened in the next few hours, at least she would feel they had been honest with one another.

'And before you go getting angry at Clara, I wormed it out of her. I'm not stupid, Seth, I could see there was something more to your trip than you were letting on, and both she and I felt it was daft that I didn't know what that was. For goodness' sake, what does it matter if I do? Who could I possibly tell?'

A muscle was working in his jaw.

'She still had no right to do that.'

'No? Given what we're trying to achieve here, I'd say she had every right.' As soon as she said it she realised her mistake.

Seth raised an eyebrow, and she held up her hand.

'Yes, I know. In all likelihood, by this time tomorrow, I'll no longer be here. Not if Agatha has her way anyway.'

'True. She certainly seemed to be baying for your blood. I don't think I've ever seen her so excited. She must think she has very good reason.'

Maddie wasn't sure whether he was teasing her or not.

'And what do you think?'

An inordinately long amount of time seemed to pass before he answered.

'Maddie, I've already had Clara bend my ear once this evening—'

Maddie stood up. 'Do you need anything else?' she asked. 'Because if not, I've probably got packing I could be getting on with.'

'It's the middle of the night…'

'Yes, it is.'

'But I could actually murder a cup of tea…'

She stared at him.

'And a couple of biscuits or something, I'm starving…'

It was hugely tempting to slam the door behind her, but it was, as Seth said, the middle of the night, and Clara, who had stayed in case she was needed, would hopefully be asleep. Maddie pulled open the door and was just about to close it behind her when he spoke again.

'You could get yourself a cup too, and then I could tell you what I said to Clara… about how you were set up…'

She turned around. There was a soft, but weary smile on Seth's face. She smiled a reply.

★

'So, you knew all along. You total bastard!'

Seth grinned at her. 'Look, believe me, it was a hell of a lot easier just to get rid of Agatha than to enter into a conversation. If she knew I'd already had an email from her niece there would have been no stopping her. Besides which, when I got it, all I did was just poke around a little, ask a few questions of a few people… Agatha's niece is not the only one with contacts in London and I thought it best to check out the facts before I returned home… I'm still not actually sure what happened of course, what I learned was mostly hearsay.'

Maddie took a biscuit from the plateful she had brought back to Seth's room. She felt rather like a naughty schoolgirl having a midnight feast after lights-out, but at least they both seemed to be feeling a little better.

Seth had perked up somewhat after a huge mug of tea, or perhaps the painkillers were kicking in. Either way at least he had been at pains to put her mind at rest as soon as she had reappeared, even if he had teased her about it first.

'I'd settle for positive hearsay if that's all I'm going to get. At least it means the gossip about me is not all bad—' She broke off suddenly. 'Not that I'm looking to go back, you understand, not now… It's just that it's been a tough few months.'

'So tell me what did happen. I don't believe Natalie's version of events, I've come across her sort before, but she did seem very sure of her facts.'

Maddie drew in a breath. It still wasn't an easy subject for her to speak about. And she could imagine very well how Natalie would have phrased her email to Seth; it would have made for damning reading.

'Well, essentially the facts she told you were true. I was sacked from my last job for gross misconduct. Supposedly I stole another colleague's ideas and passed them off as my own, and when I was found out I made up some cock-and-bull story about how it was, in fact, the other way around. I mean, the sheer audacity of it.'

'And your references?'

'Ironically, were absolutely true. Except that when you put that together with the fact that I was fired from my job, it completely invalidates them of course.'

'But why give you references in the first place?'

Maddie sighed. 'Because I threatened to take the company to court for unfair dismissal. I doubt I would have won. In fact, I would probably have been crushed like a bug on a windscreen, but it's an industry that's only as good as its reputation and, while there was the tiniest bit of doubt that any mud would stick, they couldn't risk it. So I was promised a pay-off and good references if I kept my mouth shut. I really didn't have any choice. Win or lose, no one would employ me with a history like that, not in London anyway.'

Seth gave an amused smile. 'And so here you are.'

'Indeed.'

'Still causing trouble…'

She looked up sharply.

'Just kidding!' There was a glimmer of something in his eyes as she held his look but then he dropped his gaze, shifting a little in the bed, straightening a leg, and grimacing at the pain the movement caused. 'It can't have been easy.'

'It wasn't. I was betrayed by someone I thought was my friend. I even trained her, taught her everything she knew, and then when the time came for promotion she won out over me. And even that was fine; her presentation was honestly better than mine, and I didn't mind, I was happy with the clients I had and I wasn't precious about sharing my ideas either. That really is what's ironic about the whole situation. If she was struggling I would have helped her out. She only had to ask.'

'So your boss *did* steal your ideas?'

'Not only that but she managed to make out I was spectacularly useless as well. I'm not sure which was worse.' She pulled a face. 'My boss, Nina, had just lost out on an account – it happens, you can't win them all. But when the next client came along looking for ideas, the head of division asked four of us to submit, and Nina wasn't one of them, although as client liaison manager, our presentations would still have to go through her. That happens too, it doesn't mean anything, it's just rotation of workload. So, I got started on my ideas, along with three of my other colleagues, when all of a sudden Nina pulled me off the job, telling the client that I was no longer available, which, incidentally, is code for my ideas were shit and it would look bad for the agency if I were to submit them. Lo and behold, Nina then submits them as her own, and the client goes for it. I knew they would; they were bloody good ideas.'

'But you called her out on it.'

'Of course I did! But according to her I was obviously resentful of her, and jealous of her success. She did such a fantastic job of convincing people, she should be on the stage. Hell, I almost believed her myself.'

She ground to a halt, and took a bite of her biscuit, chewing deliberately slowly. She could feel her blood pressure begin to rise. In the beginning when she thought about what had happened it always made her cry. Now it just made her angry...

Seth watched her for a moment. 'Natalie's email didn't say who it was she'd had lunch with, but it's my guess it was Nina. I did a bit of fishing and Natalie's firm have done business with them in the past so it would make sense.'

Maddie nodded. 'And I can only imagine the spin that would have been put on it.' She shivered suddenly. 'What I don't understand though is why she would go to all that trouble to drag my name through the mud again. I mean, isn't once enough?'

'My dressing gown is on the back of the door,' he said. 'Put it on if you're cold.' He was watching her intently.

She was about to refuse when she realised that she was feeling quite chilly. There was gentle breeze blowing through the window and she was wearing only thin cotton pyjamas. More than this though, was a feeling that the comfort a dressing gown could bring would be most welcome, even if it was Seth's. She crossed the room, taking down the soft blue robe from its hook, and swinging it around her, shrugging her arms into the sleeves. A soft, almost spicy scent rose up around her, and she immediately felt a warmth settle over her.

The dressing gown was huge on her, and she pulled the belt tighter, hitching the folds of the gown beneath it before tying. She looked back at Seth, feeling a little embarrassed at wearing something of his that was so intimate, but he looked relaxed, an amused expression on his face. She was about to resume her previous position when Seth wriggled, shifting his legs to one side of the bed. It was almost subconscious but its meaning couldn't be clearer. She caught his eye, but apart from a raised eyebrow, his expression hadn't altered and without saying a word she climbed up onto the bed beside him.

He offered her the plate of biscuits. 'I don't suppose women like Nina suffer too badly from attacks of conscience,' he said. 'I guess having told her story once it mattered little to repeat it. Either that, or she wanted to make damn sure you never came back to London.'

Maddie turned slightly to look at him better. 'Do you honestly think that's what she was doing?'

Seth shrugged. 'I'm no expert on the female psyche, but you said yourself that if you made a success of things here, it would stand you in good stead for returning to your old hunting ground. Nina wouldn't want that under any circumstances I would have thought, however small the risk. Perhaps by scuppering your chances here also she sought to nullify it. Where would you go from here? Not back to London, that's for sure. Chances are it would be somewhere even further away.'

Like Yorkshire, thought Maddie, with a fresh surge of anger. To a friend's house in the middle of nowhere where she would pose no threat whatsoever to anyone.

There was silence for a moment. Maddie wasn't sure what she was thinking and Seth had closed his eyes.

'Is this what you want, Maddie?' he said, after a minute. 'Think about it properly before you give me an answer.'

Her eyes flew to his. 'What, here, do you mean? Joy's Acre?'

He gave a small nod and swallowed.

Maddie didn't need to think about it. She had hated it at first. She would have done anything to leave the dirt behind, and the animals with their mess and their hair and slobber, but, although she wasn't sure when it had crept over her, Joy's Acre had her well and truly in its spell. From the gentle morning skies that greeted her when she woke, to the soft sigh of the wind in the trees, the scent of the earth, and the flowers, the warmth of the sun on her skin. Even Rumpus, with his vibrating purr and velvety paws, had stolen a march on her heart.

She opened her mouth to speak but, to her horror, nothing came out. Her anger had left her as quickly as it had come and in its wake came a wave of longing and sadness that took her completely by surprise. She nodded instead, lifting a hand to her eyes to wipe away the tears that had sprung from nowhere, looking at Seth and nodding again in case he had misunderstood her silence.

He nodded his own reply. 'I know what it's like to have something you love taken away.' And his hand touched hers, the fingers closing over her own. 'I'm glad you want to stay…'

When Maddie dared to look at him again, his eyes were closed and his mouth slightly parted, the dark stubble of his beard encroaching on his lips. He looked peaceful, the release from his pain finally overwhelming all else. He slept.

Chapter 17

Maddie's eyes flew open as she wondered what on earth had woken her and then she stopped, confused, staring around her in bewilderment. She took in the rumpled bedclothes, the plate still lying on the covers beside her, and the picture on the wall opposite which was in the wrong place entirely. The noise sounded again, and she realised it was exactly the same pounding that had been meted out against the front door the day before. The dogs began to bark.

The side of the bed next to her was empty and she groaned inwardly. How on earth was she still in Seth's room? She must have fallen asleep, but she didn't remember anything beyond his asking her if she wanted to stay, or the look on his face when she told him that she did. She touched a hand to her eyes, knowing they were dry, but recalling how her tears had spilled down her cheeks at the thought of having to leave. She sat up with a shock, suddenly realising what the noise meant.

She swung her legs over the side of the bed and stood up abruptly, swaying slightly as her body protested at the speed with which she moved. She yanked open the bedroom door and flew down the landing, her ears tuning in to the voices she could hear. She was absolutely right; one of them belonged to Agatha.

She realised her mistake the minute she marched into the kitchen. Seth gave a low groan, Clara's eyes widened in surprise and Agatha's mouth settled into a hard line. Maddie dropped the cord of Seth's dressing gown as if it was on fire.

'I see,' declared Agatha. 'Well, that certainly explains things.'

Dear Lord, could it get any worse? She threw Seth a look of abject apology, clearing her throat and turning to face Agatha squarely.

'I know what this looks like, but it's not what you think. I was cold and I don't own a dressing gown if you must know. Seth very kindly lent me his.'

'How chivalrous,' Agatha replied, looking her up and down. 'However, what you get up to no longer concerns me, Miss Porter. I made my position very clear yesterday, and despite being treated in a disgraceful manner, I was prepared to overlook it as I could see that Seth was somewhat inconvenienced. However, clearly not as incapacitated as I thought.'

Maddie was about to defend Seth when he jumped in first.

'And, as *I* said, Agatha, the accusations you made yesterday were simply not true. Maddie has explained what happened in her previous position, and I believe her. Apart from anything else, however, what is important is that her work since she's been here has been of the highest standard. Surely that should figure in to your considerations, not the lies of someone who set out to discredit Maddie simply to save her own skin.'

'Are you suggesting that my niece hasn't checked her facts, Seth? Because I can assure you, she has.'

Seth squared his shoulders. 'No, I merely suggested that she was taken in by a class act, someone with no morality to speak of. Fortunately, I'm able to provide some clarity on the situation, having spoken to the person in question rather than listening to gossip. Surely that provides a much better basis on which to make a judgement.'

Agatha's mouth opened and closed, her lips pursing together as she gave Maddie another once-over.

'Yes, well I can see very clearly how you've made your own judgement.'

Maddie's hands went to her hips. 'Erm, excuse me. I am still in the room!' She glared at Agatha. 'I know you're my boss but you could have at least done me the courtesy of coming to talk to me if you thought there was a problem. And then, even worse, when you're informed that there is no problem, you basically accuse me of lying. Then, not content with that, of sleeping with Seth as well; which I did not!'

'Well, technically speaking you did.'

Maddie whirled around to find Seth grinning at her. 'We did actually sleep together. What we didn't do is play three rounds of hide the sausage, which is what Agatha here is suggesting, I believe.'

There was a snort as Clara collapsed into giggles behind them.

He took a step forward, still favouring one leg, Maddie noted.

'I've had just about enough of this, Agatha,' he said. 'You did, as you say, make your position quite clear, as I believe did I. Now it's really very simple. You have sacked Maddie, and despite information which shows you to be in the wrong, you are persisting. As of today therefore, Maddie has been informed that her job with you is terminated. Given that she is still within her probationary period, you are required to give her only one week's notice, which is paid I might add, during which time she will be a house guest at Joy's Acre. At the end of this week, provided she accepts my formal offer, she will, instead, be employed by me.' He took a breath. 'I can't make it any clearer.'

Agatha drew herself up to her full height, lifting her head so that she couldn't look any further down her nose if she tried.

'Then I withdraw my funding. Forthwith.'

Maddie stared at her. 'What? You can't do that! Oh for goodness' sake, this is ridiculous… Look, I'll bloody well go, if it's that important to you.'

'Stay where you are,' growled Seth. He turned to Agatha. 'You really are the nastiest piece of work I've ever had the misfortune to come across,' he said. 'And you're prepared to throw all this away because someone pointed out you're wrong. How much more arrogant can you get?'

'It's my prerogative, Seth, although you seem to be forgetting who I am.' She fixed him with a glacial stare. 'I will not stand by and watch you make a mockery of everything that Jen—'

'Don't you *dare* bring her into this!' spat Seth, his eyes flashing. 'This is my house, my farm, and as far as I'm concerned you are not welcome to set foot in here ever again. Do I make myself clear? Now get out!'

Agatha opened her mouth to speak but no words came as she and Seth locked eyes. The seconds stretched out, the threatening silence becoming more and more unbearable, until abruptly, thankfully, Agatha turned and stalked from the room.

There was silence for quite a few minutes while the air settled back down around them. Maddie's face was burning with a multitude of emotions, none of them good, and Seth looked utterly distraught. She picked a spot on the far wall and stared at it resolutely, her jaw clenched together.

'I can't believe you said "hide the sausage",' said Clara into the silence. 'That's the funniest thing I've heard all year…'

Maddie swung her gaze to where Clara was standing, her hand covering her mouth as she tried her hardest not to laugh. A small burble escaped her.

'Sorry,' she said. 'I just can't help it…'

Maddie watched in horror as Seth turned to face her, his hand also lifting to his mouth. But instead of the explosion of anger she expected, his lips curved upwards slowly, and a strangely high-pitched giggle erupted from them, a noise so incongruous it made it even worse, until he clutched his sides in an agony of laughter, which was echoed by Clara.

'Guys, it's not funny!' Maddie protested.

'Oh, yes it bloody well is!' he blurted. 'I've never seen Agatha so angry. I thought her eyeballs were going to pop out of her head.'

At this, Clara laughed even harder.

'Oh, don't,' she cried. 'The poor woman. I bet she doesn't even know what it means.'

Seth stared at her. 'Of course she does! I bet she was a real goer in her day. You know what they say, it's the quiet ones that are the worst.'

'Mind you, there's nothing quiet about Agatha…' mused Clara, sobering suddenly, as she looked between the two of them. 'Shit,' she said. 'What are you going to do?'

'Not give a fuck, that's what I'm going to do,' said Seth. He was leaning back against the edge of his table, legs stretched out in front of him, crossed at the ankles, his arms folded across his chest. 'I'm honestly sick of the sight of that woman and her demands. I've spent too many years having to grovel round her, going to her cap in hand for anything I wanted and being grateful for any scraps she deigned to throw me. Nope, from now on, we make our own futures.'

Maddie looked helplessly at Clara. Who the hell was Jen? There was something else here that went way, *way* deeper than what had just happened on the surface, and she hadn't a clue what it was.

'I'll go and apologise,' she stammered. 'It was my fault after all, and I'll beg if I have to. I don't care about my job, just as long as you get your money back so you can carry on.'

Seth unfolded his arms. 'You'll do no such thing. We're done prostituting ourselves.' He gave her a long slow look, from head to toe, his lips curling upwards at the corners. 'It looks better on you than me,' he said. 'Did you sleep okay in the end?'

She flushed bright red, pulling at the belt of Seth's dressing gown. How on earth could he just change the subject like that?

'I didn't think... I'm sorry. I realise what it looked like.'

'You didn't answer my question,' he said.

'No,' she replied. 'I didn't... answer your question, that is, but yes, I think I did sleep well.'

She gave Clara a furtive glance, wondering whether she was finding the conversation as strange as she was, and suddenly remembering Seth's final words to her of the night before.

'And you?' she asked. 'How are you feeling this morning?'

'What, apart from poor, you mean?' He held up a hand. 'Just kidding... gallows humour, sorry.' He shifted his legs. 'Bit sore still. My own bloody fault of course, but better, thank you. Nothing that a couple of days' distance won't cure.'

Maddie swallowed. 'I think it's an amazing thing you've done,' she said. 'I understand why you don't want to talk about it, or have a fuss made... I just wanted you to know.'

His gaze softened as he held her look. There was acceptance there, slight embarrassment perhaps, and something else that Maddie couldn't quite put her finger on, but something which brought an unexpected heat.

'We probably ought to get some breakfast,' he said after a moment. 'And then get the battle plan underway. We're going to need one.'

Clara came forward, touching Maddie's arm as she passed. 'Right, kettle first, and a mighty pot of coffee and then what would everyone like? You didn't eat much yesterday, Seth, are you up for the full works?'

'I might be able to manage that,' he said. 'Maddie?'

'I should go and get dressed,' she muttered, not quite meeting his eyes. 'I'll just have whatever's easiest,' she added, slipping from the room before anyone could say anything further.

★

Her bed stared accusingly at her, the sheets still rumpled where she had abandoned them. Rumpus was long since gone, off to find breakfast of his own. She stared at her reflection in the mirror, not quite wanting to look herself in the face for fear of what she might find. She smoothed a hand down the soft fabric of the borrowed dressing gown, her fingers splaying across her flat stomach. What had she done?

The shower was far too hot to stand under comfortably, but Maddie let it play over her skin, gulping in the steamy air. She had never felt like this before and the sudden force of her emotions shocked her. It was ridiculous that this should even be happening, and worse, she wasn't entirely sure what had triggered the feelings in the first place. Things had been far from simple up until now, but this would only complicate things further still and under the circumstances it was the last thing any of them needed.

There was only one thing she could do. Despite all that happened, and all that had been said, she was still left with only one choice. If she packed now, she could be away in under an hour. She could slip away and all the things that had happened since she arrived would slip away with her, go back to normal, leaving lives and futures intact. She turned off the shower and stood, water and tears dripping from her body.

Back in her bedroom she dressed quickly, marvelling at the irony of finding herself packing to leave yet again. She was about to start throwing her clothes into her case, when there was a soft knock at the door.

'It's Clara. Can I come in?'

Maddie froze. She could pretend she hadn't heard the door, but then Clara would only knock again. She might also be able to pretend she hadn't heard that either, but after that? It wasn't as if she could hide anywhere. They would have heard the shower in any case, and where else would she be but in her room? Reluctantly she opened the door.

Clara took one look at her face and in an instant pulled her into her arms, where Maddie stood, fighting hard to keep the tears at bay.

'I feel so foolish,' she said once Clara had released her. 'Everything's my fault.'

Clara gripped her arms, holding her back a little to see Maddie's face. She cocked her head to one side.

'What are you referring to, Maddie? The fact that you might have, unwittingly, set us all free, or the fact that you've strayed too close to Seth and now realise what a gravitational pull he exerts?'

Maddie gulped. 'How did you know?' she managed. 'I've been trying to convince myself it was my imagination, but…'

'You've never felt like this before?'

She hung her head.

Clara pulled her into a hug again. 'Come on, come and sit down.' She led Maddie over to the bed, patting the top of the duvet cover and then, once she was seated, taking up a place beside her. 'The only reason I know is because I've been right where you are now, don't forget. Only in my case, I really was crazy.'

'But this was never supposed to happen, it's the last thing I wanted, you have to believe me.'

'You make it sound like it's a bad thing,' said Clara, gently. 'But it doesn't have to be. I've already told you that Seth's a very special person. Ordinarily he keeps his cards very close to his chest, but if that changes it's almost impossible not to be drawn in by it. And you honestly don't need to look like that, I'm not cross with you.'

There really was nowhere for Maddie to hide.

'I feel as if I'm standing in an asteroid field. Just when I think I've dodged one hulking great ball of rock, along comes another. The trouble is it was me that drove us in here in the first place, but I really am sorry… for everything. I can't believe I didn't think about what I was wearing before I blundered into the kitchen this morning. That wasn't fair either, on Seth, or on you…'

'Maddie…' warned Clara. 'Don't apologise. It honestly was the funniest thing, like something out of a French farce. That aside, I know nothing happened between you and Seth other than you being there for him when he needed it… and possibly the other way around. But it honestly wouldn't have mattered if it did. I told you there's nothing romantic between us, and when I said don't hurt him, I meant just that, not stay away from him altogether. I see how he looks at you. Come on, let's go downstairs; we've got a lot of things to talk about.'

Maddie wiped her eyes, pulled her shoulders back, and inhaled. 'I know, but there's something else too. Who's Jen?'

Clara put her finger to her lips. 'No one you need to worry about just now. All in good time, Maddie. All in good time.'

Now what kind of an answer was that? She was about to frame another question, but the look on Clara's face stopped her.

'Are you sure it's going to be okay?' she asked instead.

'Positive.' Clara smiled. 'We're in this together, come what may, so let's focus on what we really need to right now. Whatever happens we have a lot of decisions to make and it's time we started making them.'

Chapter 18

'So we have about five weeks to get everything finished in the first cottage if we want to stick to schedule. Building finished, inside and out, gardens sorted, website up and running—'

'And how are we supposed to do all that with absolutely no money?' asked Maddie. 'We can't just ignore that fact.'

'I've been thinking about that a little,' put in Clara. 'Seth, coming to work here has been the best thing I've ever done, but you know how reluctant I was in the first place. And because of that you went to great lengths to convince me how much you needed a gardener, which we both know you only did to ease my conscience so I wouldn't feel like I was taking something in return for nothing. But the truth of it is that I have been. I have no ties and no dependents, and I've managed to save a bit. So I have no real need for the salary you pay me at the moment, not when right now, Joy's Acre needs it more.'

She sat back, a defiant glint in her eye. 'And don't you dare bloody argue, because if you do I'll withdraw my services.'

'Oh for goodness' sake, Clara,' said Seth, rolling his eyes. 'What would be the point in that?'

'Absolutely none,' she replied. 'So you had better agree with me, hadn't you? Otherwise you're going to lose the best gardener you've ever had.'

'In that case, I make the same demands,' said Maddie. 'You can't afford to employ me once my notice period is up with Agatha, so I shall work here as a volunteer. That's non-negotiable by the way.'

Seth opened his mouth and then closed it again. 'And what if I refuse?'

'Then you'll be doing everything yourself, which put bluntly you have neither the aptitude for, nor the time to accomplish it. Your dream for Joy's Acre will wither and die like the uncared-for garden that will surround it.'

'Jesus, Clara,' flinched Seth. 'And I thought you were nice,' he said, weakly.

'I am nice,' she announced. 'Which is precisely why I've just made you the offer I have.'

'I wouldn't mess with her, Seth, if I were you. In fact, I wouldn't mess with either of us…'

'No, I'm beginning to see that. I really don't know what to say…'

'You don't need to say anything actually,' said Clara. 'And if you do it will only be taken down and used in evidence against you. We're all grown adults here, we understand how it works, and I think it's true to say that we are also very aware of what we're about to get ourselves into.'

She gave Seth a rather fierce look. 'This isn't a time for pretending, or being anything less than honest with each other. It's going to be hard work, and we will all need to be able to rely on each other one hundred per cent.'

Seth looked a little sheepish.

'Trixie will be here shortly, and although I've briefed her a bit on the phone, things have changed rather substantially since she was offered a job. It's only fair that we give her the option to change her mind, once we've made it clear how things could pan out. It might be some while before we can even think of paying her a proper salary, and I don't want us to hide those possibilities from her. If, after all that, she still wants to stay, then I think we've found our perfect combination, don't you?'

Maddie and Seth both nodded.

'Right then. Maddie, you made a list of costings recently, didn't you? Let's have a look at those while we wait for Trixie and then we can think about how we're going to slash our costs.'

Maddie gave Seth a cautious glance. 'I never knew you were quite so bossy, Clara,' she said, a small smile gathering at the corners of her mouth.

'Oh, you'd better believe it,' came the reply.

★

Trixie stood with her hands on her hips in the middle of the kitchen while three faces regarded her anxiously.

'Bloody good job I couldn't hear you properly on the phone yesterday,' she said.

'Yes, I'm sorry, it's come as a bit of a shock, I know,' replied Clara.

'And that's my fault, I'm afraid,' said Maddie. 'But now you know the whole story I hope you can see that this alteration in how we're going to have to do things here has come a bit out of the blue for all of us.'

'I didn't say I was angry,' said Trixie. Her face broke into a grin. 'Story of my life actually…' She looked between them. 'There are a few things I want to check though,' she added. 'Just to be absolutely clear.'

'Of course,' said Seth. 'Ask anything you want.'

'So, even though you're not actually gonna pay me anything, you are gonna let me live here for free? In this awesome house…'

Seth nodded.

'And I get to cook whatever I want, and I won't have to pay for anything I use?'

'Yes… and no!' Seth grinned.

'And more than that, you'd like me to work on a list of menus I can create for guests, and also think about creative ways we can sell what we already produce… and that's entirely up to me?'

'It is,' said Clara. 'You can really go to town… cakes, pies, preserves, anything we have in abundance and can add value to.'

Trixie's eyes were shining. 'Would I be able to help in the garden too?'

'I'll bite your arm off.'

'And lastly. Do you all promise not to grope my bum at every available opportunity?'

Clara giggled. 'Well I do,' she said. 'I can't speak for the others of course.'

Maddie held her hand over her heart. 'I solemnly swear…'

Seth grimaced. 'Bugger… and it was all going so well…'

'Yes or no?'

He held up his hands. 'Okay, okay, I promise…'

The four of them grinned at one another.

'In that case, you've just knocked spots off my last job, money or no money. I'll put the kettle on, shall I? Start as I mean to go and all that.'

★

An hour later and they were still sitting around the table, looking at the long list that Maddie had produced. What had started off as a typed sheet was now adorned with crossings-out, notations and quite a few doodles. They had begun by striking from the list anything that was not an absolute necessity to get them up and running. All of the swanky extras (as Maddie had put it) had been removed, as had things which could be considered a little further down the line. What they were left with was still a rather daunting and expensive-looking piece of paper.

'So, first things first, we need to get on to sorting the website,' said Maddie. 'We really can't afford to leave this any longer or we run the risk of being ready for nothing. We need immediate occupancy and, if possible, a run of bookings.'

Clara frowned. 'But is that even possible? I thought you said it could take several weeks, and come at quite a price.'

'Ordinarily yes, *if* we outsourced as I'd first intended. The original brief for the site would have been for something very flash, but I can put us together something more in keeping with what we're trying to achieve here at very little cost by using a free service to create our own site, and then just paying for our own domain name. It'll cost about twenty quid, that's all.'

'Won't that still take ages though?'

Maddie shook her head. 'I can sort out the website in a day or two once I know what I'm putting up there. But that's the tricky bit. I want us to look different from all the traditional holiday cottages you can see online. You know the sort of thing I mean: rows and rows of photos which all look pretty much the same. I want our website to draw people in and make them want to stay... So, we need a brand or a concept; anything we can hang a hook on to say this is Joy's Acre and this is what we're all about.'

'You said before that we should use Joy and Edwin's story, so why not?' interrupted Seth, running a hand through his hair. 'It's a great love story...'

Clara shot him a look. 'But that's not what—' She broke off suddenly, a guilty look on her face. 'Sorry,' she added.

Seth gave an almost imperceptible shake of the head. 'When Maddie mentioned it before I wasn't sure it was right, but I've had some time to think about it…' He nodded at Clara. 'And now I think it makes more sense than anything else.'

'Are you sure?' asked Clara, eyebrows raised.

'I'm sure,' he replied, giving her a very pointed look.

Inexplicably, Clara broke into a broad grin. 'He's right… I think it's a brilliant idea.'

Maddie gave them both a wary look. 'Well in that case I think I do too… if you're definitely happy?' she finished.

She received two firm nods in reply.

'Okay… Now that would work as an overall theme of the site, like the blurb for a book if you like, but now we need the individual cottages to be like chapters of the book, so that they each tell their own story while at the same time contributing to the overarching theme of the book.'

'Go on,' said Seth. 'I think I see where you're going with this.'

'Well, this first cottage, the gardener's one, what's different about that for example?'

'What did you call it?' Clara looked up from the table where she'd been toying with the edge of a place mat. 'The gardener's cottage?'

Maddie looked at Seth, confused, trying to recall what she'd said. 'Well yes, but I didn't mean that's what it should be called, only that it's how I think of it in my head. Probably because you were going to move in, but also because of where it sits; after all, it's practically in the garden.'

Clara sat up a little straighter. 'No, wait a minute, I think you've got something here… Going back to Joy's Acre for a minute, which was a Victorian farm, wouldn't it make sense to have the cottages echo their past rather than try and be something they're not? So you could have a gardener's cottage, and a… blacksmith's cottage.' She held her hands up, inviting comment. 'I'm thinking of traditional craftsmen and the like, what every respectable Victorian farmer would have on his payroll…'

'Well, a thatcher, obviously,' added Seth, grinning.

'And a woodsman… woodcutter, something like that…?' suggested Trixie.

'Yes, brilliant! This could work perfectly. We could even…' She trailed off, looking between Clara and Seth excitedly. 'Oh God, I've just had the most brilliant idea, at least I think I have. Come with me a minute.'

Maddie jumped up from her chair. 'I've just remembered something I found a while ago—' She stopped suddenly. 'No, it wasn't. It was only yesterday afternoon…! It was what I was doing when Agatha first hammered on the door, but it feels like it was ages ago. I'll show you.'

She led them down the hallway to the room she had been trying to sort out ready for Trixie's arrival. The boxes and piles of magazines were exactly where she had left them.

'Had you any idea what was in here, Seth?'

'Not really,' he admitted. 'Most of it was here when I moved in, up in the attic. I brought it all down because I was worried it was a fire hazard. I've been meaning to go through it all one day but… well, you know how it is.'

Maddie knelt on the floor, picking up some of the catalogues and holding them up for the others to see. 'Because I found these, and it rather got me thinking. See for yourselves.'

She waited while they all looked at what she had passed them – Seth almost in awe, but Clara and Trixie with a growing excitement.

'They're amazing!' Clara exclaimed. 'So beautiful.' She turned one of the seed catalogues over in her hand, opening it carefully and peering inside. 'Are they authentic?'

'Well I've no reason to doubt it,' Maddie replied. 'Yesterday I thought they might come in useful. Today I'm thinking they might be just what we're looking for.'

She had Seth's interest, she could tell, but as yet he couldn't see how they might be useful.

'Originally we thought the cottages would be furnished sympathetically, but essentially still with top-of-the-range, brand-new fixtures and fittings. Is that right?' At Seth's nod she continued. 'And all that would have come at a price, which thanks to me, we no longer have the money for.'

She held up her hand. 'No, let me finish. I'm not being a martyr, or trying to elicit sympathy, what I'm trying to be is a realist. And the simple fact of the matter is that while the type of furnishings we had in mind for the cottages might have brought in top money in terms of rental value, it would have cost a fortune in the first place. Now we have to find a much, much, cheaper option.'

She held up a catalogue. 'Why don't we go for a complete about-face? The covers on these are stunning and we could use them in a variety of ways, but what they've made me think is whether we could make a feature of the real heritage of each of these cottages. Furnish them completely with salvaged items that fit the themes we've come up with, and make them a Victorian home-from-home if you like. We'd need to be very resourceful, not to mention creative, but I reckon we've got the right combination of people here that could make this work. What do you think?'

Clara was still marvelling at the artwork on the seed catalogues. Bright floral combinations, enchanting scripts, swirls and scrolls. Just the sort of thing that was fashionable in vintage stores up and down the land. Except these were the real deal.

'These would be perfect for the gardener's cottage and look stunning against the whitewashed walls. Or we could even use them to cover furniture, like decoupage, then they could go on any old mangy chest of drawers for example. No one would be any the wiser and they'd look beautiful.'

'Or we could sell them,' said Seth. 'They must be worth a bit.'

The three women turned to him, horrified.

'No!' they chorused.

He grinned. 'Only kidding. I can't believe I'm hearing this from you, Maddie. Miss, *I want everything ultra sleek and covered in glass*, Porter.' He winked at her. 'I'm incredibly pleased though. Joy's Acre has worked its magic after all, and I love the thought of what you've described. I think it would be absolutely perfect here.'

He looked about him. 'I suggest before we go much further that we look through the rest of this stuff with a fine-tooth comb. It's got to be done anyway, let's see if we can turn up any other gems, particularly ones we might use in the other cottages. We're going to need to come up with some similarly brilliant ideas for those as we go along.'

Maddie slowly unclenched her muscles. She hadn't realised how tense she'd been until she'd heard Seth's final words, but now she could feel the relief flowing through her. However generous he and Clara had been about the situation with Agatha, and the loss of their funding, she still felt an enormous responsibility to put things right. They had to succeed here. Whatever happened from this point forward there would be no second chances, no room for mistakes. They simply couldn't afford to get it wrong.

Chapter 19

It was one of those perfect spring days, when the air felt alive with promise. At least, that's what Seth had said to her as they headed outside first thing, and he was right. Maddie pondered his statement and realised that since coming to Joy's Acre she had begun to think about the weather more and more.

When she lived in London, the only thing the weather often determined was how bearable or unbearable her Tube journey was likely to be. Rain, and it was a juggling act of umbrellas and papers getting wet. Cold, and it was a case of dressing according to the weather outside, forgetting that once underground she would swelter in too-thick jumpers. And heat, well, heat was the worst; jammed up against sweaty armpits, with her make-up running and thighs sticking together.

Here though, things were different. Here, the sun made certain flowers open in the morning and close by dusk. Even the humble dandelion tracked its passage across the sky. Here the sun had brought a smattering of freckles to her face, and lifted the colour of her hair so that it glinted with a coppery hue. The rain by turn brought a beautiful freshness with it, a smell of earth and sky, catching the light like diamonds as it dripped to the earth below. Even the wind brought treasures, fragrancing the washing blown on the line, rustling through the trees, the noise a constant lilting companion to the day.

And Seth was right, today was perfect. She had slipped on another of Clara's soft tunics, a gentle sage green, which she wore over pale blue jeans. Her sleeves were rolled up, and the warmth of the day felt like a tender caress on her skin. The air seemed delicate, an invitation to what was yet to come, and as they walked down the path, Maddie felt her heart lift.

Tom was already hard at work, whistling a catchy melody and surprisingly in tune. He lifted his hand in greeting when he saw them, bouncing on the ladder as he shimmied to the ground.

'Are you ready for this, Maddie?' He grinned. 'I reckon you're going to be a natural, what do you say, Seth?'

Seth raised an eyebrow. 'Probably. But let's face it, she can't be any worse than I was when I first started to learn how to make spars. How long did it take me, Tom?'

'About six days too long if I remember right.' He chuckled. 'And just remember, whatever Seth tells you, there's a technique right enough but the hazel can smell your fear just like a horse can. You have to show it who's boss, so no sidling up to it, you've got to meet it head on.'

Maddie gave Seth a look, but he looked just as serious as Tom did. She had a horrible feeling she was being made fun of. The next thing she knew they'd have her going to buy a tin of striped paint.

'Right, let's crack on then,' said Seth. 'We'll take the bundles over to the garden if that's okay. We might as well be comfortable.' He stopped to pick up two huge bundles of twigs bound with twine. 'You might want to bring those gloves as well,' he added, motioning to Maddie with his head. 'The hazel will rip your hands to shreds, but to start with you're better off without them; you'll get a feel for the wood then.'

'Sounds fabulous,' muttered Maddie, but she was smiling. When Seth had first mentioned giving Tom a hand with the spars she had asked if she could help. To her surprise, he had agreed immediately, saying it wasn't the easiest thing to learn, but if she could master it, Tom would be eternally grateful. The quicker they got the thatch finished the quicker they could attend to some of the other jobs that needed doing.

Once on the grassed area, she waited while Seth took a knife and sliced through the twine holding the twigs bound together. They tumbled to the ground like an oversized version of the child's game, pick-up sticks. He sat down cross-legged on the grass.

'Have a seat,' he said. 'And make yourself comfortable. You need to be relaxed.'

She followed his lead, realising that this was probably the first time she had sat this way since she was at school. It took her a minute to adjust her feet into the best position, but then she looked up expectantly.

'So the object of the exercise is to bend the hazel twigs through ninety degrees, so that they have a perfect turn or twist in them.' Seth picked up one of the sticks and with a deft flick of his wrists did just that. 'That done, what you have is a spar; a spring-loaded "pin" for want of a better word. And it's important that the twig is twisted not broken. If there's no spring it won't hold the straw against the roof.' He let go of one end of the spar and watched as it pinged upwards and outwards. 'See, if you simply break the twig you won't get that effect.'

He picked up a second twig, and although to Maddie it seemed as if he performed exactly the same movement, she could see that the end result was very different. The twig didn't spring anywhere and although it wasn't broken in two, once Seth let go of it, both ends simply hung limply in his hand.

He turned to smile at her. 'Now it's your turn,' he said. 'Pick a twig, any twig.'

Maddie held it just as Seth had done, her thumbs braced a little distance apart, almost in the centre. She flexed it experimentally. It was much tougher than she thought, and she wondered whether she'd even be able to break it. She looked down at the completed spar now lying on the grass, checking the shape, trying to copy in her mind the twist in the wood. She held the twig up slightly, adjusted her grip and… The twig snapped clean in two with a sharp crack.

Seth handed her another. 'On you go,' he said. 'There's plenty more where these came from.'

Maddie grimaced. 'Seriously, how long did it take you before you could do it?' she asked.

'About an hour,' Seth replied. 'I told you I was rubbish, and I got through about forty or fifty twigs before I got it right as well, so don't worry. If nothing else, it will give us plenty more kindling for the fire come winter time.'

She gritted her teeth. 'Right,' she said. 'Now I know what my target is I feel better. Half an hour or less is what I'm aiming for.'

'Have you always been this competitive?' joked Seth. 'I'm not sure I should help you now.'

Maddie stuck out her tongue. 'Spoilsport,' she said. 'Come on, top tips… I want to know them all.'

Seth got to his feet and crossed to kneel behind her. She could feel the warmth from his chest jump the gap between them. He gently took hold of her elbows, pulling them out to the side a little.

'A bit more leverage might help,' he said. 'Then pull your elbows down and to your sides as you twist, as if you were pretending to flap your wings.'

'Do I have to quack as well?' she asked.

'Whatever it takes,' came the voice from behind her, a breath on the back of her neck.

She waited until Seth returned to his original position before trying again. There was no way she could even attempt to bend the twig with him in such close proximity.

A loud squawk echoed around them as another twig snapped, but at least it had them both hooting with laughter.

'I might try it without the sound effects this time,' she said.

Twenty minutes later she gave a frustrated groan. 'Arrgh, what is wrong with me?' she moaned. 'Apart from being spectacularly useless, that is.'

She dropped another broken twig onto the lawn. Her hands were smarting from where the wood had rubbed against them and her thumbs felt like they were going to snap themselves. She really didn't think she would be able to do many more.

Sighing, she got to her feet. 'I need a stretch,' she said. 'I'm too tense now, I think.'

She lifted her arms above her head, feeling the pleasing pull of her muscles as she raised them higher.

Seth joined her. 'Skip,' he said. 'It's great for relieving tension.'

Maddie gave him a sideways glance. 'Yeah, and for looking like a total prat,' she answered. 'I am not skipping anywhere,' she added firmly.

'Shame!' said Seth, launching himself forwards, his long legs taking wider steps, his knees rising higher and higher as he skipped across the grass in front of Maddie, both arms swinging wildly by his sides. He careered in front of her.

'Come on in, the air's lovely,' he said.

'Will you come and sit down,' Maddie hissed. 'Someone will see you.'

Seth stopped, suddenly looking around him. 'Like who?' he said. 'The only one around is Tom and he's facing the other way.' He held out his hand. 'Come on,' he said. 'After all, the clock's still ticking and you haven't got all that long now…' His head dropped to one side. 'Or are you chicken?' he said, grinning.

Maddie's mouth set in a hard line. 'Out of my way,' she said. 'I'll show you how to skip properly.'

And with that she completed a perfect circle, setting off again once she'd done so. As she came back around for the second time, she realised Seth had done the same so that they were both coming towards one another from different directions. Without thinking she linked arms with him as they passed, dropping them again after completing a loop so that they spiralled around each other. By the third 'pass' she was laughing so hard she had to stop.

Seth put his hands on his knees, panting. 'Right, now, grab a twig and go for it, and remember to show it who's boss!'

Maddie bent to the floor, snatched up a twig and swiftly brought her elbows out and then in again. The air was filled with the delicious sound of wood splintering, not cracking or snapping, but wrenching apart; a crunching sort of a noise. She looked down at her hands. They held a perfect, twisted spar.

'Woohoo!' she yelled, brandishing the twig. 'I did it!'

She grinned at Seth, rushing towards him, his arms opening wide as she did so to receive the hug he was going to get whether he wanted it or not. He pulled her in tight, the two of them rocking together in an excited dance. She could feel his heart beat, his warm breath in her hair, and then his head automatically dropped into the side of her neck, just as hers did to him…

They sprang apart. 'Oh God, sorry,' she said.

'It's okay,' he replied, his lips parted in a grin. He nodded towards the spar in her hand. 'You beat me,' he said.

'I did, didn't I?' She laughed. 'Just as well, or I'd never have heard the last of it.'

'Ah, but can you do it a second time? That might have just been a fluke.'

Maddie's face fell. 'I bloody well hope it wasn't.'

She dropped to the grass again, crossed her legs, wriggled her bottom into the ground and took up another twig. Tongue between her teeth, she lifted her elbows.

'Yes!' she exclaimed. 'I can do it!'

Slowly Seth sank to the floor beside her. 'You can put the gloves on now,' he said. 'We've only another four hundred or so to do.'

Once she'd found the knack it was hard to see how she hadn't been able to achieve it before, but the fact that she'd been able to do it at all made a ripple of excitement run through her. The spars she and Seth were making would be used to fix the straw onto the roof of the gardener's cottage where they would stay for the next thirty or so years with any luck, possibly longer. They would become a little part of its history, and Maddie had never before made anything that was likely to stick around for that length of time. How many people could say that about their lives? Her conversation with Tom from the other day had started her thinking about tradition and heritage and now she totally understood how vital it was not to lose these things. And, just like making the spars, it was hard to believe that she had ever thought any differently.

She looked up at the garden in front of her; at the house with its warm red brick and handsome lines, and she smiled. It had taken only a matter of days, but once she had allowed her heart to open, the magic that was Joy's Acre had begun to seep in, and now she had fallen completely under its spell. She couldn't imagine being anywhere else.

'Penny for them?'

'I was just thinking,' she said, smiling again, as she dropped another spar onto the pile in front of her.

'I can see that.'

She blushed. 'It gets under your skin this place, doesn't it? Draws you in, wraps its gentle arms around you and then refuses to let go.'

Seth cocked his head. 'You get more and more poetic by the day,' he said. 'But you're right, that is its magic. I like to think it's Joy herself, keeping a watchful eye on us all, just as if we were her guests from all those years ago.'

'Would she approve, do you think?'

'I'm certain of it. In fact, now more than ever.' He ran his thumb along a groove in the twig he was holding. 'I know you still feel responsible for what's happened, and I'm not pretending it's going to be easy, but honestly, Maddie, I feel happier about things here than I have for a long while… and a large part of that is down to you.'

He peeped up at her from under his lashes. 'I'm not sure who you were when you first arrived. An angry, uptight young woman with something to prove. I'm not being critical by the way; I understand perfectly how it was for you before you arrived, but that was never the real you, it was a persona you'd adopted to get you through the world you were in at the time. But it didn't suit you, it didn't quite fit.'

He smiled warmly. 'The person sitting beside me now is the real you; the one who doesn't wear so much make-up, whose hair just tips naturally onto her shoulders instead of being bound up tight, the one who likes the feel of the sun on her arms and who, even though she knows she looks very silly indeed, is still prepared to skip around the garden because, why the hell not…'

Maddie looked up into his dark eyes. She didn't know quite what to say. His gaze was very open, but she couldn't tell what he was thinking and she found it a little unnerving.

'I do feel different,' she said, eventually. 'Better. Like none of what I had before in my life meant anything.'

He nodded. 'A big enough improvement that you might want to stick around for quite some considerable time?'

'Oh, God yes.'

That smile again. 'I'd like that,' he said. 'And Joy would definitely approve… You see, when I look at you, Maddie, it reinforces everything I believe about this place, that my instincts are worth trusting, and right now I very much want to trust them…'

She daren't look at him. His voice was light, he could have been talking about the weather. And yet there was something about his words that sent little shock waves through her, because she wasn't entirely sure whether he was still talking about Joy's Acre, or whether he was talking about her…

He expelled a breath, uncrossing his legs and stretching them out, a slight flicker of pain crossing his face for an instant.

'I should have thought,' she said. 'I'm so sorry, that's awful of me. Are you still in a lot of pain?'

He waved a hand. 'Much better than I was, don't worry; besides, I'm still drugged up to the eyeballs. I wasn't thinking myself, maybe cross-legged wasn't the best idea in the world…' He looked around him. 'I tell you what. Could you give me a hand with the bench? We could move it over here for the time being. I think legs straight will be better than legs bent.'

Maddie helped him carry the bench back to their original spot and waited while Seth settled himself onto it. She was about to sit back down on the grass when she realised he would now tower above her and so instead she sat next to him. He bent to pick up a couple of twigs, and handed one to her. She forced it quickly into shape and leaned forward to collect another pair, stopping only when she saw that Seth was still holding his twig, rolling it absentmindedly between his fingers. He was staring into space.

'Are you okay?' she asked, thinking. 'Would a cushion help, or—'

'No, it's not that. My hip's fine, honestly. I just…' He turned to look at her. 'There's something I ought to talk to you about, something very personal, but it's knowing quite where to begin that's the issue.' He blew out his cheeks. 'It was partly something Clara said yesterday, which, if I know Clara, was aimed directly at me, but she's right of course.'

Maddie frowned, trying to think back to the day before. 'I'm not sure I follow.'

'Clara said it wasn't a time for being anything less than honest with each other, and I've been holding something back from you, something which Clara, and Tom, both know. It doesn't seem fair not to tell you.'

She could sense his reticence and held out a hand towards him. 'Seth, it doesn't have to be now, not if it still makes you feel uncomfortable. There'll be a right time, some day. It can wait.'

'It can't, for all sorts of reasons, but I appreciate that, thank you. It's not something I talk about, but it's also partly why I didn't discuss this with you either.' He tapped his hip. 'The two are inextricably linked.'

He scratched an eyebrow. 'I'm also very aware that, once you'd learned how I helped Clara, if you'd had wanted to, you could have very easily found out what I'm about to tell you. The internet was awash with it at the time. The fact that you haven't is something I'm also grateful for.'

Maddie blushed, knowing how close she'd come to doing that very thing.

'How do you know I haven't?' she asked, trying to lighten the conversation somewhat. Seth was looking very sombre, and she was beginning to feel a bit anxious about what he was about to share with her.

'I'd know,' he said. 'Believe me, I'd know.'

The look on his face made it clear he was telling the truth.

'I don't know much about bone marrow donation,' she said, trying to find an in-road for him. 'Is it like blood, something you can do repeatedly?'

His Adam's apple bobbed as he swallowed. 'No more than four times is recommended. My body replaces what's lost, but less so as you get older. Plus it's rare to match with a recipient as it is. Clara took eighteen months; I got lucky.'

It seemed an odd choice of words. 'Or *Clara* did,' she replied. 'She told me how poorly she was.'

Seth looked down at his feet. 'Yeah... We both got lucky. With Clara I was able to donate the stem cells via my blood; that's actually the more usual method,' he said. 'But this time around I donated bone marrow itself, hence why I was away for a few days. It's done under general anaesthetic.'

Maddie nodded, wondering if Seth was going to say anything else. He seemed to have got stuck. She was about to ask what had inspired him to become a donor when he suddenly snapped the twig he was holding clean in half. Then he looked up at her.

'Sorry,' he said. 'I still find this really hard.'

'Seth, honestly, you really don't need to—'

'My wife died,' he said bluntly. 'Six years ago. She died because she needed a bone marrow transplant and we couldn't find one in time.'

He exhaled a long shaky breath, raising his eyes to hers and holding them there even though hers were already filling with tears. She couldn't look away even though she wanted to.

Her hand found his, the slight movement causing a silent tear to spill over and run down her cheek.

'I'm so sorry,' she said.

And suddenly it all made sense.

'Jennifer and I had only been married eighteen months when she became ill. It all happened so fast, one minute she was fine and then in less than a year she was dead, and almost all of that year was filled with endless tests, horrible treatments, waiting, hoping and praying. None of it made any difference.'

'So you decided to help Clara…'

'I decided to help anyone I could. Anything to stop someone else having to go through the living hell we did. It was a way of coping with the grief, I know that, but the only sense I could find in any of it was to try and save someone else's life. So like I said, *I* got lucky, because without it I don't know how I would have coped at all.'

Still Maddie didn't move. 'And did it help?' she whispered.

'I was desperate to meet Clara, but they wouldn't let me for two years. I understand why now of course, but at the time they were the longest two years of my life. It's testament to the kind of person Clara is that she put up with me. I think I made things quite difficult for her.'

'That's not how she sees it, Seth. I think things were just as tough for her. You helped each other through what must have been a horrendous time for you both.'

Seth gave a wan smile. 'We went through every emotion on the planet I think, but in the end we both came through it. We put each other through the mill *while* doing it, I might add, but now we've ended up in a place that suits us both.'

'And is that why you've become a donor again; because you felt able to?'

'Well of course I'd been contacted about a possible match, but essentially I think it was kind of a test,' replied Seth, for the first time breaking eye contact with her and staring out across the garden. 'For me, I mean. To see if I was ready.'

She studied his features, frowning, surreptitiously wiping her face free from tears. 'I'm not sure I follow.'

'I was nineteen when I met my wife, Maddie; in my middle year at uni. Jen and I studied together, partied together and before we knew it we were twenty-two, sharing a flat, and struggling to pay rent, find jobs, and feed ourselves. We were barely adults but that didn't matter; we had each other and that was enough.'

He turned back to look at her, his eyes roaming her face for a few seconds. 'And it probably would have been enough had her grandfather not died and left her this place. He and Agatha were the first of the family to fall in love with Joy's Acre. I think they always intended to renovate it themselves, but shortly after her grandfather bought it he fell ill himself and so it remained as it was—'

'Wait a minute,' interrupted Maddie. 'Does that mean that Agatha is related to you...?' She searched his face. 'Oh, now I get it! That's why she has such an interest in this place...'

Seth nodded. 'And one of the reasons why she dislikes me so much. You see when Jen's grandfather left her this place it was on the stipulation that the farm be restored to its former glory, and Agatha

The Little Cottage on the Hill

made a promise to her husband that she would help that happen by
supporting us financially. It was everything we could ever have wanted.
We came to live here and as we learned of Joy and her incredible story,
we began to build our dreams around it. We got married of course, but
then shortly after Jen fell ill, and so at the age of twenty-six I became a
widower and my life has effectively been on hold since then.'

'But why does Agatha dislike you, I don't understand...'

'Because like history repeating itself we both made a promise to
Jen on her deathbed that we would do everything we could to make
our dreams for Joy's Acre come true. But for me that's proved to be
easier said than done. I was felled by grief to start with and incapable
of doing anything much beyond renovating the farmhouse, but then
once I decided that I needed to become a bone marrow donor, almost
unwittingly I made it even harder for myself to carry out my promises
to Jen. I lost so much time caught up in Clara's health issues and the
subsequent problems it caused us both that Agatha despises me for it.
She thinks I've betrayed Jen's memory even if she does recognise the
good that's been done.'

Her hand was growing decidedly hot in his.

'I see, so the test?'

'Was to see if I felt the same emotions after donating that I did the
last time. Whether I would become consumed by a desire to know the
recipient, to see if I would need another person to act as a crutch to
help assuage my grief or not... or whether I am now ready to move on
and finally start making Joy's Acre something we can all be proud of.'

'And, what do you feel?'

'Nothing,' he said. 'Beyond a relief that it all went okay and a
pleasure in having acted selflessly for someone else's benefit, I feel
nothing. Or to be more precise, I felt something else, something I

wasn't expecting. I only realised what it was yesterday when I woke up to find you asleep next to me.'

'Oh.' The sound came out before she could stop it, before clear and conscious, rational thought could take over and provide her with something sensible to say. Before she could stop her heart from leaping upwards and her stomach dropping away in shock, and even before she identified the emotion chasing around her head as joy. In the seconds that followed, all these things became known to her, as did the overwhelming certainty of her place in the world.

Even in the bright sunshine, Seth's eyes were dark as he searched her face for clues as to how she felt.

'It's been a long time since Jen died, Maddie, and nothing will ever take away how I feel about her. She's a part of this place too, she always will be and, in the beginning, I wasn't sure if I could ever bear that, to be constantly surrounded by her memory…'

'But now?'

'All I feel is acceptance; an understanding that where I am is the right place for me to be, and possibly the right place for you to be too…' He was leaning in towards her…

Her mouth parted, just a tiny bit, as a loud shout rose up from the bottom of the garden. It was Clara waving madly, and running full pelt towards them.

'You have to come with me,' she panted as she neared them. 'You won't believe what we've just found!'

Chapter 20

As interruptions went it was about as poorly timed as it possibly could be, but as Maddie's heart sank, she and Seth rose from the bench in one fluid movement.

'Blimey, Clara, you'll give a man a heart attack. What on earth's the matter?'

'You might have a heart attack yet,' she said. 'Don't rule it out.' She grinned at them, chest still heaving from her exertion and general excitement. 'Come on!'

She pulled at Seth's shirt and they had no choice but to follow at top speed as Clara led them back into the house and along the hallway. Maddie nearly tripped over Bonnie as the dogs, infected by the sudden change of mood, charged up and down the confined space. Eventually they came to rest back in the room they had begun to clear a couple of days ago.

Since that time, every box had been sorted, every cupboard and drawer emptied. They had salvaged a few things that would come in handy, mostly quirky household items which would provide interesting decoration, and importantly a few papers which gave an added insight into the history of Joy's Acre. But although Maddie had been poring over these for interesting snippets she could use for the website she was putting together, there had been nothing else which had caused heart rates to rise. Until now, it would seem.

Once things had been emptied and either stored or thrown away, Trixie had ferried her endless boxes of books into the room. The huge dresser would house some of them, and the others in time would fill bookshelves that had yet to be installed. The room itself was looking far more appealing than it had in the past and there were plans to turn it into a second sitting room. As such, both Clara and Trixie had been wielding polish, cloths and various other cleaning implements to give the room a thorough spring clean, and as Seth and Maddie burst into the room it was still in a certain amount of disarray.

'We pulled the dresser out from the wall to dust and hoover behind it, and look…' Clara held out her hands towards Trixie, who was holding a small rectangular object.

'Careful,' she warned. 'I've dusted it off a bit, but hold it by the edges for now so that it doesn't mark.'

Clara did as she was asked, passing it over to Seth as if it was made of the most fragile porcelain.

'What do you think?' she asked. 'Is it one of hers?' She looked practically fit to burst.

Seth's head shot up. 'Where was this?' he asked.

'Wedged down the back of the dresser,' replied Trixie. 'I think it must have fallen behind the shelves in the bottom section. When we moved it, I think it slid out where the back board had become bowed. We had to tip the dresser forward quite a bit to fish it out.'

Seth nodded, looking first at Maddie, then at Clara, and finally at Trixie before dropping his gaze back down to the picture he held in his hands.

'I don't believe this,' he said. 'It's been here all the time.'

'It is hers, isn't it?' said Clara. 'I knew it was.' She was practically jumping up and down in excitement. Seth just looked shell shocked.

Maddie stepped forward and Seth wordlessly handed her the picture. Even in its dusty state the vibrant colours were instantly recognisable, as was the subject matter.

'Oh my God,' she intoned. 'It is, it's one of Joy's!' She stared at the picture a moment longer, heart pounding, before handing it back.

'Light,' said Seth suddenly. 'We need more light.'

He shooed the dogs out the way and marched back down the hallway to the kitchen, where the sun was painting the walls with gold. He laid the picture down carefully on the table and stood back to look at it.

It was slightly bigger than the one which hung in the hallway, painted from the other side of the garden looking back towards the house. The greenhouse, resplendent in bright sunshine, was filled with all manner of fruit and vegetables and to the other side sat the thatched cottage, tall stems of hollyhocks waving from the side of the path to the front door.

'What do we do?' asked Maddie.

Seth looked at her, but it took a moment before her words registered. 'Clean it up a bit, I suppose, but—'

'No, I meant, shouldn't we tell someone? When I found the auction catalogue that time it mentioned that she was considered an important artist of her generation, not least of all because her work is so scarce. I know it's not a van Gogh, but aren't we supposed to say we've found it or something?'

'I don't see why.' Seth frowned. 'What business is it of anybody else's?' He narrowed his eyes at her. 'The only reason we'd need to do that was if we were thinking about selling it, which we're not.'

Clara gave an audible tut. 'Before you go getting on your high horse, Seth, no one's suggesting that we sell it, but Maddie's right. We should at least get it checked out to make sure Joy painted it, that way at least we know what we're dealing with.'

'And then we sell it?'

'No!' Clara said. 'Stop putting words in our mouths. I'm as excited about this as you are, but the more practical part of my brain is also thinking about insurance and the like.'

Seth inhaled slowly. 'I'm sorry,' he said. 'Yes, of course, you're both absolutely right. I can't afford any insurance of course, but that's probably beside the point. Perhaps we should give the guy at the auctioneers a ring in the first instance and see what he says.'

'I'll go and get the catalogue from the last sale,' said Maddie. 'I think the chap's number was inside.'

She hurried from the room, thinking fast. An idea had just come at her out of nowhere but she would need some time to think about it first. There was no way she could mention it just yet.

When she returned, the three were exactly as she had left them, although Trixie looked up as she entered and caught her eye with a rueful grin.

'I probably shouldn't say this but I'm gonna anyway… I'm just playing that devil's whatnot, what do you call it?'

'Advocate?' suggested Maddie.

'That's it! Devil's advocate, because I know I've only just got here and everything so I don't really know what's going on, but you guys are seriously strapped for cash, and we've just found a painting which you're all making sound like it's worth a fortune… So why aren't you going to sell it? It's pretty, but I'm not sure it's worth making a massive fuss over.'

Maddie grimaced. It was a valid comment, and there was a good deal of truth in what she said, but somehow she didn't think Seth was going to see it that way.

'Don't shoot the messenger…' sang Clara under her breath.

A few poignant seconds passed before Seth opened his mouth to speak. Neither Maddie nor Clara dared to answer on his behalf.

'I should shoot you on the spot for treason,' said Seth, his face sliding into a grin, 'but fortunately for you I've taken my sidearm in for servicing. What you suggest is, of course, what every sane person would do in our position, but what on earth gave you the idea that we were sane, in any way, shape, or form?'

'Hmm, I'm beginning to see that…' muttered Trixie. 'But listen, you're talking to a woman with bright pink hair – conforming to how everyone else thinks I should behave isn't exactly top of my list. I'm quite happy to be added to the insane list.'

'Consider yourself added in that case, the only rule being that you never, ever mention selling this painting again. We should probably tell you why though, I guess that's only fair.'

Maddie handed Trixie the story of Joy's Acre that she had brought from the other room.

'A little bit of bedtime reading,' she said. 'Make sure you've got a tissue to hand though, it's heart-wrenching in places.'

Then she handed the auction catalogue she had also brought to Seth, and turned over the front cover for him.

He paused, looking at the page in front of him where the auctioneers' contact details were listed.

'I should go and do this now, shouldn't I?' he asked.

'Yes,' chorused both Clara and Maddie together.

'Otherwise we all know that you'll put off every opportunity to do it for the next millennium,' added Maddie. 'Strike while the iron's hot and let's find out whether Joy really has left us another gift.'

Seth's eyes stayed on hers for quite some time before he dropped his gaze; at least it felt that way to Maddie, who had suddenly become hyperaware of everything that Seth said or did. She was, as Clara suggested, completely under the influence of his gravitational pull.

How on earth was she ever going to broach her idea with Seth? She wasn't entirely sure what there was between them yet, or even that she had read the signs right, but whatever their relationship was, this ran the risk of blowing it wide apart. So wide that they might never recover from it. The trouble was that Joy's Acre probably wouldn't exist much longer without this intervention. With her project manager's head on, she knew, perhaps more than any of them, what they were up against here. They might make it, but common sense told her there was a good chance they wouldn't. She looked across at Clara who was busy studying the painting again; she was probably the only one who would understand, but whether Maddie would have the nerve to talk to her about it, now that was another matter.

She could see Seth through the kitchen window, pacing up and down in the yard with his mobile to his ear. A few weeks ago, this would have been an impossibility but the arrival of broadband had been a definite step in the right direction. Wi-Fi calling was another benefit they were all getting pleasantly used to, but that, like everything, came at a price. She took a step to one side as Clara came to stand beside her.

'What do you think?' she said. 'Right decision?'

'As opposed to?'

'I don't know,' sighed Clara. 'Burying our heads in the sand?'

'Seth would call it loyalty and commitment,' she commented, keeping her eyes on the yard. 'But I think you're right. It's not being disloyal and it might never come to it, but I think if we ever had to sell the painting, I'd like to know where we stand. All we're doing is checking our facts.'

'I think Seth understands that. I know he can seem a bit blinkered at times, but once he's had an opportunity to think things through he usually makes pretty sound judgements.' She elbowed Maddie very gently in the ribs. 'You seemed very close out in the garden,' she said.

'Did we?'

'Hmm, you did...' She was grinning now, Maddie could hear it in her voice. 'And I thought you were supposed to be helping Tom.'

'We were!' Maddie protested, although she knew there was little point in trying to pull the wool over Clara's eyes. 'It took me a little while to learn how, but once I'd got the knack, we made no end of spars.'

'Well there wasn't much that Seth was doing except for making eyes at you...'

Maddie batted her arm. 'Oh give over,' she said. 'You're just imagining things.'

A voice spoke from behind them. 'I'm probably not supposed to say this either, but this is far more exciting than some bloody picture. Are you and Seth—'

'No!'

Trixie and Clara exchanged looks. 'Protesting far too hard, I'd say...'

'Definitely,' confirmed Clara.

'Although I would, given half the chance. He's pretty nice to look at... smouldering dark eyes, tousled hair, and a bit of rough with the beard... just how I like them.'

Maddie rolled her eyes. 'Ladies, please.' She still had one eye on the front window. 'Shh, for goodness' sake. He's coming back.'

'Right, well I don't know whether that was good news or bad news,' announced Seth, coming back into the kitchen. 'The chap who dealt with the sale before has left the company, but they have a new man who's a specialist in Victorian art. Rather surprisingly he knew Joy's name, although under the name she painted of course – CJ Davenport – and he has declared that he'll be very happy to give us an assessment on our picture's authenticity.'

He pulled a face. 'Although, seeing as this was her house and the picture was rammed down the back of her dresser, I fail to see how it can have been painted by anyone else.'

'Did he seem interested?' asked Maddie.

'Very,' said Seth, frowning at her.

'So, just to play the devil's whatnot again,' said Trixie, 'did he mention how many gazillions it might be worth?'

'No, Trixie, he didn't, and before you ask, no I didn't mention it either. Anyway, he's coming on Friday, so we'll just have to wait and see.'

Friday was two days away. 'So, what do we do now?' asked Clara.

'Well, Maddie and I still have hundreds of bloody spars to make, and I guess you two can just carry on as you were.'

'That wasn't exactly what I meant,' she replied.

'No, I know,' he said, grinning. 'But that's the only answer you're going to get.'

Chapter 21

Maddie looked up and smiled gratefully as Clara set down a cup of tea beside her. She'd been hard at it since dinnertime, working on their new website.

'Ah, you're a lifesaver,' she said.

Clara peered at the screen. 'How's it going?'

'Coming together,' she replied. 'I know what I'm doing, for most of it anyway, but it's time-consuming getting the detail right.' She sat back slightly so that Clara could see better. 'What do you think? It was the design that took the longest amount of time.'

'May I?' Clara said, pulling up a seat and sitting down. 'That's amazing, how did you do that?'

She was looking at the home page which Maddie was just finishing off. The background to the page was designed to resemble one of the seed catalogues that they had been looking at previously, with the border of the page a beautiful riot of pansies, sweet peas, nasturtiums and hollyhocks, all in a fabulous vintage style. Superimposed over this was a gilded picture frame, the 'picture' itself featuring the title *Joy's Acre* in a glorious swirling Victoriana font, together with details and links to the other pages. These would hold information about Joy's Acre itself, the individual cottages, booking forms and the like.

'They're just stock photos,' Maddie replied. 'But there's so many of them, you can spend days looking through them all to pick the perfect one.' She grinned. 'And then just when you settle on one, you think, *I'll just check a few more to be on the safe side*, and before you know it another couple of hours have gone.'

'Well, those look perfect.'

'Do you think so…?' Maddie tilted her head, looking at the screen from a different angle. 'I think it works.'

'I love how it tells the story without even trying. It's captured the essence of what we are here brilliantly, and using the picture frame is inspired.'

'Yeah, well let's just hope it inspires truck loads of people to want to come here, and not just artists.'

Clara gave her a warm smile. 'I'm sure it will. Visually, it's about as appealing as you can get, and so different from the run-of-the-mill holiday cottage sites.' She stared at the screen again, pausing for a moment. 'How are things looking?' she asked. Her manner was casual enough, but Maddie wasn't fooled.

She pulled a folder that was sitting on the edge of the desk closer to her.

'Honestly?' she said. 'Not great. There were still quite a few contractors that needed to be paid off for work already done, and even with taking over the painting etcetera ourselves, there are things we just simply need to pay for. Sanitary wear, a new kitchen, carpets… even with everything we save on recycling furniture and decorations, there's still a huge list.'

'So have we run out of money, or are we still limping along?'

There was no point in hiding the truth, Clara was too much of a pragmatist for that. When it came down to it, Maddie knew she would much rather hear the truth.

'The pot's virtually empty,' she said. 'Which means that while we might make it to the finish line, it will only be because we've cut so many corners the house will no longer look square. I love what we're doing, Clara, you know that. It feels absolutely the right approach for the cottage *and* it will look stunning. Bottom line though? If people are going to part with good money to come and stay here they will want certain things to be in place, and of a sufficiently high standard. If they're not, we'll be crucified.'

Clara nodded. 'And we'll have nothing left in reserve to carry on work on the other cottages or the barn,' she said.

Maddie gave no reply; she didn't need to.

'Today's news couldn't have come at a better time then?'

She groaned. This was something she really didn't want to have to think about, and sitting in the office, out of the way of everybody else, had almost allowed that to happen. Almost, but not quite. Besides, if anyone could spot what Maddie was thinking without her having to say anything, it was Clara.

She wasn't the only one who had held her breath the whole time the expert from the auctioneers was with them. Earlier that afternoon, the chap had been seated at the table, a cup of their best coffee put in front of him and the picture placed reverently on the table. All the while, four people hung on his every word.

There was never any doubt in Maddie's mind that he would declare the painting to be an authentic CJ Davenport. What made her more anxious than she could say was the value he was prepared to place on it. This was crucial to her plan. Of course, she had to look interested, but not unduly so; delighted to have found one of Joy's paintings, but in a totally non-materialistic way, and at the same time supportive of Seth's plan to hang the painting straight on the hallway wall beside Joy's other picture.

When the valuation had come, she'd had to clench her fist under the table to keep from shouting out. Of course, there were no guarantees. If the painting ever came to sale, the auctioneer's job would be to try and raise the price as high as possible, and while on the one hand that was exactly what Maddie wanted, on the other it wouldn't work in her favour at all. The question was, should she tell Clara, or not?

'Do *you* think it's come at a good time?' she asked, batting the ball very firmly back into Clara's court.

A stern finger was waggled at her. 'Oh, no you don't,' said Clara. 'I asked first. So, I'll repeat the question. Given the opportunity that has now presented itself to us, and taking Seth's opinion out of this for the moment, do we need to sell the painting?'

Maddie took in a deep breath. 'Yes,' she said sadly. 'But you can't remove Seth's opinion from the equation, because it's a huge issue. He's invested such an enormous amount in Joy's Acre, physically and emotionally, that this would be a huge blow to him. He sees this as confirmation from Joy herself that we're doing the right thing.'

'I know,' nodded Clara. 'But he's not stupid. Given the choice of Joy's Acre or no Joy's Acre, even he would compromise his principles.'

'He might have to,' replied Maddie. 'Getting him to accept that, though, is an entirely different matter.'

Clara smiled suddenly. 'You're just going to have to sleep with him, you know. Soften him up a bit – all for a good cause though, obviously.'

Maddie, who had just taken a sip of her tea, nearly spat it out across the desk.

'Oh, will I now? Honestly Clara, say what's on your mind why don't you. Plus, he's my boss, in case you hadn't forgotten.'

She giggled. 'Just a thought… although, like I said before, you were looking very close the other day in the garden. Have things, er, developed in any way?'

'No, they have not!'

It was an automatic protest, but the truth of it was that Maddie had been a little disappointed. Seth and she had duly gone back outside on the day they found the painting and had indeed carried on making the spars for Tom, but, despite the fact that they took up their original positions on the bench, there had been no return to the previous topic of conversation. In fact, anything and everything but. Whatever the moment was, it had gone. She had harboured thoughts that perhaps the opportunity might present itself again, but it hadn't and now, knowing what she did, and what her plan would entail, there was a very real risk that Seth would never want to speak to her again, let alone sleep with her.

There was only one way she was ever going to know if her plan was a good one.

'Can we just forget about my non-relationship with Seth for a minute. I've had an idea about the painting and, if I'm right, I think it might solve all our problems. The trouble is, I will probably need your help, and if you agree to it, life's going to get very tough for a while.'

★

Maddie sat and stared at the computer for a few moments after Clara had gone, slowly sipping her tea until it was finished. She was glad to have Clara's support, but that still didn't alter the fact that somebody needed to speak to Seth about selling the painting, and soon. Despite Clara's protestations it was also clear to Maddie that she was the obvious person for the job. She had all the facts and figures at her disposal and it was probable that Seth would be more likely to listen to logic than emotion, at least she hoped so…

She saved her work on the website, logged off from the computer and, collecting her mug, rose to return to the kitchen where she was hoping to find Seth. No time like the present.

He was sitting reading at the table as she entered the room, or rather perusing a brochure on kitchen fittings, but at least when he looked up he was smiling.

'How's it going?' he asked.

Maddie crossed to the sink where she began to rinse her mug. 'Yeah, good thanks. Well I've had Clara's seal of approval anyway, but actually I'm pleased with how the site's turning out. I think it will do the trick.'

Seth closed the brochure. 'Shall I come have a look?'

'Oh.' She wasn't expecting that. 'I've logged off now,' she replied. 'Never mind, I can show you another day. It's not finished yet anyway, I've just been working on the overall design, but now that I'm happy with it I can start to add in the detail. And more importantly get the booking form on and work on optimising the site through different search engines as soon as possible.'

'Hmm, we're going to need it.' He sounded somewhat absent-minded, but there was no mistaking the seriousness of his words. His attention had been drawn back down to the catalogue momentarily, but then he looked back up at her, pulling a face. 'In fact I wondered whether you were coming in here to tell me we need to sell the painting, you looked so serious when you arrived.'

Maddie fought to keep her face under control as Seth kept his eyes firmly on hers. She knew she probably wasn't going to get to pick the perfect opportunity to say exactly that, but she had hoped nonetheless for it to be as non confrontational as possible.

'Ah… I see I got it right after all. But then I already knew how you were thinking. It was pretty obvious considering the expression you had on your face the whole time the auctioneer was here.'

'It was not! What expression did I have on?' She could feel the heat rising up her neck. 'That's not fair, Seth. Why else were we all listening to what he had to say? So that we could consider our options, that's all. And that's exactly what we should be doing. Not only is it sensible—'

'So you do agree that it should be sold then?'

'I didn't say that.'

'Did you need to?' His look was not far off a sneer. 'I'm not stupid, Maddie. I know you have a spreadsheet that can tell you just how empty the coffers are, but I have one of my own, up here.' He tapped the side of his head. 'I can do the maths too.'

'Then why are you getting angry with me?'

He sighed. 'I'm not, not really… I'm just disappointed that after all the plans we made and how right everything feels, and we get the biggest confirmation that there is from Joy herself no less, and then almost within hours we're prepared to cash it in seemingly without another thought.'

Maddie could feel her frustration rising. 'But perhaps you're looking at it from the wrong point of view. You're seeing our discovery of Joy's painting as a good luck omen, one we should keep with us, but given everything we feel about her, what if she's provided for us right at the very moment we need it most? Doesn't that make sense too?'

'Oh, very convenient…'

'No, just as plausible a reason as you're suggesting.'

They were practically glaring at each other.

'So I'm just being stupidly sentimental, am I?'

Seth looked tired and somewhat defeated, and Maddie would have loved to put her arms around him and tell him everything was fine, but despite what his words were doing to her insides she knew that wasn't the answer. She had to do what was right for Joy's Acre.

'You're being sentimental about a painting, when what you should be being sentimental about is Joy's Acre, the whole of it. That's your choice, Seth, I can't make it any clearer. It's one or the other, you can't have both.'

His head dropped to his chest as he inhaled a huge breath.

'And you know I'm right…'

'Fine.' He breathed out. 'We'll sell the painting.' His voice was no more than a whisper.

Chapter 22

Tom was his usual cheerful self, but it didn't make up for the fact that Seth was ignoring her at every opportunity. He pretended not to of course; he was civil and to outward appearances it was business as usual, but none of this fooled Maddie. He no longer stayed to chat with her if she was washing up; more often than not he left the room if she entered it, claiming he had to get on with something; or, he simply found ways to be elsewhere when there was something to discuss, saying that he would leave any decision to her superior judgement.

The irony of this last statement wasn't lost on her, but, in a way, it was also true. Seth *did* accept what he had been told. He understood their financial situation fully and, given the options, he had agreed that the only possible and logical way forward *was* to sell Joy's painting. Except that somehow, it seemed however hard he tried, he couldn't overcome his disappointment that it was Maddie who had been the one to persuade him this was their only course of action. They had bonded over their shared love for Joy's Acre, but now it was as if she had revealed herself to be nothing more than a business woman looking for a fast buck. It was no surprise to her that he thought this way, but it still hurt.

Maddie adjusted her grip on the tray she was carrying. This was the second pot of tea that she had brought out to Seth and Tom today, along with some fresh brownies that Trixie had made, and yet, what would hopefully be a day for celebration, was, for her at least, tempered by Seth's attitude towards her. In all likelihood the roof would be finished today and all along this had been the signal that they were on the final stretch, the home straight; a sign that they were almost ready for business. But her excitement level was far below where it should have been, and it saddened her.

'Tea's up!' she yelled as she neared the cottage. 'And more cake!'

It had been somewhat of a running joke that since Trixie moved in they seemed to be constantly devouring huge chunks of cake, but to be honest, some days it was all they seemed to live off until their evening meal. Not perhaps the healthiest of lifestyles, but physical exercise was in plentiful supply too, as a catalogue of aching and bruised limbs would testify.

Tom immediately shimmied down the ladder, wiping his hand across his brow as he reached the bottom.

'Blimey, it's warm up there today,' he said, coming forward. 'Might have to take my top off soon.' He winked at her.

'You'll scare the birds away, Tom,' she replied, handing him a mug. She shielded her eyes from the sun and looked up at the roof, where Seth was still working away. 'Is he coming, do you think?'

Tom put two fingers in his mouth and gave a sharp whistle. 'Oi, guv'nor,' he shouted. 'Get your backside down here for a drink. I don't want you keeling over on me, not when we're this close.'

'Are you really going to finish today?' she asked while they were waiting.

'I reckon so,' Tom replied. 'Wasn't sure we would, but then we've had such a run of good weather, and Seth's been like a man on a mission, so...'

She looked away at the slight inflection in his voice and pretended to be studying the thatch. Whatever Tom had noticed was not something she was prepared to discuss; she really didn't want to know what Seth had been saying about her. Joy's painting had been included in an auction that would take place in two days' time, and then it would all be over. Until that happened she would bide her time.

'It looks amazing, Tom,' she said. 'And to think that just a few weeks ago I thought thatch was a waste of time. I feel ashamed to say it, but I can't believe how naive I was. Now I know the skill and work that goes into it.'

She ran her eyes along the roof line, to the far end of the ridge where two straw hares leaped in joyful play.

'Is that your signature?' she asked. 'I've seen them before but never really considered why it was done.'

'A bit of whimsy, maybe. Some thatchers don't hold with finials, thinking them arrogant, I don't know, but where I trained all of us did them. It lets folk know who thatched the roof for one.'

'So why are yours hares then? Why did you pick those?'

Tom tapped the side of his nose. 'Ah, well that's the thing, isn't it. There's always a story in there somewhere. Mine came about a few years back when I was playing with the band at a wedding. A right do, it was. Very posh, but man they could put away the booze. At the end of the night, we were playing a fast jig and it got to my solo bit on the banjo. Folks were totally piddled by then, but one lass, a farmer's daughter I reckon, got a fit of the giggles and couldn't stop. She said all she could see was hares running and chasing in the fields.'

He rubbed at his chin. 'I didn't think much of it at the time, she was probably seeing unicorns and all, but afterwards I got to thinking about it myself. Have you ever seen mad march hares, Maddie? It's not just a saying, but if you've ever seen 'em you'd never forget 'em. Nothing like it for letting you know that spring is on its way. It seemed right that I should use them after that.'

Maddie gaped at the roof. 'Why don't half of us know these things?' she said. 'What an amazing story.' She looked over at Seth, who had finally come to join them, and smiled. 'Well, that's definitely going on the website,' she said. 'What do you think, Seth?'

He gave her a quizzical look. 'About what?'

'The finials, and the reason why Tom picked hares.'

He shrugged. 'That old chestnut. I thought it was just a chat-up line to be honest.' Maddie tutted, but Seth was actually smiling. 'Well, whatever it was, Tom, it's still a good story, and, more importantly, it will become part of the charm for folks who come here.'

'Which shouldn't be long with any luck,' added Maddie. 'Our click-through rates on the website are going up every day, and the more we get it's only a matter of time before someone makes a booking. Once we're done here I can add some more photos as well, internal ones too.'

She wasn't really fishing for compliments, but it would be nice to hear some positive feedback. Seth hadn't exactly been gushing with praise recently.

'Well that's what it's all about, isn't it? Translating this lot into cold hard cash.' Seth drained his mug, replaced it on the tray and took a brownie from the plate, biting it in half. At no point did his eyes meet hers. He waved the other half of the cake at Tom. 'See you back up there, mate.'

Tom bit into his own cake, shuffling his feet. 'Ignore him, Maddie,' he said so softly she almost didn't hear it. 'You're doing the right thing.'

She looked up at him, his face unusually sombre, but she had nothing more to say. It didn't really matter what anyone else thought.

For some reason all she cared about was what Seth was thinking. She nodded, rearranging the items on the tray so that Tom could replace his mug too.

'Thanks,' she said quietly, smiling as best she could.

★

Logging into the computer took all of thirty seconds, but Maddie stared at the screen far longer than it took for the system to boot up. She didn't need to add the latest costings into the spreadsheet to know what the end result was, but she was going to do it anyway. She had purposely left the folder with all the information in it on the kitchen table last night, knowing that if Seth opened it he would be able to see the current state of play within a minute or so. She didn't really need to prove her point, but it was there for the taking.

She had also kept a list of savings they had made over the last few weeks, thinking that this was just as important for them all to know. It made the hard work seem all the more worthwhile. It justified the time and effort they had all put into it and, she hoped, provided further proof, if any were needed, of how well they had all worked together as a team.

In two days' time, provided the painting sold for a good price, she would know where she stood, but she hoped with all her might that the outcome was the one she desired. Joy's Acre was so much more to her now than just a job, but if things didn't go according to plan, that's probably what it would become.

The email program booted up automatically, and she stared at it as it loaded, willing the inbox to show new mail had arrived. Her heart leaped as a tiny ping announced the arrival of a message, but sank just as quickly when she saw it was simply junk. How was that even possible? The site had only been up and running a couple of weeks. She completed her task and pushed the chair back from the desk. The information could stay on the screen for the time being, it wouldn't hurt.

She wandered back through to the kitchen, almost flinching as she passed the painting that hung in the hallway; the one that Seth had bought at auction years before, the one that had suddenly made her realise what Joy's Acre was all about. To its left was a bare hook, empty of the new picture that was now safely delivered to the sale room. She walked on by.

Trixie was still baking, up to her ears in dough which she was pounding relentlessly on the table. Every time Maddie had seen her during the course of the day she had been doing the exact same thing.

'Can I have a go?' asked Maddie, grimacing. 'I could do with giving something a good thrashing.'

Trixie flashed her a grin. 'Be my guest,' she said. 'My bloody arm's about to drop off.'

Maddie had actually been joking, but as Trixie raised her hands from the ball of dough and stepped away she realised the truth in her own words.

'I've never done this before,' she admitted. 'You'll have to show me how.'

'Easy peasy,' replied Trixie. 'Just imagine it's Seth's body there on the table and you're trying to tear him limb from limb.'

Maddie looked up and groaned. 'Is it really that obvious?' she said.

Trixie just looked at her. 'Limb from limb,' she repeated. 'Go on, try it.'

And so Maddie did, stretching at the dough furiously, pulling it this way and that.

Trixie gave a low whistle. 'Jeez, remind me never to get on your bad side,' she quipped. 'Quite therapeutic though, isn't it? And when you're done tearing limb from limb, you can pick the dough up and then roll it around – use the heel of your palm to push the dough into the table, like you're trying to grind someone's face in the dirt.'

Maddie stared at her. 'That's awesome.' She grinned. 'Remind me never to get on *your* bad side either. Where *do* you get your analogies from?'

Just as Trixie was about to reply the front door banged and Seth came storming through into the hallway, Clara hot on his heels.

'And don't you bloody walk away from me when I'm trying to talk to you! You really are the most pig-headed, stubborn man I know—'

'This is my house, I'll walk where I damn well like.' He swivelled to face her. 'And as a topic of conversation I am not prepared to discuss it under any circumstances, have I not made that clear enough yet? Give it up, Clara.'

He continued his march down the hall.

'No! I won't!' she shouted at his retreating back. 'Because you're making the biggest mistake of your life and you know you are. You're just too bloody proud to admit it…'

The shouting match continued up the stairs and along the landing, at which point another door slammed. Maddie walked to the kitchen door, holding her floury hands aloft, and nudged it closed with her hip.

'That's better,' she said. 'Now where were we?' And with that she renewed her attack on the helpless piece of dough under her fingers. She continued for several more minutes. 'If I haven't ruined it, what are we making?' she asked eventually.

'They're for the farmers' market tomorrow,' Trixie explained. 'I'm making bread samples, eight different loaves in all, which we're going to try out on punters and see which ones go down the best. Then next month, we'll make tons of them and hopefully a nice tidy profit at the same time. All part of our cunning plan.' She paused for a moment, looking slightly uncomfortable. 'Shouldn't we go after them?' she said.

'Nope,' said Maddie, firmly. 'Whatever they're arguing about, I'm staying well clear. Besides, by the sound of it Clara has things well covered.' She softened her mouth a little. 'I'm sorry though,' she added. 'You've only just arrived and it can't be very nice for you at the moment. Things are a bit intense, aren't they?'

'They often are when passion's involved. My mum and dad fight like cat and dog, but their marriage has outlived all of my mates' parents' and they're still going strong. I've learned that it's just the way some people are. They love each other, that's what counts in the long run. Seth's no different; he loves this place and so he fights for what he believes in. Underneath that doesn't stop him from knowing that he can get things wrong too, and when he realises that, he'll have learnt from it and the bond will be even stronger still.'

She gave Maddie a sideways glance. 'I know,' she said. 'I'm amazing. It comes with being a barmaid. We're fully trained to give advice on anything and everything, but marriage guidance is usually a speciality. There's quite a lot of call for it.' She raised an eyebrow.

Maddie laughed. 'Oh, I bet there is.'

'So, in your case, whatever happens at the auction on Friday happens, and life goes on, and it will go on. Plus, Seth will realise that his passion for this place… and other things… also goes on, unaltered.'

'And in the meantime?'

'In the meantime, we bake…'

★

Maddie hadn't intended to stay and help Trixie at all, but it was wonderfully cathartic and before she knew it they were on to making another batch of bread. A honey and sunflower loaf this time. It was good to get away from figures, work schedules, fittings lists and decision making. There in the kitchen it was just them, a few ingredients and the strange alchemy that was bread-making. The noise had continued upstairs for a little while, but all had been quiet for some time now, and neither Seth nor Clara had reappeared.

As the afternoon turned to early evening, Trixie's attention switched to preparing dinner; a mushroom, spinach and nut pie, which sounded mouth-watering. Given that she had been baking most of the day, Maddie offered to stay and give Trixie a hand, and first on the list was the washing and clearing up after their bread-making session.

Maddie turned the tap on full and waited for the water to heat, adding a generous squirt of washing-up liquid into the huge butler sink. Trixie had gone out to the garden to gather some of what she needed for their meal and for pretty much the first time that afternoon the kitchen fell silent. Maddie stood staring out the window as the sink filled, lost in thought. Her time with Trixie had been good for her, taking her mind off her troubles, but now she was alone once more the list of things that still needed to be done began to crowd her head. Pulling on the lurid yellow washing-up gloves, she turned to fetch the mixing bowls from the table.

Her hand flew to her mouth.

'Christ, you made me jump!' she exclaimed. 'How long have you been standing there?'

In fact, Seth wasn't exactly standing, he was leaning up against the table, his legs stretched out and crossed at the ankles. His arms rested lightly in his lap.

'Not that long. You didn't hear me come in.'

'No, really? For God's sake, Seth, you nearly gave me a heart attack.'

'You were staring out the window. I wondered what you were thinking.'

'Just stuff,' she said noncommittally, her eyes dropping automatically to the floor before raising them again briefly. Seth was staring at her.

'I see. Good stuff… Or bad stuff…?'

She didn't answer him.

'I see,' he said again.

All of a sudden, his discomfort made her angry.

'Well what do you suppose I *was* thinking about? Eh, Seth? It doesn't take a genius to work it out, now does it? One minute you were confiding your innermost secrets to me, hinting that… well never mind, but friendly at least, and then the next minute you can't bear to be in the same room as me. I know what I've done, Seth… No, wait a minute, that's not right. I know what *we've* done, Seth, and I know why we've done it. The only I in this equation is there because it was me that drew the short straw and told you we have no choice other than to sell the painting. But it's not like we didn't know it was coming, any more than we think it's a terrible idea. So, pardon me if I find it a little upsetting now that *I'm* being treated like a pariah, when everyone else is still top of your Christmas card list.'

Her eyes blazed at him as he stared at her calmly and quietly. It was more than a little unnerving. She wanted him to retaliate, to at least try to defend himself so that she could denounce his words and throw more bile at him, but he just stood there, eyes locked on hers, his face unreadable. And those big brown eyes, dammit, so dark they hid his emotion from her.

Slowly he uncrossed his legs and straightened. Then he took a step towards her, and another. In the second before his hand snaked around the back of her neck she wondered if she'd pushed him too far, but then he pulled her head closer and laid the gentlest kiss on her lips; a soft sigh, as his breath mingled with hers.

'I don't blame you,' he murmured. 'I blame me…' And then he kissed her again.

'Do you think everyone would like salad with—' Trixie's voice from the doorway stopped suddenly. 'Oh.'

Seth pulled away, but not before she had time to see that she had got it wrong before; she didn't need to see his emotion after all, she could feel it very clearly indeed. The next instant he had flashed Trixie an apologetic smile and fled the room.

Trixie's hands went to her hips. 'Now what the heck was all that about?' she said.

Maddie's fingers touched her lips. 'I have absolutely no idea,' she said.

Chapter 23

It was utterly ridiculous to think that she would sleep, and it was a weird sensation lying there knowing that there were three other people in the house, none of whom were probably asleep either. Yet the house was silent. No opening doors, no creaking floorboards, no sighs of frustration or cisterns flushing, but the building itself was suffused with an expectant air. Maddie could feel it pulsing in the silent night, pressing down on her and imprisoning her thoughts, allowing no others into her head save those of tomorrow's auction.

All five of them had been restless today. Clara had dug over the new flower beds she had created around the cottage, even though they had been done the week before. Tom had spent the morning helping two lads to fit the new kitchen for the cottage, banged a nail into his finger and finally disappeared off down the pub. Trixie had decided to go through her vast collection of cookbooks to reacquaint herself with favourite recipes – the last time Maddie had looked in on her she was sitting in the middle of the carpet with them heaped up around her – while Seth had spent the entire day popping up everywhere that Maddie was. This was totally by coincidence of course, but once in her vicinity he watched her surreptitiously, wearing a haunted look.

Dinner had been subdued until Maddie, not able to stand it any longer, had got up and fetched an extra place mat and cutlery from the drawer which she made a great show of placing on the table in front of a spare chair.

'For the elephant in the room,' she said casually before sitting back down again.

It broke the ice, sort of; there were giggles, furtive looks, a short conversation about the mechanics of the forthcoming day, and it looked for a time as if the atmosphere might improve, but then the chat died away again and the remainder of the meal had been eaten in virtual silence.

Maddie turned to look at the clock on the bedside table. At last the sky was beginning to lighten and she got up to throw open the window, breathing in the cool morning air which was rapidly filling with the dawn chorus. She padded across the room to where Seth's dressing gown still hung on the back of her bedroom door. Quite why that was she couldn't say, but she had hung it there the day after the disastrous visit from Agatha and, somehow, there hadn't seemed to be an appropriate moment to return it. Pulling it on, she inched open her door and crept down the landing to the stairs.

Passing the kitchen, the two dogs lifted their heads lazily from their baskets, tails thumping against the floor, but neither were inclined to investigate any further and she reached the front door without incident.

She realised she had never been up early enough to see the dawn here before, but as she made her way to the bench she had first sat on all those weeks ago, it seemed fitting that today should be the day. One way or another it would herald a change at Joy's Acre; just how much of one remained to be seen. The painting would sell, she was sure of it, and that in itself was out of her hands. But, if she was lucky, fate would smile on both her and Joy's Acre; if not, then perhaps it was never really meant to be. Either way, Joy's Acre would be the winner, and that was the most important thing.

Closing her eyes, she offered up her face in the direction of the sunrise and tried to remember the feeling of completeness she had experienced the day she had found the first of Joy's paintings.

'I still think it looks better on you than me.'

Her eyes flew open.

Seth was standing on the path in front of her, wearing jeans and a tee shirt. She felt distinctly underdressed despite the heat now surging through her body.

'I saw you come out,' he added. 'I guess we're all having trouble sleeping.' He nodded towards the bench. 'Do you mind?'

Maddie moved a couple of inches to her right. There was plenty of room to sit down.

There was silence for a minute or so. Maddie couldn't think of a single thing to say. She was about to make some banal reference to the weather when Seth got up again.

'I'm sorry,' he said. 'You probably wanted to be on your own.'

'No.' Her reply was immediate. 'Don't go, please. It's just that I don't know what to say to you, Seth. I feel closed off, like there's some invisible barrier between us, and try as I might I can't get over it, or around it, or under it for that matter… and it's driving me mad! I know you feel let down, betrayed even, but no one feels it as much as I do, Seth.'

She dropped her head. 'Sorry, I promised myself I wouldn't get angry, but I feel so responsible for everything that's happened here. You have no idea what that guilt feels like.'

His eyes reached hers, tired, but filled with pain at her words. 'I've lived with it every single day since Jen died, Maddie. Guilt because she got ill and I didn't. Guilt because I couldn't be the one to save her. Guilt because I couldn't find anyone else to save her, and guilt because in my desperation to keep her alive I know she suffered.'

Even in the pale morning light she could see his face drain of colour.

'I'm sorry,' he said again. 'I thought I was ready for all this… whatever this is, you and me…' He trailed off.

Maddie held out her hand, entwining her fingers with his and pulling him back down onto the bench.

'No one can ever change how you feel about Jen, not me nor anyone else. I don't know why we would want to. But one thing I do know, is that for you to love her as much as you do, Jen must have been a very special person, and there's no way she'd want you to feel like this. It's not your love that's tethering you to the past, Seth, it's your guilt, and you have nothing to feel guilty for.'

'She used to waggle her finger at me,' he said softly, giving a rueful smile. 'Even when she knew she was going to die and it was no longer a hypothetical scenario, she still made me promise to move on with my life, to let her go…'

'And wouldn't you want the same for her if the situation was reversed?'

He smiled. 'No, she was always a better person than me. I think I'd haunt the living daylights out of anyone who tried to love her.'

'I don't think she's haunting me though, Seth… This was her home, and she loved it every bit as much as you do.'

She looked up at him, wondering whether to go on.

'When I cleared out the office a few weeks ago, just before I first found out about Joy and her paintings, I came to sit in the garden… I felt like I was dreaming, a strange sensation, but as if every part of me was suddenly connected with every part of Joy's Acre. It made me realise how much I loved it here and how much I wanted to be a part of things. I felt… comforted, accepted – loved even. I never realised at the time, but perhaps that was part of Jen's blessing, Joy's too; a message to look after this place, make it the very best it can be, in both their names.'

'I've behaved appallingly over the last couple of days…'

'No, you haven't. You need to be sure that what you're doing is the right thing and I would expect nothing less from you. I don't know what there is between us either, Seth, but whatever it is I don't want it to end. Your friendship means too much to me.'

His fingers moved over hers. 'I think it's gone way beyond that, don't you…?'

★

The memory of his kiss was still causing Maddie's cheeks to burn as they filed into the auction room several hours later. One kiss that had changed two worlds in an instant. She smiled to herself, feeling the nerves bubble in her stomach, nerves that were no longer simply due to the sale of Joy's painting. She deliberately positioned herself so that she wouldn't be sitting next to Seth. There would be no way she would get through this if he were by her side.

It seemed to take an interminably long amount of time before their lot came up. Maddie's heart was going like the clappers.

Clara slipped her hand in Maddie's and gave it a squeeze.

'I've no idea what happens now,' she whispered. 'But whatever does will be the right thing, I'm sure of it.'

She had only just finished speaking when the auctioneer's voice boomed in Maddie's ear.

'And who's going to start the bidding for me, shall we say three thousand pounds?'

She stared at Clara. 'Jeez…' she muttered.

There was silence in the room.

'Two thousand pounds,' the auctioneer stated. 'Who'll give me two?'

Still silence.

'Come on, ladies and gentlemen. Who's going to start me off? This is a rare piece, one of only four thought to be in existence…' The auctioneer leaned over to a colleague. 'I have a telephone bidder,' he said. 'One thousand pounds… One thousand pounds I'm bid.'

Maddie's head shot up as she dug her fingernails into the palm of her hand. It wasn't enough. It was nowhere near enough.

She almost missed the briefest of nods from the auctioneer. 'Fifteen hundred I'm bid, who'll make it two?'

From that moment, her head ping-ponged from side to side as she sought to keep up with the placement of bids. In less than a minute the bidding had jumped to nine thousand pounds…

'I have ten on the telephone. Do I see eleven?' He nodded. 'Eleven I'm bid, thank you…'

She almost couldn't bear to listen. Everything was riding on this. At fifteen thousand pounds she honestly thought she might pass out. She stared at a spot on the wall.

'I'll take a half then… eighteen and half, the bid's against you, sir?'

Maddie craned her neck…

'Thank you. Do I hear nineteen?… On the telephone… and a half…?'

The air seemed to ring with silence.

'Nineteen I'm bid, do I hear nineteen and a half…? Are we all done at nineteen?' The auctioneer's eyes scoured the sale room. 'I'm selling at nineteen…'

Maddie couldn't hold her breath for very much longer. *Nineteen thousand pounds!*

The gavel banged down. 'Sold to the telephone bidder at nineteen thousand pounds… Next up is lot number forty-three…'

She felt like she was at sea, floating, riding enormous waves that buoyed her up and down. They were making her feel slightly sick. Maddie closed her eyes, waiting for her blood pressure to return to normal. They had done it. Oh God, they had done it…

★

How Seth drove them home was beyond Maddie; she had no recollection of the journey at all. It wasn't until they were standing in the yard and she saw Seth hugging Clara in excitement that she began to take in her surroundings. Clara pulled away as Trixie came running out the house to meet them, and then it was her turn as Seth's arms went around her, lifting her off the ground and spinning her round. As yet there was no sign of Tom.

'Thank you, thank you,' breathed Seth in her ear.

She pulled from his grip. 'What do you mean, thank you?' she urged. 'What's it got to do with me?'

Seth stared at her, puzzled. 'You're the only one with any sense around here. If it wasn't for you, we'd all still be sitting round the table staring at our plans. Instead, we're inches away from realising our dream.' He kissed her again, an excited kiss, a chaste kiss. 'Nineteen thousand pounds, Maddie!'

She swallowed. It was a huge amount of money. It would make all the difference… She lifted her head, suddenly understanding what it would mean for all of them. She flung her arms back around Seth, nearly knocking him off balance, and then she kissed him, and it wasn't chaste at all…

Clara gave a low whistle.

'Maddie Porter!' she exclaimed, and then, 'About bloody time too!' She put her arms around them both.

'Kettle's on!' squealed Trixie, coming to join in the group hug. 'Although we should probably be drinking champagne.'

'Then I really would fall over.' Maddie laughed. 'I hope there's some biscuits somewhere; I couldn't eat any lunch and now I'm starving.'

'White chocolate and raspberry, or orange and lemon?' Trixie replied. 'What? You didn't honestly think I was going to sit here and twiddle my thumbs, did you? It was agony. I had to do something to occupy my hands.'

'Now that's my kind of friend,' said Clara.

They were well into their third cookie each by the time a loud horn sounded in the yard. Seth shot up from his chair.

'Just wait till I tell Tom,' he said. 'Cover your ears though, ladies, he'll turn the air blue.'

'I wonder if he got the job?' said Clara to no one in particular.

'I wonder...' echoed Maddie innocently, winking at Clara behind Seth's back.

Trixie gave her a puzzled look. 'What are you two up to?' she asked. 'Don't tell me this job was another of Tom's concerted efforts to acquire a little love action?'

Clara snorted with laughter. 'No, nothing like that. You'll see...'

'What?' asked Trixie, frowning. 'Oh, that's not fair, tell me.'

Maddie could see Seth and Tom in the yard, slapping each other's backs. 'You might as well,' she said. 'She's going to find out soon enough anyway.'

Trixie's head was swivelling between the pair of them.

'Only that Tom hasn't really been to see anyone about a thatching job today, Trixie. That was just a ruse to get him out of the way.' She tapped the side of her nose. 'He's been on a secret mission instead...'

Maddie grinned at her. 'And you're just about to find out what...'

Tom's smiling face greeted them as he came through the door with Seth. 'Well blimey, that was a result and a half, wasn't it?'

'I'll say,' agreed Clara.

Maddie eyed him up and down.

He made to sit at the table and then jumped up again. 'Oh bugger, I've left something in my truck. Pour us a coffee, Maddie love, my mouth's really dry for some reason. Back in a minute.'

Clara looked at Seth. 'Well that was rather restrained for Tom,' she said.

'Hmm, maybe... I think it's just a bit hard to take in, that's all. I mean it is, isn't it?'

Maddie nodded slowly. 'Yep,' she said. 'It certainly is.' Out of the corner of her eye she could see Tom hurtling across the yard... and back again.

She got up to pour him a cup of coffee like he'd asked, and was just adding two spoonfuls of sugar to the mug when she heard the front door bang. Tom's voice floated through the kitchen doorway.

'Where do you want this picture, Maddie?' he called.

Her back was still to the door as she replied, 'Just pop it on the hook in the hall please. Thanks Tom.'

It was almost as if Tom's words were dropped into a pond – she could feel the ripples spreading out across the room. And then a screeching noise as Seth's chair scraped across the floor. She turned slowly.

When he came back into the room, Seth was holding Joy's painting in his hands. He looked up at her.

'How the hell...?'

'I couldn't bear to lose it,' she said simply. 'It belongs here.'

'But...'

Clara dragged a bemused Trixie from the room, as together with Tom the three of them left.

Seth was still looking at her, his Adam's apple bobbing up and down. 'I don't understand...'

Maddie smiled. 'It's really very simple. I bought Joy's painting this afternoon. So now it's ours.'

'But the money?'

'I think I mentioned it before; I had a pay-off from my previous company—' She stopped suddenly when she realised what she'd said. 'Ah, that wasn't exactly what you meant, was it? But yes, the money I paid is yours... For Joy's Acre, to do with as you please.'

Seth paled, and swallowed, looking horrified.

'You can't have,' he managed. 'Maddie, I can't let you do this...'

'What are you going to do, buy it back off me?' She smiled again. 'I'm sorry, the painting's not for sale.'

They stared at one another.

'I can't believe you've done this, Maddie, I... don't know what to say.' He took a step closer.

'Well, it's really very simple...'

'Is it?'

'Oh yes.' And she took a step closer too. 'You see, you were absolutely right about me. I didn't know who I was before I came here. I'd pretended to be something I'm not for so long that I'd honestly started to believe it.'

She cocked her head on one side. 'And then again, perhaps I did know who I was, but I was scared – afraid to show the real me in case I didn't fit in. But here... here it's all so different. Here things matter, people matter, and they're prepared to stand up for what they believe in… and so am I.'

She held his look. 'I'm sorry I didn't tell you what I was planning, but I know you would have tried to talk me out of it, and I couldn't let that happen.'

'But you've put yourself through hell the last couple of weeks. Why did you do that, when once we decided that the painting had to be sold you could have just bought it?'

Maddie shook her head. 'No, I couldn't,' she said. 'Because whatever happened, I needed to be sure that the painting sold for the best price it possibly could. The only way it could do that was at auction. It was a risk – I could have lost the painting – but one I had to take. If I lost, then Joy's Acre would still have ended up with as much money as possible, and if I won…'

'But it cost you more money!'

She dipped her head. 'I know, Seth, but it was worth it. I've honestly never been so sure about anything in my life before.'

'No?'

'No,' she said, swallowing.

The corners of Seth's mouth were beginning to turn upwards.

'And this certainty,' he said. 'Does it extend to other things as well…? Other people?'

'Oh, it does.'

'Well that could be a bit of a problem…'

Maddie gave him a puzzled look.

'I'm your boss…'

'Yes, you are,' she murmured. Her face now only inches from his. 'You could sack me?'

'What, again? Miss Porter, your employment record is a downright disgrace...'

'Yes, it is,' she said, as his lips finally met hers.

She was just sinking into the most exquisite feeling when Seth suddenly broke away. She looked up, startled.

He still held the painting in his hand. 'Let me just put this somewhere safe,' he said, laying the picture down on the table, 'so that I can do this properly...' Both arms drew her in close. 'Now where was I...?' he murmured.

Seconds later there was a shriek from down the hallway.

'Honestly?' muttered Seth, smiling. 'Again? I really am going to have to talk to Clara about her appalling sense of timing.'

'I suppose we'd better see what the problem is,' said Maddie, grinning. 'Just in case it's something as important as last time...'

The kitchen door flew open.

Clara and Trixie stood there, both doing a remarkable impression of the Cheshire Cat.

Clara slapped her forehead. 'I've done it again, haven't I?' she said. 'But I'm sorry, this really couldn't wait.'

'We've had an email!' squealed Trixie. 'From a lady who wants to rent the gardener's cottage!'

'She's a musician,' put in Clara. 'And she doesn't just want to rent the cottage, she wants to rent it for *six weeks*!'

Maddie stared at Seth. 'Did you hear that, she's a *musician*... and she's coming for virtually the whole summer. It's happening just the way you said it would...'

'On today of all days...' He turned away to look at the painting on the table.

'Yes,' murmured Maddie. 'It's almost as if they knew; like they've given us their blessing.'

Seth pulled away from Maddie, his eyes shining. 'Where's Tom?'

'Emailing the lady back,' replied Clara. 'She wants some peace and quiet apparently to finish a composition she's working on. And with his knowledge of music he's the perfect person to see if she has any particular requirements in that regard.'

Seth laughed. 'Yeah, I bet he is!' He swung around to look at Maddie, his eyes bright and shining. 'You know what this means, don't you…?' he asked. The others exchanged glances. 'Joy's Acre is now officially open for business!'

He opened his arms so that Clara and Trixie could join them in a group hug. They clung together, jumping up and down, everybody kissing everybody else. Maddie thought her heart was going to burst with joy.

It was Clara who pulled away first, but not before whispering a soft thank you in Maddie's ear. She straightened up, pulling at Trixie's arm.

'Come on,' she said. 'Let's go and see what Tom's found out.'

She gave Maddie and Seth a knowing look.

'Great idea!' said Seth as they both reached the door. 'Keep us posted… in a few minutes.'

Clara looked back and grinned, taking the hint.

Seth caught Maddie's hand. 'Oh and Clara?'

'What?'

'Close the door…'

A Letter from Emma

I just wanted to say a huge personal thank you for reading *The Little Cottage on the Hill*. I hope you enjoyed making friends with everyone at Joy's Acre as much as I did. If you want to stay updated on what's coming next then please sign up to my newsletter here:

www.bookouture.com/emma-davies

I'm typing this letter from my little shed in the garden where I do all my writing. It's the middle of winter, I have my heater on and a rug on my knees, plus my fluffy socks! Who said writing wasn't glamorous? It's freezing cold outside, but it's always so heart-warming to know that people have read and enjoyed my books. Your comments really make my day, so thank you also for taking the time to leave a review, or a post on social media. Even a recommendation to anyone who'll listen at the hairdresser's is very much appreciated!

From my shed I also have a wonderful view of the bird table with my little robin to keep me company as I look out across the garden. We haven't long moved in to this house, so I'm really looking forward to seeing the changing seasons here from my little window on the world, and I think that's one of the nicest things about writing a series of books, particularly ones which are seasonal – it gives me a wonderful opportunity to share all the things I love about each time of year with all my characters who, of course, by now have become firm friends. So, I hope you'll join me for the next book in the series, where you can catch up with old friends, and make some new ones too. It's been huge fun seeing what they've all got up to through summer, autumn and winter.

I love hearing from readers, so do come and say hello. You can find me on Twitter and Facebook, or pop by my website where you can read about my love of Pringles and sign up to my newsletter, among other things…

Hope to see you soon,
Love Emma x

🐦 @EmDaviesAuthor

📘 www.facebook.com/emmadaviesauthor

🖥 www.emmadaviesauthor.com

Acknowledgements

The brilliant author, Paul Auster, once said about his writing that he was 'just a man, sitting alone in a room, putting words on pieces of paper'. I've always loved that quote – it captures the very essence of what we writers do in a very humble way, but of course once the book is written then we welcome in a team of wonderful people who do wonderful things with the words we've put onto paper. I've very lucky to have such a team in Bookouture, and so huge thanks are due in particular to my brilliant (and very lovely) editor, Jessie Botterill, and the most amazing marketing duo out there, Kim Nash and Noelle Holten, whose dedication and support knows no bounds.

Thank you also to the wonderfully supportive Bookouture authors who, just like any family, are always there through good times and not so good times. You really are the best – and funny too!

Thanks of course also must go to my family, without whom, I like to joke, this book would have been written a lot faster, but who also put up with me disappearing to my shed in the garden at regular intervals, having to eat far too many pizzas and never complaining when it's chips again for tea. They also very kindly remind me to come and join the real world every now and again.

And lastly, thanks to my friends, and one in particular who is possibly, despite our conversational topics, the sanest person I know.

Warm, witty and wise, your musical suggestions have rocked my writing cave on more than one occasion and our trips to Middle Distance and beyond have been some of the most memorable I've taken. Keep up the good work!

.

Printed in Great Britain
by Amazon